STRANGERS WHEN THEY MARRY

The air of the barroom was dense with the reek of liquor. The nine men drinking at the bar turned unsteadily and scowled.

"If my car is ready, we'll start now, Señor," Kay said with a quaking air of authority.

"Oh, but why you go on? Why not marry here? We will have what the **americanos** call a wedding party, yes?"

"No, no not here. We must go on."

The bearded officer drew an automatic from his belt and twirled it casually.

"Señorita, eet make me sad to say not so. I have a pistol. You weel be married here."

Kay glanced up at the stranger who was to be her husband. She had never seen a face so white.

Bantam Books by Emilie Loring
Ask your bookseller for the books you have missed

STARS IN
YOUR EYES

Emilie Loring

BANTAM BOOKS · TORONTO · NEW YORK · LONDON

*This low-priced Bantam Book
has been completely reset in a type face
designed for easy reading, and was printed
from new plates. It contains the complete
text of the original hard-cover edition.*
NOT ONE WORD HAS BEEN OMITTED.

STARS IN YOUR EYES

*A Bantam Book / published by arrangement with
Little, Brown and Company*

PRINTING HISTORY

Little, Brown edition published October 1941
2nd printing ....March 1942   3rd printing ....January 1943
Grosset & Dunlap edition published May 1944
2nd printing ....July 1946
Bantam edition / March 1966
2nd printing ....April 1966   6th printing ....June 1968
3rd printing ...September 1966   7th printing ....June 1969
4th printing ...March 1967   8th printing ....July 1969
5th printing ....January 1968   9th printing ....September 1970
New Bantam edition / June 1976

ISBN 0-553-06618-8

Published simultaneously in the United States and Canada

Bantam Books are published by Bantam Books, Inc. Its trademark, consisting of the words "Bantam Books" and the portrayal of a bantam, is registered in the United States Patent Office and in other countries. Marca Registrada. Bantam Books, Inc., 666 Fifth Avenue, New York, New York 10019.

PRINTED IN THE UNITED STATES OF AMERICA

STARS IN
YOUR EYES

I

A tire burst with an ear-splitting explosion. Kay Chesney maneuvered the skidding sedan to a stop. . . . Now what? She jumped out and examined a rear wheel. Flat as the proverbial pancake. No wonder on a bumpy dirt road like this. Along with the rude sign by the paved highway, LAREDO DETOUR, ROAD AHEAD UNDER CONSTRUCTION, why hadn't the Texas authorities warned AT YOUR OWN RISK—AND WE MEAN RISK?

According to her wrist watch she should have been crossing the Rio Grande at this moment. Hugh would be waiting for her at Nuevo Laredo, on the Mexican side, wild with anxiety if she didn't appear as per schedule. She shook the wheel as if by some magic in her touch the tire would inflate automatically. Nothing doing. Looked as if she would have to change it herself —no chivalrous, accommodating male in sight to do it for her.

If they could see her at this minute, her friends in Massachusetts would be gleefully caroling, "I told you so." They had to a man—Bill Hewins in particular and a girl or two—prophesied dire complications if she drove alone to join her stepbrother at a United States Consulate in Mexico.

She had cockily assured them that after four years in college, a year in Defense training and singing at innumerable relief benefits, she craved adventure. Suppose she did get into a jam, hadn't she brains enough to get herself out of it? Think of what women were up against in Europe.

She hadn't admitted to her advisers that back of her defiance of their counsel was the determination not to be a leaner. Devotedly loving the mother she had lost two years ago, often she had been exasperated by her dependence. She would call on her stepbrother, Hugh, for help at the least complication. Kay herself had decided that she would build her life on independence and that she wouldn't yell to a man for help each time she came up against trouble.

The plan was fundamentally sound but a bit superheroic when one found oneself with a crippled car on a rough, strange road with night settling down swiftly and all sorts of queer, uncanny squeaks and rustles seeping from the bushes. A low laugh rose in her throat. Her decision didn't necessarily mean that she wouldn't welcome male assistance at the present moment. Thank heaven for the stars. They looked friendly.

How about snapping out of this attack of jitters? In the Volunteer Service Mechanics course she had passed with an A hadn't she been taught to tear down and assemble any sort of car motor, to say nothing of such a run-of-the-mill job as shifting a wheel? Her beige-and-white print suit wasn't designed for motor-repair work but standing in the road regretting wouldn't change it. She reached for the tools.

"Sure'd like to help if I kin, Marm."

The drawled male voice was like a powerful grip on her shoulder. It twisted her around. Her heart shot to her throat and pounded like a pile driver on a resisting log as she stared at the mounted man who had spoken.

Ragged blue trousers, a torn shirt—faded to a dirty tan and wet with sweat—covered his lean, rangy body which slouched in the saddle. One leg was thrown over the saddle horn. A businesslike rifle lay across his lap. His face, below the gallon hat tilted back on his rough dark hair, appeared to be split by a wide, semi-toothless grin, to be dotted with two burning black eyes. His piebald horse must be on the phantom side. She hadn't heard the sound of hoofs. A Texas bad man if she knew her movies—and she did. She had to swallow her heart before she could release her voice.

"Thanks. Is there a garage between here and Laredo?"

"Sure, Marm. 'Bout fifty yards ahead. Jest round that curve. It belongs to a quick-lunch place, Casa Fresco. You kin wait in there while the mechanic comes here and changes this wheel."

She glanced at the sedan, thought of the ducky clothes, sports, prints, do-dress and don't-dress costumes in the wardrobe cases on the back seat—"Bring the clothes that will be comfortable in a moderate, even temperature," Hugh had advised—of the small automatic with her jewelry, real and costume junk, in her alligator-skin dressing case and shook her head.

"Only fifty yards? The car can hobble that far. I'll stick with it."

"Suit yerself, Marm. Me an' Mose'll amble 'longside yer, so if yer git stuck we kin give it a haul."

She would much rather he would stay behind. Each time her eyes met his her heart did a wing-overwing. The sedan bumped over the rough road to the accompaniment of the creak of saddle leather. "Mose" minced along companionably with an occasional roll of enormous brown eyes at her as if wondering why she was there.

"Here we are, Marm."

One moment there had been nothing but cacti-spotted fields and shrubs and the pungent smell from sage, mesquite and damp leaves; the next she was looking at a rambling adobe building with a string of red-and-green electric lights outlining the roof.

The rider slid from the saddle. His mount whinnied and joined the horses tethered to a rail. A door opened and let out a burst of dance music, let out also a beam which illumined the sedan like a floodlight. Her self-appointed guide took the two steps to the porch in one and whispered to the shirt-sleeved fat man, apparently the proprietor, who was peering from the doorway.

"Sure, we can change that wheel," mine host encouraged in a voice alcoholically cordial and far-reaching. "Send a man out to at once. Sure, Marm. Come in. Make yourself to home while you wait." He tightened the embossed-leather belt which accentuated the size of his paunch and bowed from what in an earlier day doubtless had been a waist.

Kay clutched her dressing case and slowly mounted the steps—nothing else to do though instinct warned her that she was walking into one of those jams through which she had boasted her brain would carry her victoriously.

Just inside the door she stopped. Pin-point carbonation pricked through her veins. The air of the large room was dense with tobacco smoke and the sickening reek of liquor, noisy with blatant music from a juke. The men, nine, she counted hastily, who were drinking at the bar opposite the door turned unsteadily and scowled. Their libations had reached the fighting stage apparently. Rather a pity that Bill Hewins' taste in movies had run to Westerns. He had taken her to so many that memory set her imagination off to a terrifying start.

Four of the men might have completed a set of quintuplets with the man who had brought her here; they were alike to a tooth gap and gallon hat. The others were undoubtedly Mexicans, bronzed, slim, in shabby uniforms and tall boots with tarnished-silver spurs. A man in light-gray tweeds at a table at the end of the room raised his head and glanced at the mirror above the smoke-blackened fireplace. Thank heaven! An American, almost as dark as the Mexicans, and decent—no mistaking the type. Her appealing eyes met his in the glass. Yelling for help so soon, was she?

"What is this? A movie company on location?" she asked in a voice, pitched to reach him, which, she fondly hoped, was tinged with laughter.

With an exclamation he was on his feet striding toward her. She had time only to notice the red of lips, the gleam of white teeth below a small mustache, black as his hair, two lines, deep as if inked between his brows, before he caught her in his arms.

"At last. I've waited and waited. Began to think you had lost your courage—darling, and were letting me down." He bent as if to kiss her, whispered:—

"Name's Drex. Danger."

No need to tell her that last, or that she could trust the man whose voice had melted the ice in her heart. His brain must work like a steel trap to have thought up that yarn. With a supreme effort she forced a laugh and drew away. Her valiant eyes met his.

"Don't kiss me *here,* Drex. This gal likes privacy. Why did you think I had lost my courage? And why select this sort of a place for our rendezvous?" She shrugged dainty disdain and looked around the smoky room, at the staring, incredulous men at the bar. The music faded away. "Nothing very romantic about this."

"Say, what's it all about, Mister? The dame came here with me." The man who had guided Kay to the place took a menacing step forward.

The others, all save the barman, who was assiduously polishing glasses, and the tallest Mexican, with a beard, dark spectacles and the insignia of a major on his shoulder, closed in about them.

The man in tweeds drew her close with the arm he had kept about her, so close that she could smell the scent of tobacco on his coat.

"Your mistake, Texas," he corrected lightly. "She didn't come with you; she came to meet me." Kay wondered how he could laugh when the arm about her was tensed like steel. "To let you in on a secret, we're eloping."

"My family had someone else picked out for me, they protested, 'Kay, don't marry and go so far away.' Being free, white and twenty-one I declared I would stick to my man and here I am. We're planning to be married as soon as we cross the border, aren't we, Drex?"

She had a shaky feeling that she hadn't helped by her interruption. She had started to provide her fiancé-for-the-moment with a name for her and then her sense of the dramatic had lured her on.

"So that ees how it ees, Señorita? You lof heem? You marry heem, yes?" Gloating was the word to describe the quality of the soft Castilian voice.

The men gave way as the man who had spoken, the Mexican with a major's insignia, came forward. He held his body with the rigidity of a person who knows himself to be drunk. The fingers of his left hand were clenched around his leather belt as if to steady his arm. His thin, severe face with its untidy Vandyke beard had the imperiousness of a Spanish grandee, but the black spectacles gave a demonic touch. Was he disguised? If so, why?

"Of course I intend to marry him. Would I come all this way just to say 'Good-by'?" Kay's valiant voice belied her sense of terror. There was something about the bearded face which sent icy chills slithering through her veins. She swallowed hard before she added:—

"And, proprietor, if my car is ready we'll start *now.*"

"Oh, but w'y you go on? W'y not you marry here? We weel have w'at the *americanos* call a wedding party, yes? In thees room—is eet not so, Señores?"

The smooth suggestion of the bearded officer was greeted with a burst of ribald laughter from the others and loud hand-clapping which shook the rafters.

"No. *No,* not here." The arm around Kay tightened. Was this Drex person prodding her to protest? Did he think she needed urging? "You wouldn't like that would you, darling?"

"Like it! Not for a minute. It's a hideous suggestion. We must go on."

The bearded officer drew an automatic from his belt and twirled it casually. He braced his shoulders in drunken dignity. The barman ducked and disappeared.

"Señorita, eet mak' me sad to say not so. *Tengo una pistola.* In English, I have a pistol. You weel be married here. You weel pay us well, Señor, or the Señorita weel not leave this place except, but perhaps, with me—*bueno,* eet might be better that way, *sí?"*

Kay glanced up at the man beside her for a cue. She had never seen a living face so white. His eyes were like flames as they met hers.

"Why not, darling? The sooner the better. Strike up the band, Señor— Perhaps it's Padre! You are a padre in disguise, aren't you, or you wouldn't suggest a marriage ceremony?"

"Me padre? *No es probable!* It ees not likely. Joe!"

To Kay's horror the man who had guided her to

Casa Fresco swayed forward on a wave of laughter from his companions.

"*Bueno,* I give you American Justice of the Peace, you call heem. The marriage must be made to hold tight, eh, Señores? Eet may pay us well. You want to marry, Señor?"

"Sure, crazy to marry. Right—Kay?"

"Right, Drex."

"*Está bueno.* It ees well you say that. Then *naturalmente* weetnesses swear you marry of your own free will. Queek, Joe."

Amid a burst of applause and tipsy laughter the Texan stepped forward. He administered a resounding clap on the Major's shoulder:—

"Yo' shore picked a good idee, *amigo.*"

Someone dropped a coin into the juke. To the accompaniment of "Marquita, Marquita," "Joe" droned the formula of a civil marriage service. Kay whispered her name. The man beside her gave his as Drexel Hamilton in a clear, unfaltering voice in which there was no intimation of the fact that his grip crushed the fingers she had laid in his when, at the command of the Justice, he pulled a ring from his hand and slipped it on her finger.

This is a dream, she kept telling herself, in a minute I'll wake up. It can't be real, nothing like this could happen in the state of Texas, in the United States of America. Couldn't it? Weren't more improbable things happening all over the world? She felt a hysterical urge to sing *The Star Spangled Banner* at the top of her voice. Would that break the spell? Her thoughts snapped back to her surroundings.

"*Está bueno,* you have your bride, Señor Hamilton," the master of ceremonies exulted. "The reech Señor Hamilton, *un gran caballero,* I know you now. You pay well for her, much moneys—queek. You an' she both. All the moneys you have. Eef you give us w'at the *americano* calls the ha-ha, eef you hide thees marriage—eet mak' more pay for us, eh, Señores? Now give w'at you have. Queek." The automatic twirled suggestively.

Hamilton put his hand to his breast pocket.

"I don't carry much. American Express cheques and . . ." His hand came out with a revolver.

"All up," he thundered. "Get behind me, Kay."

The surprised Major's pistol dropped with a clatter. His left hand tightened on his belt till the knuckles shone white. His face—what skin was visible between spectacle rims and beard—turned a pasty yellow. He's nothing but a cheap four-flusher after all; so are the others. Why, oh why didn't we defy them, Kay asked herself, as the outlaws stuck unsteady hands high above their heads.

The room was so still that the ponderous ticking of a clock sounded like the knell of doom, so still that the tramp of footsteps on the porch reverberated like the thunder of an approaching army. Two men in olive-drab uniforms burst into the room. Three more blocked the door.

"What's going on here?" the Captain demanded. "I'll take over. Lieutenant, cover them. What's it all about, tall fella?"

The man who had called himself Hamilton thrust his revolver into the shoulder holster under his coat.

"A holdup, Captain. Detour sign a way back to switch travelers from the highway, and a crop of long, sharp nails for tires to pick up. Not a big haul tonight, first me and then the girl. Now, if you'll excuse us, we'd like to get out of here."

"Sure. Give me your names. We may need you as witnesses when we jail this bunch." He grinned sardonically at the group of Mexicans. "And we've orders from your Government to keep you rebels there a long, *long* time."

His face was noncommittal as he glanced at the card Hamilton handed him. When he had burst into the room Kay had imagined that his eyes had wire-lessed a message to the man who was shielding her with his body. Must have been wishful thinking on her part.

"Come." Hamilton touched her shoulder.

She drew a deep breath of the clear, sage-scented air when she reached the porch which was flooded by the lights from an army car and truck. The tied horses were kicking and yanking at their tethers.

"That was a nightmare, wasn't it? It wasn't real?" she pleaded. "That phoney marriage couldn't happen in this country. Say it couldn't."

"Is that sedan yours? Come on. Even with the U. S. Border Patrol on the job we'd better make a quick getaway."

"But, the tire—"

"The wheel has been changed. Didn't you notice that the barman was absent for a while?" He hurried her across the rough road. "Hop in. I'm driving you to Laredo."

"But you came in a car, didn't you?"

"The Captain will take care of that."

He didn't speak again until they were back on the glistening paved highway, under a field of stars which seemed so near that one had but to reach out to pluck a bouquet of them, until she asked:—

"Who are they?"

"A bunch of American cutthroats who have joined up with a few rebels who left Mexico shortly after the latest election to continue their planning to place their candidate in the presidential chair. The U. S. and the Mexican Governments have been co-operating in every way possible to nab them; the Consuls on each side of the border work together in the most friendly spirit. The boldness and elusiveness of the bandits have been the pest of the two nations. They have operated on both sides of the river. Have stolen, kidnaped and haven't stopped at murder. They hit the nail square on the head when they named themselves 'The Scorpions.' I swallowed their detour bait intentionally, but you . . ." He ran his hand under the collar of his blue shirt as if it choked him.

"Do you realize what a jam you were in? My God, when I looked up and saw the glint of your coppery hair in the mirror, the fear in your enormous brown eyes, your slight figure drawn up as if facing a firing squad, I thought I had hallucinations. What in thunder brought you to that dive? How did you happen to be driving alone in this country at this time of day to get into a mess like that?"

She told him that she was on her way to join her stepbrother whose wife had left him, that he had written her that his little daughter, Jill, needed her.

"Hugh rather let himself go in that letter. It isn't like him. I was up to my ears in Defense training but when I read it I realized that he felt the situation was desperate. I've always believed that one owed help to one's family first and I had a chance to demonstrate that belief, so here I am.

"Hugh is a consul, a career man; he has been in Mexico two years. The moment I heard of his appointment I began to study Spanish, thinking that someday I might visit him. I hope this night's adventure won't in any way react to hurt or worry him. Of course that absurd marriage wasn't legal, *was it?*" Something in his silence had strained her voice to breaking point.

"Take it easy. To be honest, I don't know. If you noticed, the gang leader got our consent before the ceremony went on. I thought we had put that elopement act across when I declared we were crazy to marry and you agreed. . . . If the marriage had been performed under duress, that's the legal term, it would be invalid, but he had witnesses to prove we agreed to it. If the Justice of the Peace was a fake that ceremony isn't worth the powder to blow it."

"What did the poisonous Mexican mean by 'Eef you hide thees marriage—eet mak' more pay for us'?"

"Blackmail. He knew we hadn't planned to meet there and called our bluff. We'll thumb our noses at him and keep the secret until I find the truth about that alleged Justice."

"Won't the others talk?"

"Not if they are smart. They're thinking, if just about now in jail the Señores are thinking at all, that they've feathered their nests for years to come with a chance at blackmail."

"They were nothing but a bunch of cowards masquerading as Bad Men. Why didn't you defy them before that hideous ceremony instead of after? Why? Why? *Why?"*

"Have you forgotten they were fighting drunk? I wouldn't take the chance of leaving you alone in their clutches. Don't judge Mexicans by the bunch of black sheep you saw tonight. They are cultured, patriotic, charitable; they have taken in homeless Spanish children, have welcomed exiled Spanish scholars. They're lovable and altogether likable. . . . Here we are at the International Bridge. It's crowded as usual. Americans, Mexicans, Indians and Europeans, they're all here. Not afraid to cross alone, are you, if your brother is to meet you at the other end?"

His calm, matter-of-fact voice infuriated her. Didn't he care that she had been through a terrifying experience?

"Afraid after that Casa Fresco horror? What could be worse than to be tied up in a marriage ceremony to a man you never saw before in your life?"

He stepped from the car. As he closed the door he suggested:—

"Think it over and answer that question yourself. Worse things have happened and while you're at it you might consider the fact that it may prove as much a horror to me as to you. By the way, forget that I said I had swallowed their detour bait intentionally. Keep mum about what happened at Casa Fresco tonight until you hear from me. If you confide in anyone the result may be serious. All spies are not in the service of foreign countries. *Don't talk!* Good-by."

II

Consciousness penetrated the blurred dream world. Kay lifted heavy lids and frowned at the bar of sunshine across the foot of the bed. Were the sounds outside the chatter of birds? Did she smell flowers? *Flowers* at this time of year in New England . . . New

England! She wasn't in New England; she was at her brother's home in Mexico.

The memory brought her sitting up, wide-awake. She thought backward through the last forty-eight hours, back from her arrival at this house yesterday. Thought of the motor trip from the Rio Grande, visualized Hugh's white, anxious face when he had greeted her in Nuevo Laredo: "I had begun to think you were lost, strayed or stolen, Kay" (he hadn't known how near he was to the truth); thought back further to the narrow, crowded International Bridge, to the stop of the sedan; heard a man's voice saying:—

"If you confide in anyone the result may be serious. All spies are not in the service of foreign countries. *Don't talk.* Good-by."

He had disappeared in the dusk before she could give him the ring, with its coat of arms cut in brown onyx, she had jerked from her finger. She shivered as she heard the bearded Major hiding behind dark spectacles say:—

"*Està bueno.* You have your bride, Señor Hamilton."

That brought her out of bed with a jump . . . *Bride!* She dashed for the shower. Its prickly cold might break the spell of memory. The marriage ceremony couldn't be real. It must be a nightmare. Why kid herself? It wasn't. Could she have done anything different in the face of that brandished pistol? Could she have refused to consent with the Mexican Major's sinister alternative: "The Señorita weel not leave thees place except, but perhaps with me—*bueno,* eet might be better that way," and those drunks ready to back it to the limit?

What good to wonder now? She hadn't known then that she was up against a bunch of yellow cowards, had she? She had been sure that she was terribly near the verge of tragedy and had acted accordingly. If she were in a state of jitters what must be the condition of the man, Hamilton, who had had a strange female wished on him? He had reminded her curtly that the marriage might prove as much a horror to him as to her.

Whether it was or was not a legal marriage it had twisted her life forever out of the conventional pattern. The Casa Fresco episode would always lurk in the back of her mind affecting her sense of values, her reactions to persons and ideas.

"Now, Miss Jill, honey. You put down that book while I braid them pigtails. Allus readin', you is, allus readin'. Your pappy gits turrible put out ef you's late to meals, sure does."

The rich Negroid voice drifted into Kay's room. . . . Breakfast time. Hugh would be annoyed if she were late. She knew from a visit in another Consulate that he expected his family to be at table before he left for the office. As she zipped the front of her green-linen frock she listened to Jill's high, impatient reply to Verbena, the portly black nurse, who had taken care of the child since she had come into the world.

"I hate my pigtails, Beeny. I hate everything about myself—spectacles like owl's eyes and teeth like the Wolf in Red Riding Hood, *'Woof! Woof!* The better to eat you, my dear,' and my nose that turns up at the tip like a hook. Why couldn't it have been a perfect shape like Kay's? Why can't I have hair like hers, soft and wavy and shiny and reddish like the copper kettles in Morning Glory's kitchen?"

"Now, honey chile, don' you fret. Yo' nose is agwine to unhook in time, sure is. You's agoin' to be be—e—utiful, jest lak yo' auntie am. Jest yo' wait till yo' grows up. P'raps yo'll be prettier—but I reckon de Lord don't mak' 'em much prettier. Dat Miss Kay, she hav' a smile dat would coax dem Seraphims an' Cherumbims right down from Heaven, sure has. An' her brown eyes, dey shine jest lak stars—mm—mum. Now run out an' git to de table 'fore your pappy begins to fuss."

At the tall, grilled window of her room in the two-story stucco house Kay watched the blue-frocked child, pigtails bobbing—"Mr. Pickwick," white-coated, black-spotted Dalmatian at her heels—run across the patio. Its paving was patterned with dancing shadows; its walls quivered as the soft breeze stirred the masses of glowing magenta bougainvillea that covered it. Its furniture was of natural, polished pigskin, stretched over rattan frames. In the flower border, tall yucca shook its creamy bells above luxuriant rows of yellow, pink, blue, red and white blossoms that filled the air with fragrance.

She thoughtfully regarded her stepbrother as he rose from the table to greet his daughter. He dropped a kiss on top of her smooth head as she wriggled into the chair the Indian boy in his native white pajamalike outfit drew out. Hugh's impeccably tailored beige-shantung suit gave his figure a trim military appearance. He had changed during the last two years. The hair at his temples, which had been brown, was frosty; his once-smiling mouth was set in a grim line; his hazel eyes which had been so ready to sparkle with laughter were the somber eyes of a man who had been tragically disillusioned.

Darn that wife of his! How could Blanche have left him and their child? "My own money," and the fact that she had been rotoed and headlined as one of the South's ten most beautiful, best-dressed women was the answer. Money undoubtedly made the mare go, but, in a matrimonial partnership where the bulk of the income was possessed by a selfish wife who craved only adulation, and the social merry-go-round of an international set, that same money was pretty sure to goad the aforementioned mare into a runaway. Would Blanche have deserted family and home so indifferently had she been dependent on a husband's pay? No . . . a colossal no . . . Kay reached that conclusion and the patio at the same moment.

"*Buenos días, Señorita Jill, buenos días, Señor Consul,*" she greeted gaily. She tweaked the silky ear of the Dalmatian squatted on his haunches beside his mistress. "*Buenos días,* Mr. Pickwick. How'm I doin' with my Spanish, folks?"

Her brother smiled as he sat down. Jill slipped back into her chair and frowned at her aunt through the big lenses of her horn-rimmed spectacles. The native boy grinned as he drew out her chair.

"*Buenos días, graciosa Señorita.* Yo' doin' fine."

"Rested after the trip, Kay?"

"On top of the world, Hugh. For an hour or two last night I felt the motion of the car. Then I slept so deeply and soundly that it took me a few minutes to orient myself when I woke. I smelled garden flowers and thought, 'Flowers at this time of year in New England?' At home Boston Common will be just beginning to be misty with diaphanous green."

"What's orient mean?"

"Realize where I was, Jill."

"Kay doesn't speak like the other Americans here, does she, Daddy?"

"No, honey. Jill is accustomed to Southern voices, Kay. Yours is quite as charming but it's crisp and sure, as if you know exactly where you are going and are on your way."

"Just what I was thinking," agreed a voice.

Startled at the unexpected interruption Kay turned to look at the man who was crossing the patio. Mr. America wins the beauty contest! She swallowed the chuckle the thought inspired. And does he know it! A profile that properly belonged on a Greek coin, eyes at the moment large, dark, kindling with the old where've-you-been-all-my-life light, though for a split second when they first met hers they had been cold, calculating. . . . Hair light, with a wave of satin sheen —as much a movie male-star trade-mark as the MGM lion—a tanned skin set off to perfection by a white-linen suit. . . .

Even as she thought all this, he was bending over her hand in response to her brother's introduction.

"Kay, this is my senior clerk, Gordon Slade, and late as usual."

Hugh Chesney resumed his seat. With a laugh Slade dropped into the chair Felipe drew out for him. He winked at Kay.

"The Chief won't step out socially, insists that I do it for him and then beats me up, figuratively speaking, because I'm late for breakfast. Have to sleep sometime. Didn't get in until four A.M. It was a large and wet evening. Herr Von Haas was paying his social debts with a ball at the Club.

"Coffee and one of Morning Glory's popovers,

Felipe, if I can stop at one. Your brother upped the reputation of the whole State Department when he installed Verbena's daughter as his cook, Miss Chesney. Sweetheart—how *can* you do it so early in the morning?" He shuddered theatrically and pointed to the sizable mound of oatmeal, in the midst of a sea of rich cream, Jill was attacking with enthusiasm.

She scowled at him over the shell rims of her spectacles. "It isn't early and I wasn't out all night drinkin' an' carousin', that's what Beeny says you do. I'm hungry and I'm *not* your sweetheart, Gordon Slade."

"That gets me down, all right." He grinned at Kay. "I know who your sweetheart is, honey child. Jealousy's tearing my heart up by the roots. That reminds me, heard the news about Drex Hamilton, Chief?"

"No. What is it?"

Kay's heart took off with a jump and fanned its wings chokingly in her throat. What had happened to Hamilton? Had the story of that nightmarish ceremony at Casa Fresco leaked out? He had warned her that if it did the results would be serious for him.

"He has opened his town house. His sister moved in from the country yesterday. Wonder if the irresistible Señorita Amelia Mansilla has refused to bury herself on that hacienda of his."

"Planning to live in the city? He's crazy. When did he return from the States?"

"Sometime yesterday. He was at the party last night as smiling and debonair a bucko as you'd care to see; all lit up inside, as it were. You're positively shocked white, Miss Chesney. That doesn't mean what you think. Hamilton doesn't drink, but he sure is a glutton for trouble. He eats it up."

"Wonder what Drex has up his sleeve now? If he'd only let me in on some of his plans." Hugh's voice sounded worried.

Why hadn't the man admitted that he knew her brother when on the way to Laredo she had told him where she was going? That Señorita! Did he love her?

Was that why the marriage ceremony might prove a "horror" to him?

"Sorry to interrupt, Hugh, but I can't stand this tantalizing conversation another minute. It's like waiting for next week's installment of a who-dun-it serial, your comments are so drenched with mystery. Information please. *Who* is the reckless Drex Hamilton? *Why* shouldn't he open his house in town? *How* does the irresistible Señorita what's-her-name fit into the scenario?"

Her brother frowned as if deliberating an answer. Gordon Slade's smooth voice slipped into the breach.

"Drexel Hamilton, Drex for short, came here as a small boy with his mother when she married Señor Gonzalez de la Cartina, a Mexican magnifico. Mexicans like American women as wives, I'm told. Better watch your step, Miss Chesney. He was educated in the United States and returned to this country permanently when his stepfather, whose holdings were to a small extent only expropriated by the agrarian policy, became seriously ill and unable to administer his property. Drex took it over.

"Later, de la Cartina died leaving him a big fortune, a super-hacienda and a colossal cattle ranch where a famous strain of fighting bull is bred. Their bulls are as sure to fill a plaza as the most renowned matador. He had a mother and a half-sister to look after. The mother died a few years ago. The half-sister, Mercedes de la Cartina—'Chiquita' to her family and friends—doesn't need much looking after; she's a civic power. She's fighting against removing trees and razing the Spanish Colonial buildings here."

"While you stop for breath I'll carry on, Slade. Señorita de la Cartina is right. The beautiful old homes, courtyards and squares shouldn't be destroyed or dwarfed by tall apartment houses. So far she has succeeded, has prevented spoilation and this small city remains one of the best examples of the Spanish Colonial Period."

"She must be a super person, Hugh. Is she old?"

"Old! No. She's five or six years younger than Drex."

"Youth. Wealth. Beauty. An unbeatable triumvirate," Slade cut in dramatically. "She is all for Mexico but her half-brother has retained his American citizenship which doesn't increase his popularity in some quarters of this country. How'm I doing as a gossip columnist?"

"Fine. But it doesn't sound-real. It has the Hollywood flavor. Do you know this gay and reckless 'bucko' well, Hugh?"

"Sure. Though he is younger than I, he is my best friend here. He has been invaluable helping me steer clear of the quicksands of prejudice. I'm sorry to have to admit that the Mexicans are not completely sold on Americans; they are being harassed by propaganda. There is a foreign element here which loses no opportunity to create ill-feeling between them. One of its jobs is to convince Americans that any harm that comes to them or their property is directly attributable to a Mexican. Part of my work is to knock the spots out of that devilish viewpoint whenever I meet it and to prove that the United States is sincere in its desire and determination to be a friendly neighbor. Jill, if you've finished breakfast, run along to Beeny and get ready for school. I'll leave you there on my way to the office."

"Goody, goody, that will be dandy, Daddy. See you later, Kay. Good morning, Mister Slade." She made a little face at her father's senior clerk who blew a kiss in return.

Kay waited until girl and spotted dog had disappeared into the house before she prodded: "Good as far as it goes but that doesn't explain why the glamour lad is 'crazy' to live in the city."

"Cut out that glamour stuff, Kay," Hugh Chesney ordered impatiently. "Slade has given you the wrong slant on Hamilton. Those two hit it off about as well as a Hitlerite and a Churchillite——"

"You've got me wrong——"

"I have the floor, Slade," Hugh Chesney interrupted his senior clerk's indignant protest. "Drex is trusted and liked by the present Government; that's why he has been mysteriously warned by unprincipled malcontents to keep away from the city, that his number is up. The country is settling down but all is not yet sweetness and light."

You're telling me, Kay thought.

"El Señor Hamilton," Felipe announced.

She caught her breath . . . Now what? For a brief instant her eyes met the deepset, heavily lashed eyes of the man standing between the grilled gates of the house portico. She had forgotten he was so tall; hadn't realized he was so darkly handsome. In her excitement that night at Casa Fresco she really hadn't seen him. His hair was black, as was his slight mustache. His features were clear cut. His skin was a rich bronze—perhaps his light-gray clothes accentuated that effect. His eyes which had burned like coals in the dim, smoky room were really a clear, dark blue; she remembered the two deep lines between his brows. . . . Well-knit compact body. Lean hips and waist. A man who would get things done.

"Drex, you crazy coot." Hugh Chesney's voice was warm with affection. "I hear you have opened the town house. It's suicide."

"Keep your shirt on, Consul." If she lived to be a hundred never would she forget his laugh. For her that horrible night it had held gaiety and tenderness and invincibility.

"Greetings, Slade." He glanced at her, then inquiringly at her brother. "You have a guest. Am I intruding?"

"Don't be a dumbbell; you couldn't intrude. My guest is my sister; you should recognize her, you've seen her photograph often enough. If you hadn't been out of the country for the last two months you would have known she was coming. I hope she lives through the festivities planned for her; the series opens this afternoon. Kay, Drex Hamilton. Felipe, coffee for *el señor.*"

"And one of Morning Glory's popovers, Felipe," Hamilton added before he sat down.

Kay softly let out the breath she had been holding tensely. His bow in acknowledgment of Hugh's introduction had been as impersonal as if they were meeting for the first time. He had no intention of revealing their coadventure. Relief flooded her in a stimulating tide. Her eyes laughed; her lips tilted up at the corners.

"I've been hearing the most breath-snatching stories of your recklessness, Mr. Hamilton." What had she said to make his face darken redly, to strike two little sparks in his eyes?

"Have you? Facts get frightfully exaggerated in this country; people have so little to talk about. I haven't done anything which will compare in recklessness with the exploits of some American girls I've met during the last two months. Brainless, I calls 'em. Consul, can you spare me a few minutes before you go to the office? I need your advice."

Brainless! . . . The word pricked at Kay's mind like a burr. Was that a crack at her? She wasn't the only American girl who had motored across-country alone, was she? It hadn't been her fault that the cutthroat gang had set up that fake DETOUR sign, had it?

"Time to burn for you, Drex. Kay, how'd you like to drive into the city with Gordon and give my official headquarters the once-over?" Her brother's question cut off her angry mental tirade.

"I'd love it—if your senior clerk wants me?"

"*Want* you! You bet. Come on, let's go. You can see the town and get back in time for a long siesta before you knock out the eyes of native *caballeros,* and your less picturesque compatriots, at the garden party this afternoon."

"In just a minute, Mr. Slade. Sorry you've been so unlucky in the type of American girls you've met, Mr. Hamilton. We're not all brainless, though I admit even the most intelligent of us may have our crackpot moments. It's been nice meeting you. Good-by."

Her brother stared at her as if doubting he had really heard her curt dismissal. His lips parted. Before he could speak Hamilton slipped a hand under his arm.

"Come on, Consul, we're detaining these young people. I can see that Slade's fairly champing at the bit. Good morning, Miss Chesney. I don't like that word good-by; sounds as if we wouldn't meet again and often."

"Kay," her brother called from the doorway. "Find Jill and take her along with you. Tell her I won't have time to drop her at school. Come on, Drex."

"Kay, you don't mind if I call you Kay, do you?" Slade inquired, as the two men entered the house.

She shook her head vigorously. The implication in Hamilton's voice had sidetracked hers.

"Don't stare at that portico as if the guy had hypnotized you. No use falling for him. He's gone off the deep end, ready to sign on the dotted line of matrimony."

"You mean that Señorita somebody? Is she beautiful?"

"As a dream. Hasn't much comeback. Goes down better with Mexicans than Americans, though she's had Hamilton big-timing her. I like 'em more peppy, myself. . . . No money but fabulous jewels and one of the oldest, most historic haciendas. As a child she was affianced, that's the classy word here, to a cousin and then along came our hero and cut him out."

Kay drew the stem of a big pink rose through her green belt.

"How did the cousin like that, Mr. Commentator?"

"He didn't like it. He was all burned up, all set to pick a quarrel with Hamilton for another reason. But, just as he was ready to order pistols for two, he got into a political mess and skipped the country. He is related to the de la Cartinas; both families go back to Cortes. There is a newspaper printed across the border that carries a column, 'Air Waves,' which is devoted to Mexican socialites and their scandals. It is suspected that he pays back slights or feuds by sending items to that. Only a suspicion, mind you, but, boy, it's strong enough for his friends and acquaintances to stop, look, listen, before they affront him."

"What is his name?"

"Señor Edouard Rafael Castello."

"Suppose he returns before the marriage. If Mr. Hamilton is an American citizen a row over a woman might cause international complications, mightn't it?"

"I doubt it. Complications or not, Hamilton will

take what he wants. These *hacendados* still rule like
ancient barons in their castles, but he's always ready
to pay what it costs, understand. He's that kind of a
guy. What's the matter? You look fussed."

"It's that darn car. I've driven so many miles that
every little while I feel the motion of it; my head spins
like a top. . . . All right now. Off to the big city. What's
the first sight worth seeing?"

III

Four long windows opened from the library onto a
balcony.

"Let's talk outside where we can't be overheard,
Consul," Drex Hamilton suggested.

Hugh Chesney glanced at him quickly before he
stepped through the open window. Below them, set in
green hills, lay a lovely stretch of lake clear as a blue
mirror reflecting a snow-capped mountain peak, bordered with water hyacinths and lilies.

"This do?" Hamilton nodded and perched on the
iron railing. "What's on your mind, Drex? I knew you
were troubled the moment you appeared in the patio.
Those sharp lines between your eyes are always a give-
away. If you have any—any unpleasant news to break
about Blanche, get it over with. I can take it. I can
take anything after her walkout." He cleared his gruff
voice. "Shoot."

"You've got me wrong, Consul. I haven't heard
a word from or of your wife since she left." He selected a cigarette from a gold case, snapped a lighter,
looked over the top of it. "You complain that I don't
tell you my plans. Here's where I lay my cards on the
table—part of them. What I have to say is about your
sister."

"About Kay? *Kay!* She didn't arrive until yesterday. You didn't meet her until this morning. What can
you have to say about her?"

"Hasn't she told you what happened before she reached the International Bridge?"

"Not a word. What are you trying to get across, Drex?"

"Good girl. I warned her not to talk, but I thought after I left her that it was like putting her in a strait jacket after what she'd been through."

"Been through! What is this, a guessing game? What had she been through?"

"She got tangled up with the Scorpion gang and to get her out—we—we—she and I were put through a marriage ceremony—of sorts—at gunpoint."

Amazement doubled Hugh Chesney's knees and dropped him into a gaily cushioned rattan chair.

"You! Kay! *Married!* You're crazy!"

"I wish I were. I wish the infernal experience were a nightmare, but it's a fact. This is what happened. I'll have to go back a bit. I went to the States as one of the goodwill ambassadors bent on wiping out past disputes and to open the way for economic and defense collaboration. Now it can be told. Those high in authority here felt that because of my life in Mexico my point of view would count with the committee in Washington. It was mighty inconvenient to leave the ranch just then but I decided that if I could help this administration, which, I am convinced, will do big things for the country, my personal affairs would have to wait. As you know the plan went across. In consequence bank deposits mounted, Government bonds went up, financial circles saw the light."

"It's a big step toward the prosperity and welfare of this Western Hemisphere. But what in thunder has that to do with you and Kay?"

Hugh Chesney watched an Indian toiling along the thread of bridle path near the shore of the lake, balancing a pole across his shoulders from each end of which a bucket dangled . . . Kay married? It couldn't be true. He brushed his hand impatiently across his eyes; he must be dreaming. No. The peon was real. Drex's voice was real.

"On my way home, when within a hundred miles of the border, I was informed, never mind by whom, that a certain commodity produced in Mexico, and war metals drastically needed here, are being secretly sent to one of this country's Pacific ports, from which they are unlawfully rerouted in foreign vessels to a foreign country."

"I've suspected it. The agents whose activities were curbed for a while are getting busy again in other ways than that. This country is a superbly placed vantage ground from which to strike at the United States. There have been some American shops looted; all evidence has pointed toward Mexicans as the offenders, but I'll eat my hat if those same foreign agents aren't responsible and I intend to prove it."

"But you haven't suspected, have you, Consul, that there is someone in this city who is covering up for them? That the person or persons are linked with The Scorpions? I was told that the gang would round up that night at Casa Fresco and was asked to go there and find out, if possible, who the ring-leaders are. That'll give you an idea of what your sister and I were up against."

"Why pick on you, already in wrong with certain elements, to put your head in a noose?"

"I seemed to be Johnny-on-the-spot. My car has a two-way police radio, which would get me in touch with the Border Patrol in case of an emergency. Also, I was informed that the gang had put up a detour sign to switch travelers to its temporary hideout with a view to a holdup. I know this preamble is trying your patience, Consul, but you have to hear it to judge of what followed."

Hugh Chesney stopped his nervous pacing, leaned against the railing and packed tobacco hard into his pipe.

"My mistake, Drex. I'll stop prowling. Go on."

"After that I got in touch with a U. S. captain in the Border Patrol. We arranged that I was to walk into the trap and that he would follow, allowing time for me to get the information I was after. He followed, all right, five minutes too late."

"Then what? For God's sake go on. Just remember that I persuaded Kay to come here. I suspect she was preparing to marry Bill Hewins, a boy she's known all her life, and put him off to help me. If anything happened—"

"Nothing happened to her which can't be straightened out, so try to take it easy, Consul. To get on with the melodrama. With a few forceful remarks on the subject of detours in general and that one in particular, I walked into the smoke-filled, liquor-reeking room at Casa Fresco. My heart stopped short when I saw, leaning against the bar, disguised by a beard and dark spectacles, Señor Edouard Rafael Castello wearing the uniform of a Mexican major."

"*Castello!*"

"Not so loud, Consul. Sometimes I suspect that these stucco walls of yours have ears."

"Or had. But that's another matter. Go on. Why the uniform? He's never served in the army. Are you sure it was he?"

"I'd know that hidalgo if he had stuffed himself inside a bearskin; there's a nervous twitch of his left arm he can't control. He did his darnedest that night but it got away from him when I entered the dive and I saw it. After that he kept his left hand clenched tight round his leather belt to control the arm. He had been drinking heavily. I was sure he didn't suspect I recognized him. When, later, he spoke, he used broken English—and I mean broken—and you know that having been educated in England he speaks English perfectly with an Oxonian accent."

"It's incredible. He was exiled. Would he dare face you? Sure this isn't all a hectic dream, Drex?"

"Quite. In the present world, when real-life melodrama has fiction licked to a fare-thee-well for improbability, it isn't so unbelievable when there's a sure-fire motive behind it. To return to my three-reel thriller. I gave an order to the Mexican bartender as I had been instructed to do by my informant—the man is there in the interest of law and order, I had run into him before—and sat down at a table opposite a mirror which reflected every move in the room behind me. There were several Mexicans at the bar and a few Texans. From their manner, it was evident they were waiting for someone before starting to do a job on me.

A car stopped outside. The Captain at last! Not a minute too soon. I was getting jittery. I had my information. I could identify every cutthroat there and I would be mighty glad to get away with a whole skin and lucky at that. Imagine my horror when reflected in the mirror I saw your sister enter. I've looked at her photograph on your desk often enough to know her if I ran into her in the Antarctic. I could tell by her eyes as they met mine that she realized her peril, but there wasn't a hint of fear in her voice as she wisecracked:—

'What is this? A movie company on location?'

"My God—a movie! After that, things happened with a speed which made my head spin."

He told of what had followed to the moment when Castello had said, *Està bueno*, you have your bride, Señor Hamilton.

"Why didn't you give a false name, Drex? Then there would have been no possibility of the marriage being legal."

"A false name with Señor Edouard Rafael Castello looking on, hating me, twirling an automatic in the midst of a cutthroat gang drunk enough to carry out his orders? Spark to dynamite. Not a chance of getting away with it. Didn't dare reach for the gun in my shoulder holster for fear I'd start something which would result in injury to your sister.

I had stalled as long as I could, fervently praying that the Border Patrol Captain would appear. When Castello suggested that he would take the girl with him if I didn't marry her—I wouldn't put it past him—I chose the only safe way out for her. I knew what he was up to. Married—and securely married to an American—I would lose the estate which according to my stepfather's will, would go to him as next heir in the male line unless I married a Mexican and took the de la Cartina name before I was thirty-five *or* Chiquita marries. Simple as that."

"Sure-fire motive. You said something when you said Castello had that. I'm convinced now that the improbable thing really happened. I admit that at first I thought you were suffering from a touch of the sun."

"I wish that were all there is to it. I'm in a spot. If we ignore that cockeyed ceremony there is always blackmail. I can take it for myself but not for your sister. It will begin by innuendoes in the newssheet printed across the border, of which Castello is suspected of being the power behind the scandal gun. Much as I dislike the man, I can't believe he is that type of heel—but if a hint of the Casa Fresco marriage appears in 'Air Waves' it will be proof positive that he *is* responsible for that vicious column."

"It's outrageous. I'll have that Texan held until he proves his appointment as Justice of the Peace if he's kept a prisoner till doomsday."

"The idea is O.K., Consul, but unfortunately there's a hitch in it. I haven't let grass grow under my feet, you bet. After I left your sister that night I returned to Laredo, hunted up the Border Patrol only to find—

What? *What?*

That the alleged Texan Justice had escaped from his captors; that the dove of peace had laid the olive branch at the feet of our brave Señor Castello, that he had been released by order of his Government as soon as jailed. They've been hunting for him for weeks. He has been recalled. His estate has been returned. Already his foreign-agent pal, Von Haas, has joined him at his town house. All will be sweetness and brotherly love as long as he remains a good boy and no one knows better than he how to be good. I advised that he be forgiven before I went away. Suggested to the high-ups that it would be easier to watch him here. I didn't know then that he would be a menace to your sister."

"Castello loose hating you, with that marriage ceremony up his sleeve. Trouble plus, double plus. Does Kay know who the bearded Mexican major really is?"

"No and she mustn't at present. Without intending to she might put him wise to the fact that I recognized him and we'd never find out the truth about that Justice of the Peace. Be careful that she doesn't get a hint that you're wise to what happened. Wait for her to tell you about it."

"O.K., you're the doctor, Drex. I won't mention it until you've found out something definite. Good Lord, now that Castello is free she'll meet him socially. Have you thought of that? What's our next move?"

Hamilton's blue eyes, above the flame of his cigarette lighter, met Chesney's troubled brown ones.

"First, we'll have to outguess his game. Next, fine out whether that Justice of the Peace was real or a phoney. Tomorrow I'll start to run down the truth. After—that—*quién sabe?* If I'm a judge of the female of the species, and I am, your sister will be the toast of the town's *caballeros.*" He grinned boyishly. "You'll have to agree that I'm off to a flying start with the lady, Consul. Good morning and—good courage. I'll be seeing you."

IV

Kay and Gordon Slade deposited a disappointed, sulky Jill at the school door and drove on in his black roadster. She drew a long, ecstatic breath.

"This city with its Colonial Spanish atmosphere is like an iridescent jewel dropped into a setting of green-jade mountains. I love the pink houses. Hugh told me yesterday they were built of a sort of pumice stone. Hope you don't mind my little rave, Mr. Slade."

"For Pete's sake, don't be formal. Call me Gordon. Your rave is all right with me. If you like this part of the country wait till you see Mexico City. That's som'-pin'. There you step into the real tropics."

"Perhaps, but this place is my first love. Curious the way the streets cross at right angles. That white-uniformed policeman standing on the wooden box under the huge green umbrella doesn't appear to be overworked. Your roadster runs as if on velvet instead of a paved avenue. When I arrived at Hugh's yesterday I was fed-up with motoring, thought I never wanted to step into a car again; now I'm having the time of my young life."

"Was it a monotonous trip?"

"*No.* Not a dull moment. I stopped at different cities on my way to say hail and farewell, practically in the same breath, to college classmates, which brief visits were quite exciting. Then came Texas and later miles upon miles of oil wells looking as if an epidemic of Eiffel Towers had broken out. It was the last twenty-four hours before I reached Laredo which seemed interminable." She felt his quick look at her. "See those masses of white clouds piled high against the sky. Reminds me of the drifts after a New England blizzard."

"Anything happen in that last twenty-four hours to make you breathless when you think of it?"

She'd better watch her tongue. "What could happen on a straight highway bordered by sage and field after field of cacti, pepped up occasionally with other cars, or a great sinister bird wheeling overhead? Why relive that when we are passing these beautiful homes? I imagine they are beautiful though not much but overhanging tiled roofs, a suggestion of iron balconies are visible above those vine-covered walls. How soft and fragrant the air is. Is Drex Hamilton's town house one of these?"

"No. It is on the Avenida Madero where it joins the Plaza de la Constitución. The larger estates are in that locality."

"There must be superb gardens behind some of these walls. I would love to see them."

"Don't worry, you will. Every hostess in town will throw a party. No American girls here, only middle-aged marrieds. You'll be a sensation. The merry-go-round begins today in the late afternoon. The Smalls are entertaining. I've been training my junior to take over my work that I may devote my entire time to you. Big-hearted Gordy, that's me."

He was companionable, with a suggestion of the

glib patter of a supersalesman, and good fun, but a warning gong had sounded in her mind when her eyes met his for the first time.

"Why so thoughtful? Don't tell me you are about to spurn my devotion," Slade pleaded, in the voice of a man who was quite sure that such a lack of appreciation couldn't happen.

"Me? Spurn devotion? I adore it. But, I was thinking that there was something wrong about training that junior to take over your job, Mr. Slade. How about shouldering my brother's work from now on, that he may beau his charming sister—Kay Chesney to you —in case you're wondering."

"Wondering after that gay crack? Not a chance. I can see that you have been divinely sent to be the social dynamo of our prosy lives. Besides, even had he the leisure the Chief wouldn't go with you. He was always bored to tears by the social stuff. He has cut it out entirely since—"

"Since his wife deserted? Hugh is such a grand person. Why, oh why did she do it? Was—was there another man?"

"Little girls shouldn't ask questions."

"This little girl—just to keep the record straight, I'm twenty-three—realizes quite well that she shouldn't ask questions about his wife of anyone but her brother, but I can't bear to bring up the subject to him. His heart must be raw."

"Don't ask him about that. He doesn't know the gossip about her. At times I was tempted to warn him. I have always felt that a guy named Von Haas was giving her a rush to find out, if he could, what her husband knew of deals between the U. S. and Mexico. That's the way his country works. It puts in years of groundwork before it strikes. No contact is too small to serve a strategic purpose. I shouldn't have told you that, about the gossip, I mean."

"I made a rule long ago to break a chain of gossip when it reached me."

"Thanks a million. I know I talk too much. I'm only the glad-hand man on the Consul's staff. I may be wrong about his wife. It might not have been another man in spite of the hints in the scandalous 'Air Waves' to which I referred before. She may have been fed-up with small-town life. Your brother hates the social merry-go-round and, smart as he is, he hasn't yet been sent to any important post."

"But he will be. From the time he was a boy he has trained himself for the Foreign Service in South America. He speaks the language; can discuss the art, the music, the philosophy and culture of the Spanish peoples. Watch him climb. He'll be an ambassador sometime; that is, unless his wife's contemptible desertion hurts him."

"Cheerio, perhaps he'll find someone to take her place, a woman who likes small-town life. I can't believe there is such an animal. Sometimes I feel as if I'd go berserk and smash my way to New York. Now there's a place where there's something doing every minute."

"If you are as frustrated as your voice sounds, why do you stay here? There must be plenty of men who are working up in the service who would jump down the throat of a job like yours."

"I stay because I haven't money enough to go home and live as I want to live. Here I can save my salary and there's always hope of a chance to make a little something—Forget it. I guess I've gone loco from homesickness. Making something on the side is tabu with a capital T."

His annoyance at his admission was genuine. Had he suddenly realized that she might know of the rigid rule that no consular officer whose salary exceeded one thousand dollars a year would be permitted, while he held office, to be interested in or transact any business? Was he dabbling in "a little something" on the side? She was unfair to suspect it. Anyone might make extravagant statements when homesick. Hadn't one terrific attack her first night at college made the bottom drop out of the universe for her?

"Look here, you're not thinking of that fool remark of mine about extra money, are you, Kay?"

"Good heavens, no. I'm back to Hugh and his avoidance of society. Was his wife popular? Am I likely to meet the man whom you think was devoted to her because he was after information? It might help me if I knew what complications, social and political, I'm up against. I intend to adjust my life to this new world or perish in the attempt."

His laugh told her that she had successfully side-tracked his regret at his admission of discontent.

"You won't have to die for a cause; it wasn't that bad. Mrs. Chesney was admired and copied, she was an up-to-the-minute dresser—just not liked, get the difference? Since her departure, an American woman, Cynthia Small, wife of an oil magnate, has stepped into her shoes and boy, do they fit! Watch the Lady Small's tactics and you'll be seeing Mrs. Hugh Chesney's, with the one exception that your sister-in-law didn't try to run other people's lives. With Mrs. Small it's a passion. She unearths and broadcasts domestic scandals like a dredger turning up mud."

"Thanks for the warning. I'll cross to the other side of the street when I see her coming."

"You sound scared. Why should you be afraid of her? Any dark and dour secrets in your life?"

She swallowed the gasp which might have betrayed her. "Nary a secret. My life is an open book. That's a cliché but I couldn't think of a more brilliant comeback at the moment. Go on about Blanche and her successor."

"They're both social climbers. Wealth to their minds makes a person desirable, a title makes him or her irresistible. I figured that was the attraction Von Haas, once a baron, now plain Herr, had for your sister-in-law. Here we are in the old part of town."

The black roadster jolted through the narrow cobbled streets. There were magnificent iron *rejas* over the windows of some of the old pink houses. A whiff of incense drifted from the open door of an ancient cathedral with a filagreed bell tower; she caught a glimpse of candle flames like gold dagger-points, of kneeling black figures within. The car skimmed by the plaza, which was bordered on one side by shops, gay with serapes, curious pottery and blankets bow stripes, on the opposite by the market where of all varieties and colors was displayed in neat piles.

She sniffed. "What is that pungent smell?"

"Guavas. They sure put across their own publicity when they're on the sunny side of the market."

Through more narrow streets already hot, which were crowded with playing children and sleeping dogs. Heavily laden burros stepped cautiously among them to the accompaniment of their masters' shouted: "Aye —bur-r-o!" Good-natured vendors lifted their sombreros and pushed small carts of fruits and vegetables out of the roadster's way with a smiling, "God be with you, Señorita!"

"So this is Mexico. Even more colorful than I had pictured it. It's wonderful, Gordon. I'll never be homesick here."

"That's what *you* think. I'll remind you of that someday when you'd give your eyes to see Little Ol' New York; but it would be New England which would be your Mecca, I presume."

He stopped the car in a broader street. "Here we are. Take a load of this white-stucco building. That is where your brother and I, with a few retainers, dig and delve to help 'maintain cordial relations between two countries.' That last isn't original; it's a quote."

The walls were close to the narrow walks. High windows glinted behind iron *rejas*. Lacy balconies above were gay with flower boxes crammed with yellow, orange, flame-color blossoms and dripping with vines. Over the ornate grilled gate, a shield bore the arms of the United States. A short flag staff pointed to the blue sky. Emotion tightened Kay's throat, misted her eyes. That emblem above the door meant protection, safety, to Americans in a strange land.

"End of the route, Madam." Slade's amused voice brought her back to the present.

"Why aren't the Stars and Stripes floating above the consulate, Gordon?" she asked as a white-suited Indian swung the gate open.

"The flag is displayed only on occasions of special ceremony. I'll bet if the high-ups could see you at this minute they'd order it out pronto. If you're not something special I don't know what is. Come on in."

As they entered the general office Hugh Chesney, standing by a window, looked over the top of a paper he was studying.

"We've been seeing the town," Kay announced gaily in an effort to sidetrack his annoyance at his senior clerk's late arrival—if it were annoyance which was clouding his face. Had he news of Blanche or— A voice shot up from her subconscious:—

"Sure, crazy to marry. Right—Kay?"

Had Drex Hamilton told her brother about that hideous ceremony at Casa Fresco? He wouldn't. Hadn't he warned her not to talk?

"Kay!" The voice seemed to come from miles away. "Didn't you hear me introduce my junior clerk, Johnny Shaw?"

She held out her hand. "Forgive me, Johnny Shaw. I have seen so much in the last forty-eight hours that I'm dazed."

"I sure am proud to meet you, Ma'am." The youngster had an engaging grin, lighted by flashing dark eyes and perfect teeth. Against the dull walls of the office his hair glinted as if powdered with gold dust.

Kay returned his smile with interest. "Texan, aren't you?"

"Sure, Ma'am, an' mighty proud of it."

"That word Texas reminds me. Slade!"

The senior clerk turned from the desk where he had been rustling papers.

"Yes, Chief?"

"Here's a job for you. A Texas bad man, one of the Scorpion gang, escaped on his way to jail. It is suspected that he crossed the river above Laredo and reached this country, that he is headed this way. Some stunt if he did get across. The U. S. has increased the Border Patrol by six hundred new men because immigration and smuggling problems are increasing alarmingly."

"What—what am I to do about it, Chief?"

"Do? See that he is rounded-up if he comes within our Consular district."

"But I'm up to my ears in that other assignment you gave me. Shall I drop that?"

Hugh Chesney regarded his senior clerk thoughtfully.

"So you are, Slade, so you are. Johnny Shaw, I'll turn the Bad Man over to you."

"Gosh, I'm tickled pink. Sounds exciting, Chief. I'll find him. What did you say his name was?"

Chesney adjusted his glasses and referred to the memorandum in his hand.

"Joe, just Joe, not much to go on, but he claims he's a Justice of the Peace."

V

"Did you speak, Kay? Come into my office." Hugh Chesney opened the door of a room where long windows framed glimpses of a colorful patio.

She hadn't spoken; how could she when the name "Joe" had tightened her throat like a vise. Did Hugh know of that crazy marriage ceremony? If he did he would have to bring up the subject first. Hadn't she promised Drex Hamilton that she would not speak of it?

"Did I make a sound, Hugh? Was it a sort of groan? It's a wonder I don't make more of them. I've driven so many miles since I left home that every little while I feel the motion of that darn car and my head spins like a top. All right now."

He dropped the paper he still held to his desk before he closed the door which led to the general office.

"You wrote that you needed my help with Jill," she reminded. "On our way here yesterday when I asked what I could do you answered: 'Wait until you see her.' I've seen her. I think she's a grand person in embryo and here I am ready to do anything I can for you both."

"Thanks, Kay, you always were a dependable dear." He cleared his emotion-roughened voice. "Sit in that chair at the desk opposite mine and relax. Since the moment I met you on Mexican soil I've felt that your nerves are taut with excitement. I hope I haven't thrown sand into the gears of your life by bringing you here."

Had he? Only time could answer that question. Was he giving her another chance to confide her experience at Casa Fresco? Not yet.

"Aren't we all tense, Hugh, when we realize the shattering realities in the world with which we have to reckon? But no American can permit himself to get jittery now. Hysteria is the subversive element's meat." She leaned back in the chair and held out two slender hands with rosy nails.

"See? They're steady. Do they look as if you had upset my life, as if I were on the verge of a nervous breakdown? I'm not a tender flower but I admit that though the long solo motor trip was exciting it had also its occasional blood-chilling moments. However, at this minute I'm as relaxed and spineless as a jellyfish washed up by the tide. Let's get down to cases and talk about Jill."

Beyond the open door and windows behind him, flowers glowed like many-colored jewels in the border of the sunny patio. A bright-winged bird in a split-cane cage chattered softly; a fountain somewhere out of sight tinkled and splashed rhythmically.

"Jill's mother left me six months ago," Hugh Chesney admitted gruffly, "she said forever. Her lawyer started divorce proceedings immediately. I would have contested if my wife had wanted Jill—she didn't—or had I thought it would do any good—a broken marriage is a tragedy for a child—but I knew it would be useless. That disposes of that subject.

"Since Blanche left I've tried to carry on but as the weeks passed I've realized more and more that a father isn't enough for a girl of Jill's age, that she desperately needs the companionship and guidance of a woman who cares. My own sister Sally, she's your step-sister too, is trying to get home from the Balkans. As soon as she reaches Washington she wants Jill; she will give her a wonderful home, love and devotion. It has been intimated that I may be transferred to the nation's capital. Meanwhile, Jill is unhappy. Verbena is devoted to her but that isn't enough. Do you get what I mean?"

"Yes, Hugh. Go on."

"The child is unhappy about herself. From having, I quote, a brilliant and extraordinarily beautiful mother, end quote, she has acquired an acute inferiority complex. Also, Blanche firmly implanted in her daughter's mind the belief that she was plain and uninteresting."

"How cruel!" Kay curbed her tongue. This wasn't the psychological moment in which to express her indignant views about wives who deserted.

"I understand, Hugh. This morning I overheard Jill talking to Verbena. She hates her pigtails. She is one hundred per cent right. Smart as they are on some children they are too harsh for her spectacled face till it grows up to her beautiful but, at the present moment, enormous white teeth. Her hair should be cut to frame it softly."

"Have it done. Do anything that will give her confidence in herself. She admires you tremendously. I'll leave her entirely to you. It's a lot of responsibility to load on your young shoulders but it may not be for long. At any moment I may hear that Sally has reached this country."

"I'm used to responsibility. Haven't I had it all my life? Mother wouldn't decide the most trifling matter for herself. I only hope that making decisions hasn't become such a habit that when I marry I'll be accused of bossing my husband."

Her breath caught . . . Marry. Perhaps she was married now.

"You've led up to the very subject I wanted to discuss with you, Kay. I don't mean to pry into the secrets of your love life—" it was heart-warming to see the old sparkle of laughter in his eyes—"but I would

feel relieved if I were sure I had not broken up marriage plans between you and Bill Hewins by asking you
to come here to help me out."

Had he? That was another question only time
could answer.

"You haven't. I was glad of an excuse to break
away, to go where I could take a long-distance view
of what life with Bill would mean. We've lived on the
same street for years; I've been his girl but not in a
deeply sentimental way; our kisses have been restricted
to birthdays and Christmas."

"That's what I'd call a tepid romance."

"Go on, laugh, I can see your lips twitching. Tepid is the word. Those kisses left me quite cold. Perhaps kisses always will. Perhaps I'm made that way.
I decided that I'd better STOP! LOOK! LISTEN! to be
sure that what I felt for Bill was the until-death-do-us-
part sort of love which is the only real build-up for
marriage. I don't expect married life to flow on without
a ripple of disagreement, but I do hope that mine,
when or if it comes, will be founded on ideals and ideas
that will keep it from going on the rocks. Perhaps that's
only an iridescent dream."

"Some dreams come true. Why shouldn't yours?"

"I intend to work to make it. Bill has been ordered
to a Texas camp. He'll have a chance to think also.
Am I right?"

"One hundred per cent. The fact that you're so
cold-blooded about it proves to me that you haven't
yet known love in all its depth and complexity and
boy, is it complex!"

He straightened his shoulders.

"Now I can thoroughly enjoy having you here.
No guilty conscience nagging. Unless you have something more to tell me——" His pause made Kay think
of the awful stillness at a wedding ceremony after the
clergyman's "If anyone knows just cause why this man,
etc. etc.——"

"That's the story for today. Any charge for this
consultation?"

"It's all in the family. You'd better get home before the heat increases. One of the clerks will drive

you out. I need Slade here. Want you looking your swankest at the jamboree this afternoon. The family reputation for beauty must be upheld."

There was a hint of his old lightheartedness in his voice. If only he would make an effort at normal living, see his friends, it would help him to be happier.

"I'll do my best, Hugh. You may not believe it, but I'm a bit jittery over my social debut. I read Spanish better than I speak it. I presume I'll meet a number of Mexicans who don't understand English."

"All educated Mexicans understand and speak it. The Germans speak Spanish as well as English, fluently. That's where they have the bulge on Americans."

"Just the same I feel the need of moral support. You wouldn't come along and help a frightened female keep up her courage, would you?"

He looked down at the paper on his desk and then at her. What thoughts were moving up behind his brown eyes?

"I'll go. You're right. A beauty in the family is a responsibility. Perhaps if I hadn't shirked society before—never mind that. I'm turning over a new leaf. I'll be home in time to drive you to the Smalls'."

"Sure it won't bore you?"

"Quite sure. I'll take it and like it."

Kay remembered the determination in her brother's voice as dressed in white from head to foot, in the late afternoon, in a garden beautiful with flowers, musical with the lament of guitars, she saw him standing beside a distinguished dark-haired woman. She was undoubtedly Mexican. He appeared not only taking, but liking, his return to the social world.

"With whom is my brother talking, Mrs. Small? She's adorable in that yellow frock and hat," Kay inquired of her hostess, a beautiful if slightly overblown blonde in an azure costume which was the exact tint of her eyes. The woman squinted through a *lorgnon*. Her laugh tinkled.

"One would know you had but recently arrived, my dear. That is the glamorous Señorita Amelia Mansilla. Old Castilian family. Patronizes us Americans, all but the men, but she comes to our parties. Poor as a church mouse; her ancient hacienda is practically going to seed but she won't sell—I know because my husband tried to buy it. She must make a rich marriage."

She confided behind a jeweled hand: "My dear, they tell me that sometimes she doesn't have enough to eat. The American Colony thought she had Drex Hamilton securely hooked—I've done everything in my power to make a match there—but at the ball at the Club last night he spoke to her only once."

Kay remembered that Gordon Slade had said that Mrs. Small's desire to run the lives of others amounted to a passion. She felt as if she had been exposed to poison gas and filled her lungs with the gardenia-scented air. She watched the flight of a flock of migrant birds, brilliantly splashed with crimson and gold from the glow of the setting sun, until they were mere dots above the blue lake. Her eyes and attention returned to her hostess as she confided:—

"We were all on the *qui vive* because we had expected the announcement of an engagement between them when Drex returned from the States. Here comes Herr Von Haas. My *dear*, he was your sister-in-law's ..." Raised shoulders finished the sentence.

Kay ignored the implication and watched the man approaching. . . . Tall. Straight. Military in impeccable afternoon clothes. Hair so short, smooth and light it shone like a silver-gilt cap. His slightly inflated chest made her long to stick it with a hatpin to see if it would collapse like a punctured balloon. A monocle was screwed over one of his pale eyes, eyes which did not change in expression even when his lips smiled in response to the introduction of his hostess. As he bent over her hand a mad suggestion flashed through Kay's mind. Suppose she encouraged him to like her? Suppose he tried to get information from her; could she block his underground activities?

"We have been looking forward to this moment for weeks, Miss Chesney. Your publicity agent has failed to do you justice." The rather thick voice was without a trace of accent.

"Oh, I warned him to understate," she responded gaily. "I wanted my personality to make a splash, Herr

Von Haas. Do tell me that you think it has." The hint of mockery in her voice brought his cold, inscrutable eyes to hers.

"You are laughing at me. I shall have to do something about that. I—"

"My dear," Mrs. Small interrupted the suave voice, "your brother is bringing the Señorita here to meet you. Handsome man. Pity his good looks couldn't hold that wife of his." She smiled with arch meaning at Von Haas. "Don't let the haughty Castilian patronize you, my dear; she'll try it."

Having caused a sinister narrowing of the man's eyes and shot a dart designed to spread aversion in the girl's mind, she drifted away to greet arriving guests.

"Our hostess has a nice sense of humor." In such a voice and inflection Von Haas might have ordered a victim to a concentration camp.

"Kay, Señorita Mansilla wants to meet you. How are you, Von Haas?"

Something in her brother's voice as he spoke the name, something in his eyes as he looked at the man, sent a creepy chill through Kay. Was it possible that he was not as ignorant of the gossip about his wife as Gordon had thought?

"Now I know that all your brother's praise of you is true, Miss Chesney." The charming Spanish voice sidetracked her panicky reflection. "Only he hasn't made it colorful enough."

"You see, I am not the only one who has fallen a victim to your charm," Von Haas reminded smoothly before he walked away.

Kay's eyes met the smiling dark eyes of Señorita Mansilla in which lurked no trace of patronage. She was lovely. She was likable. No wonder the men of the American Colony admired her and Mexican *caballeros* adored her.

"Hugh sees me with big-brother eyes, Señorita. He feels it his duty to keep my feet on the ground. He ought to approve of me; I've been brought up in the way he thinks I should go."

"We've been looking all over the place for you people," announced a voice which picked up Kay's heart and plunged it into a nose dive. Now what? Hamilton in white and a beautiful dark-haired girl in filmy turquoise-blue joined the group.

"Drex! I thought you were through with the social merry-go-round. How did you persuade him to come, Chiquita?" Señorita Mansilla turned to Kay. "It may be that you have not yet met Señorita Mercedes de la Cartina and her brother, Miss Chesney."

"Miss Chesney and I breakfasted together this morning at the Consul's but Mercedes, Chiquita to you, came for the express purpose of meeting her," Hamilton answered while Kay was thinking of something to say.

"How could I stay away? Your brother has been beating the tom-tom for you for weeks, Miss Chesney. I wouldn't have lived up to the reputation of my sex if I hadn't been intensely interested."

Kay liked Chiquita de la Cartina at once and thoroughly. Liked her voice, her beautiful eyes, her sparkle.

"Modesty forbids my asking if I measure up to specifications so suppose we pause here for station identification," she countered gaily.

"That comeback gets you off to a flying start." It was the first time Kay had heard her brother really laugh since her arrival. "How about a cold drink, Señorita Mansilla? I detected the tinkle of ice as I passed a marquee."

"I would love it. Drex, did you get the address I wanted of that *couturier* in New York?"

"I did. I have it here. Will you take it now?" He raised his right hand to his breast pocket.

"Drex! Where is your ring? You haven't lost it? For years I've never seen him without that ring, Miss Chesney. His stepfather gave it to him and he has always claimed it brought him luck."

Kay felt the slow blood mount to her hair. That ring was in the bottom of the white bag in her hand. She had brought it hoping there might be a chance of returning it to its owner. If she could get it out of her possession it might help her forget the circumstances under which she had acquired it.

"My ring?" Hamilton smilingly regarded his hand.

"Hung up for repairs. Stone was loose. I don't have to wear it to bring luck. I believe that wherever it is it will do its stuff."

"You still have faith in your lucky star, Hamilton?" observed a smooth voice behind them.

"You!" Señorita Mansilla's frightened eyes swept from the man in white, undoubtedly a Mexican, with a red camellia in his lapel and a broad-brimmed panama in his left hand, to Hamilton. Señorita de la Cartina slipped her hand within her brother's arm. "Where—when—"

The Mexican's brilliant dark eyes narrowed; his red lips below the thin mouth curved in a sarcastic line.

"Amelia *mía,* why the surprise?" Kay was disappointed that his smooth voice lacked an accent. He was the Spanish-grandee type; why didn't he speak in character? "Chiquita, *carissima.*" He pressed his lips to the girl's reluctantly extended hand before he released it.

"Have none of you heard that I am no longer an exile? That my estates have been returned to me for the duration of good behavior? Greeting, Consul. The same to you, Drex." His eyes rested on Kay, then flashed in speechless demand to her brother. Hugh Chesney's voice was gruff, as if reluctant to perform the introduction being forced on him.

"Kay, Señor Edouard Rafael Castello."

VI

"Oh, Miss Chesney." Slightly breathless their hostess joined the group. "I'm too late. You and Señor Castello have met. He begged to be presented. You should feel honored. He is an F.F.V. in our little community, isn't he, Mr. Consul? F.F.V., First Family of Virginia to you, Señor."

Hugh's response to her giggle was gruff to rudeness. Allowing for the fact that Mrs. Small's archness was a trifle more disturbing than her venom he needn't take her so seriously.

"Our hostess is mistaken, Miss Chesney. It is I who am honored," Señor Castello corrected and pressed his lips to Kay's hand.

"I'm not a bit overwhelmed by your F.F.V., Señor Castello. In fact I was about to suggest that we find a cool drink together. I've said 'How do you do?'—or 'It's a pleasure to meet you'—so many times my throat is parched."

It wasn't, but she had to say or do something to break up the ice forming on the wings of conversation. Chiquita de la Cartina was definitely hostile to the suave Mexican. Hugh and Drex Hamilton stood as if turned to stone and Señorita Mansilla was obviously frightened. No wonder; hadn't Gordon Slade said that he had been jealous of Hamilton, that he was about to order pistols for two when he had to leave the country?

"Your wish is my law, Miss Chesney. Shall we go? There is dancing on the terrace. May I have the pleasure after we have cooled that parched throat?"

"I'd love it. I hope the two *señoritas* will forgive me for appropriating the returned native so highhandedly," she said as they walked toward the low-spreading pink house.

"I am out of favor both with my cousin Amelia Mansilla and Señorita de la Cartina. I have been opposed to the present Government. They are idealists, old-fashioned, not modern. They make no allowance for the action of a man whose world is in upheaval."

"Perhaps they just expect loyalty and patriotism. This is the time to hold fast to both. I believe that in the end spiritual and moral values will count above all others in this crisis. Whose world isn't in upheaval now?"

His brilliant eyes between narrowed lids met hers.

"There should not be bitterness in so charming a voice. I hope that yours isn't."

"My world! It's a great big glistening globe of happiness. That wail was a generalization." She re-

garded him with amused friendliness. "You're the second surprise I've had since I arrived in this adorable
garden."

"Surprise!"

Why should her harmless statement startle him?
Perhaps a man recently returned from exile would be
jumpy.

"Yes. I had expected that old-time residents like
you, that adorable Chiquita and Señorita Mansilla—they
are two of the loveliest girls I've ever seen—would
speak broken English; for instance, 'Señorita eet mak
me sad to—' "

Fright stopped her heart, then sent it pounding on.
Those were the words of that demonic major at Casa
Fresco. Were they burned into her mind?

"You are ribbing me, aren't you, Miss Chesney?"
His laugh was as smooth as his voice. "Why should
we speak broken English? I was educated in England.
Chiquita's mother was an American and Amelia had
an English governess from childhood. There are many
anglophiles in this country. I can speak to you in English, in Spanish, but I wouldn't be good at mixing
them. You must learn the language of Mexico."

"I understand that there are fifty or more. Which
one would you advise? I can read Spanish and understand it fairly well, but I can't speak it fluently because
I have had no practice. Give me time. I arrived yesterday. Only yesterday? It seems years ago. Already I love
the place. I've read heaps of confessions about what it
means to be an Italian or an Armenian, Jew or Norwe-
gian in a strange country. I'm keeping a journal to record my experiences and impressions. It won't be long
before I'll be writing of what it means to be a New
Englander in Mexico, one descended in a straight line
from Lexington, Concord and Bunker Hill patriots."

"*Bravo! Bravo!* I have met many charming Americans but you combine beauty and brains. Shall we
dance?"

He appeared serenely unaware of the curious eyes
on him, of the whispered comments as they wove in
and out among other couples on the terrace. Kay

wished that he had not singled her out for his attention on the very day of his return from exile. A hand descended on his shoulder. A voice said:—

"Cut."

Castello's arm about her stiffened.

"I protest. We have just commenced to dance, Hamilton."

"I don't wonder that the time seemed short, Edouard, but you've had two dances. Even the Prodigal Son on the day of his return can't be allowed to monopolize the guest of honor. That's not original. I'm quoting our hostess. She wants you."

"In that case . . ." Castello released Kay. Before he turned away she saw a flash of sinister amusement in his eyes.

The musicians were playing "Night and Day." Drex Hamilton was even a better dancer than her recent partner and she had thought he left nothing to be desired.

"I want to talk to you. Come out." He led her down the terrace steps, along a palm-bordered path, down and down to a pink-stone seat so near the lake that the soft *lap, lap* of the water was audible.

"Sit in front of these shrubs. Every man here will be after you if you're seen. Von Haas was on the hunt. I sent him in the wrong direction. I presume you know that already you're the smash hit of the party. Smoke?"

"No thank you."

He opened the gold case he had taken from his pocket and snapped it shut.

"What did Castello have to offer conversationally?"

"Oh, the usual patter suited to a 'smash hit,' pepped up a bit by the Latin temperament." Was that all he had to say to her after that melodramatic act —which so easily might have turned to tragedy—they had put on together?

"You're a temperamental person, aren't you? You resented my not plunging at once into reminiscences, didn't you? Just a minute—" he held up a protesting hand as her lips flew open on an indignant retort — "I'm leading up to it. We'll skip Castello's 'patter.' What did you think of the returned exile?"

"Sartorially splendid. That queer twitch of his left arm would get on my nerves if I saw him often. A little on the movie-heartthrob, male-lead side, but entertaining. Does that answer your question, Mr. Hamilton?"

He turned the cigarette case over in his hand as if considering his reply, slipped it into his pocket and met her eyes.

"Did he remind you of anyone you had met before?"

"No. He's my first F.F.V. of Mexico and just my idea of what a modern Spanish grandee would be like. Why did you ask? You're not listening to me."

"I am; if not to your words, to your voice. Don't like the touch of frost in it when addressed to me. It's evident that we've started off on the wrong foot. You were angry with me this morning at breakfast. We've got to hold together until this mess is straightened out."

"You implied that I was 'brainless.' "

"Sorry. You know you're not, so why should what I said trouble you? My nerves were still shot from the horror of seeing you walk into that nest of cutthroats. Believe me?"

It would be difficult not to believe him with his clear eyes probing hers and that catch in his husky voice. She nodded.

"Yes. You're a supersalesman. I'm sold."

"Going to trust me?"

"Yes. 'Peace in our time—for the duration.' "

"All right. Shake on it." He pressed the hand she offered and released it.

"Now that our friendship pact has been signed on the dotted line—it's my turn to say I'm sorry," she admitted. "I understand now what you meant when you said that ceremony might prove a 'horror' to you. I didn't know then about you and—and Señorita Mansilla."

"What do you know now?" The hint of amusement in his voice sent the warm color to her cheeks.

"Only what everyone knows. That you and Señor Castello both wanted her and you *got* her."

"I never knew before that eyes soft as brown-velvet pansies could flame. Why should you be indignant because I'm interested in what the gossips are saying? I've something to tell you." There was no hint of laughter in his voice or eyes as he added: "That alleged Justice of the Peace is loose."

"I know it. I heard Hugh tell one of the clerks to watch for him. What do we do now?"

"There is nothing for you to do but trust me. I've put spotters on his trail but I can't wait for them. I'm going all out to get him myself. As soon as we know where he came from I will check up on that Justice's appointment. Even if it were true that he had one, if he's moved about a lot he has probably neglected to have his commission renewed. In that case, the marriage ceremony will be null and void."

"What a relief! You—you don't *know!* I've tried to push it out of my mind—but—but—every little while the memory of that phoney marriage jumps out at me like a highwayman lying in wait behind a t—tree. It's—it's been like living in a horrible nightmare."

"Because of Bill Hewins?"

"Who told you about him?"

"Steady, don't get indignant again. Your brother. He's troubled. He fears that by telling you he needed you he may have upset your plans. Had you set the date of your marriage?"

"No. *No.* Nothing so definite as that." Laughter flashed in her eyes. "We—you and I—seem to be in the same boat—about our matrimonial prospects, I mean."

"That's all right with me. Just remember this. If we pull together we'll keep the tricky tub afloat. If not—"

"That shrug of yours portends all sorts of disaster." The lightness of her voice reflected her rising spirits. After all, if he didn't take the mix-up seriously, why should she? "If keeping afloat means pulling together, I'm right beside you, Skipper. Now, having settled our problems, let's return to the party." She picked up the bag from the seat.

"This reminds me. Just a minute! I forgot. I brought something in case I saw you." She fumbled in the bag, then extended her hand with his ring in the palm.

"I almost had heart failure when Señorita Mansilla noticed you weren't wearing it. I hear voices. Take it. Quick!"

"Put it on."

She slipped it on his finger.

"It's safe. Thank heaven! It is about two sizes too large for me, it's a wonder I didn't lose it that—that awful night. It's been fairly burning a hole in my bag. Now you'll get your luck back."

"Where do you get that *back* stuff? I know now that the ring has been on the job every minute. Here comes Von Haas. He's tracked you down!"

"Don't you like him?"

"No. He's a mineralogist by profession, also a shrewd operative for his Government. He's here to make contacts—he had Castello tied up tight before his exile —with men who have political grievances, men in all kinds of jobs who will be of strategic importance when he gets the signal from his boss to turn on the heat."

"That's practically what Gordon said."

"You mean *Slade?*"

"Yes. Why the surprise?"

"I just hadn't thought of your brother's senior clerk as realizing the undercurrent. I'll have to readjust my estimate of him. Nothing of all this to Von Haas remember, and beware the press, my child."

"I presume you mean Señor Castello?"

"Castello a newspaperman? Where'd you get that crazy idea?"

"Gordon Slade told me he was suspected of editing a gossip column. A scandalous one, at that."

"Don't believe all you hear in this country."

"You do think I'm stupid, don't you?"

"I think you're—continued in the next installment.

After all, why not finish now? Let's bolt for the garden and give Von Haas the air while I tell you what I think of you."

"Thanks, I'd rather stay. The man is interesting. Something tells me I'm going to like him immensely."

For an instant he stared at her as if he couldn't believe his ears, then laughed and bowed ceremoniously.

"If that's the case I'm just a spare tire. Good-by."

She watched him walk away, a little catch in her throat. When she was with him she felt safe, secure—at other times she felt as an animal might wandering in a country it knew to be beset with traps. "Beware the press, my child." Against whom had he warned her if not Señor Castello? Von Haas was "a shrewd operative for his Government." Perhaps her scheme to make friends with the man who had been devoted to her sister-in-law wouldn't prove to have been such an inspiration after all.

VII

"You're a knockout in white. Your hair glints like copper below that turban. How's this for 'atmosphere'?" Gordon Slade inquired and smiled at Kay across the small table. "Like it, don't you? You have speaking eyes."

"How could I help liking this?" She glanced around the Cantina, which was like a large, candle-lighted kitchen bordered with great bubbling caldrons of food, which dispensed innumerable tempting odors. "It smells delicious. Are those people tasting what's cooking?"

"Sure, that's how you know what you want to order. You sample the stuff in the *cazuelos,* make your choices, hail a waiter and tell him. Come on."

They made the rounds sniffing, tasting and pointing out to the man at their heels the steaming caldrons whose contents pleased them. Musicians in pajamalike red trousers, white shirts, black jackets, and gorgeously embroidered serapes, strolled about strumming guitars, knuckling castanets and singing songs in the chorus of which the patrons joined.

Every table in the dimly lighted place was full by the time Kay leaned back in her chair with a sigh of repletion.

"Miguel—I gathered that is our waiter's name— did himself proud. Such sauces, Gordon. Slightly on the burn-the-roof-off-your-mouth side, but delicious. I've never tasted anything like them. I don't wonder this Cantina is crowded."

"Even with the world in a mess we have to eat. Why not eat the best and you get the best in this joint? You're apt to see big shots here, the ace foreign agents tightening friendships; writers, musicians, artists—that type. The man at the center table, entirely surrounded by gals, wrote last year's top-selling novel. Don't remember the title."

"I know the book you mean. I liked it. He's putting on the comic-cut-up act. His color is rivaling the red, red rose. In his case an author should be read and not seen. I adore watching people. The customers seem mostly native with a generous sprinkling of tourists. I've been with Hugh two weeks and I still feel as if I were in a dream. What are they playing now?"

"The prelude of a song of the mountaineers. If he's here, I'll bet Von Haas will sing it. I hate the guy, he's so darn domineering, but I hand it to his baritone. There he goes."

The beauty of the passionate voice tightened Kay's throat. She watched the tall singer whose hair was like a smooth silver-gilt cap, paid fervent tribute to his technique as he reached a perilously high note with ease and trailed off to a low, rich finale. Voices joined in the chorus. Then came silence and the singer began to speak in Spanish.

"Mis amigos." She knew those words but followed the others with difficulty. When he stopped talking she whispered:—

"Gordon, tell me quickly the gist of what he said."

He translated in a low voice: "That Great Britain is washed up; that his country is the greatest friend Mexico has; that the U. S. is its enemy, waiting for a chance to annex it by force if necessary."

Her brother's words flashed like a neon sign in Kay's memory.

"One of my jobs is to prove that the United States is sincere in its desire and determination to be a friendly neighbor."

Von Haas was trying to undo Hugh's work and he wasn't here to reply. Her eyes swept over the room. Wasn't there an American present to stand up for the good old U. S.? She would. She jumped to her feet.

"It isn't true what he has told you. It's a reflection on your national dignity." To her excited fancy her voice rang through the startled silence. "Use your judgment, not your emotions when you listen to him. The United States is your friend. You know her sympathy is wide as the world. You know that all the time she is working to cement closer cultural and economic relations between these two countries that neighboring peoples may live together in sanity and peace. We need your friendship. You need ours. Don't believe this man. Don't take his Government's money. As for our intention to annex Mexico, it's absurd. Much as we like you, we don't want to take on your problems. Would you want to tackle ours? I bet you wouldn't. We are both working for hemisphere solidarity. One America." A song rose from her heart to her lips:—

> "America, America,
> God shed his grace on thee,
> And crown thy good with brotherhood
> From sea to shining sea."

Voices joined fervently in the chorus. As the song ended the thunder of applause startled her. The room rang with shouts of *"Más! Más!* More! More!"

She sank low in her seat with a frightened desire to hide under the table. How had she dared meddle with international affairs? She met Slade's eyes burning in his white face and paraphrased sarcastically:—

"She sails into trouble with the greatest of ease, this daring young gal on the international trapeze. Have I done something terrible, Gordon? Will it hurt Hugh?"

"It won't hurt your brother. Join in this song, quick. It's the Mexican 'Home Sweet Home.' "

Kay sang the sad and lovely music with her heart in her voice. Whichever way she turned, dark, friendly eyes met hers. Would the song last forever? She must get away. Von Haas might speak to her.

"Let's go, Gordon," she whispered. He nodded and pulled her white wrap over her shoulders.

The man who had waited on them returned to the table. His eyes shone like black diamonds in his pale-golden skin.

"Señor Slade?"

"Yes. What do you want?"

Eager as she was to escape Kay resented Gordon's irritation. He needn't have snapped at the poor man who probably was carrying out orders.

"A message for you, Señor." He laid a soiled slip of paper on the table. Slade scowled at it.

"What the devil— Look here, Miguel, go back and tell him I can't come now. I'm leaving at once."

"*Sí, Señor*. I go."

"If the message is important don't mind me, Gordon. I'll sit here and hope that no one will recognize me. If anyone speaks to me I'll freeze him or her—"

The waiter returned. "Señor. He say you much better come."

"Oh, all right! All right." Slade rose impatiently. "Excuse me, Kay. I won't be gone any time at all." He dropped a silver case to the table. "I know you don't smoke but you're the only woman here who hasn't a cigarette in her hand or mouth. Pretend. You'll be less conspicuous. Your brother would skin me alive if he knew I left you alone but, gosh, I can't help it."

"Don't worry, Gordon. I'll slip out to the car."

"That's an idea. Make it snappy. Where is the guy, Miguel?"

"Thees way, Señor."

Slade strode after the waiter, resentment in the set

of his shoulders. Kay located the door by which they left. She could make that quickly.

"What good fortune to find you here, Miss Chesney."

Castello . . . She sank back in her chair. With a man at the table she would no longer be conspicuous. Hunting for Gordon's car among the many outside wouldn't be easy. She would stay here until his return.

"Good fortune for me, Señor. I am fascinated by the place."

In white evening clothes, which accentuated the clarity of his bronzed skin, the brilliance of his dark eyes, he was extraordinarily good-looking. During the last two weeks they had met often. Each time something about him had puzzled and repelled her.

"You're not alone?" He was all Latin in his shocked inquiry.

Had she outraged his sense of propriety by her speech and song? "Of course not. Gordon Slade, my brother's senior clerk, was called away for a moment."

"With your permission, Miss Chesney." He seated himself in the chair Slade had occupied. "May I order for you? A glass of wine?"

"No thanks." No need to explain that she didn't drink. "I won't taste anything that will dim the memory of those delectable sauces."

She might have saved her breath. He hadn't heard her. He was rising to bow to a woman and man who were passing. Had she imagined it or had the woman turned a disdainful shoulder? The nostrils of his clean-cut nose were pinched as he sat down. Her tense nerves relaxed. Evidently he intended to ignore her patriotic outbreak.

"There is no real political truce in this country." His voice matched his bitter eyes. "Pardon me, you were telling me that you liked the sauces here. If you and your brother will do me the honor to dine at my home I will give you a dinner that is Mexican from start to finish. What is there in what I said to make you smile?"

"Nothing in what you said, Señor Castello; it was

the way you said it. You may have learned English words in England but your way of using them, your inflection, is pure Spanish. That isn't a criticism. It's a compliment."

"Thank you. But I cannot understand why I do not speak like any of your compatriots. Your brother, Hamilton, for instance. By the way, I understand he has returned to the ranch?"

It was more a question than a statement. She couldn't answer it. Drex had dropped out of her world. She hadn't heard from him. Didn't he realize that she was on tenterhooks to know what he had discovered about Texas Joe?

"That's why we haven't seen him since the garden party at Mrs. Small's two weeks ago. Two weeks! It seems a year since I arrived at my brother's house terribly fed-up with my motor trip."

"Does that mean that it was too exciting or too boring?"

"Boring! Not for a minute. It was thrilling in spots. I was out for adventure and I got it."

Something in his eyes—was it a dilation of the pupils—sent memory rushing over her in a searing tide. It was almost as if he were willing her to tell what had happened at Casa Fresco. "Beware the press, my child." Drex Hamilton's warning echoed through her memory.

"Something tells me that romance was mixed with that adventure. Am I right, Miss Chesney?"

"Romance! Not a shred, Señor Castello." She had the breathless sense of having drawn back from the brink of a precipice. Would she have told him in another instant? *No* . . . She couldn't be such a dumbbell.

"My compliments to you, Miss Chesney. You are a valiant opponent." It was Von Haas' too-smooth voice, Von Haas' tall figure looming above them which brought the man beside her to his feet. "We would like her to be on our side, eh, Edouard?"

She knew by the color which darkened Castello's face that he was furiously angry at that "our side."

"Sorry, I'm already engaged on the other," she responded lightly to avert a quarrel. "Here's Mr. Slade at last. Conference over, Gordon? Señor Castello has kept me company during your absence and Herr Von Haas has been kind enough to forgive my interruption of his speech. Of course you three have met before?" Gordon Slade appeared constrained and awkward. The Mexican deftly took control of the situation.

"I have not had the pleasure of meeting the American Consul's senior clerk, Miss Chesney. I have been out of the country. With your brother's consent I will see you at my home soon. Von Haas, shall we go? Goodnight."

Kay's eyes followed the two men as they wove in and out among the tables to the exit, came back to Slade.

"Señor Castello's voice has me worried, Gordon. I chase it round in my mind trying to tie it up with some person I've met. Ever have that experience?"

"You bet. Think over the Spaniards and Mexicans in movies you've seen and you'll find the missing link, quick."

"Of course. Stupid of me not to think of it myself. Did you find the man who sent for you?"

"Sure. It was—an American. He got caught in a street row between two clashing political factions, cracked a few heads on his own and needed help. Let's get out. I see some people coming this way, all set to talk to you about that monologue of yours, I'll bet."

"Let's hurry."

In the black roadster she looked up at the sequined sky. "The stars seem very near and friendly here. About that tourist in trouble, Gordon. Why did he come to the Cantina? Why not go to the Consulate?"

"I dunno, unless someone who knows me told him I was there. Forget it. I don't like to be followed up by business out of office." He passed his hand across his forehead as if realizing that annoyance had furrowed deep lines. "Still keen about Mexico?"

"Mad about it except that—"

"Except what?"

"I feel useless. Shut off the radio, please. I can't think above that boogie-woogie music. At home, where the effort of every individual counts, there is much I can do and opportunities to help in Defense training are increasing daily. Here, Hugh's home runs as if on greased wheels. Nothing to do in the house but to arrange flowers—I adore that—and be a pal to Jill. That's easy and I love it. Perhaps my sense of uselessness caused that rush of patriotism to the brain in the Cantina.

> "For Satan finds some mischief still
> For idle hands to do,"

she chanted. "I shudder to think what Hugh will say when he hears of my outburst."

"Did Castello speak of it?"

"No. I wondered why."

"Perhaps he didn't come in until after your reply to Von Haas. It was a dangerous thing for you to do, for yourself, I mean. The Lord only knows what you've started."

"Danger for me? That's a cheerful thought. Would anyone here dare touch an American citizen?"

"Forget it. I didn't mean to scare you. To get back to your 'uselessness.' Your brother needs a secretary the worst way. He won't employ one. Contends that in these ticklish times it's wiser to keep everything under his hat. It happened that while his wife was here important bits of information leaked out."

"You don't think that Blanche—"

"I don't think anything. I'm suggesting that you ask for the job and help ease the strain on him. I've done a little preliminary spadework. Told him he ought to have help. You pulled a trick when you had those pigtails of Jill's chopped off. Prickly youngster. I called her 'Nettles.' She hates me like poison."

"You're a quick-change artist when it comes to conversation, aren't you? It will take me a minute to jump from Hugh to Jill. She's sensitive and you tease her."

"So does Hamilton but she'd let him walk on her. By the way, he's back in town. I'll bet his sister is relieved."

"She's adorable. It was a case of love at first sight with me. Tell me about her."

"That Señorita is a little bit of all right. She is trying desperately to make Mexico rise to its opportunities. In looks she takes after her father. Educated in a convent, she was brought up in his religion. Mother and son kept to theirs. Curiously enough Drex and she carry on together as smoothly as the two blades of a pair of shears."

"Why not? They believe in the same great truths only they follow them by different routes. How cool and delicious the air is after the shower this afternoon. Let's drive through the old part. The streets are so gay with families laughing, singing and dancing."

"Too late."

"Too late for you? I didn't know you ever slept, Gordon. You're the white-haired boy of so many hostesses."

"Your arrival changed that. The Chief has gone social. I'm now domiciled at the Consulate and supposed to be Johnny-on-the-spot at all hours, which between one problem and another means plenty of headaches. Here we are at your brother's house."

Kay stood for a moment looking down at the lake. "Feel the breeze. It's a heavenly spot. I'm glad Hugh is not obliged to live in town in that narrow, somewhat smelly street. Had I better tell him that I waved the Stars and Stripes—figuratively speaking—at the Cantina or will it worry him?"

"Don't tell him tonight. It might keep him awake. He hasn't been sleeping any too well since his wife started the divorce action. He'll hear of it in the morning; then you can explain."

"I'd like to get it off my conscience tonight. I'm that selfish. Will you come in?"

"No, thanks. Have to get back to the old grind. Told the American guy who got caught in the street brawl to meet me at the office."

With one foot on the running board of the roadster, he turned. "Don't say anything to the Consul about my appointment for tonight, Kay. I'd like to carry this piece of business through myself. Just to show I have what it takes. Get me?"

"I do. I'll be silent as a tubeless radio. Good night."

"Wait a minute! Hand over my cigarette case."

"I haven't it."

"I dropped it on the table when I went out."

"Almost immediately Señor Castello appeared and I didn't even pick it up. I forgot it. I feel terribly guilty. I hope you haven't lost it."

"Don't worry. I'll get it back. I'll phone the Cantina about it. The *cantinero* knows me. Good night."

She lingered at the gate after he drove away. Neither of them had noticed the silver case on the table. It was a beauty. Had someone picked it up? Queer that he didn't want his Chief to know of this piece of business. Was it? Devoted as she was to Hugh she'd have to admit that he had become impatient and irritable. That was the reason she had been so ready to accept Gordon's advice not to tell him tonight about her patriotic flare-up at the Cantina. Had she helped by her defense of the United States? Gordon had hinted that it might prove dangerous for her. Suppose it did? She couldn't let those insults to her country go unchallenged. She'd better push the memory from her mind or she wouldn't sleep.

Gorgeous night. Why go in? The smooth lake was stippled with star reflections. The air was fragrant and so clear she could see the thread of bridle path near the shore and the blur beyond it which was the seat Hugh had had placed there. It was the spot in which to face her problems. The major one at present being the difficulty of deciding whether she should or should not tell her brother about the Casa Fresco episode.

If anyone saw her he would think a gigantic white moth was flitting along the downhill path. Why should this three-minute dash from home to the lake set her heart quickstepping? Here was the seat . . . Now to plan.

She drew a warm sense of serenity from the dark water; its soft *lap, lap* worked to a charm. She would think the situation through, stop dwelling on the past, cut out the uncertainty of what might happen which was whirling her mind round like a weathervane on a bender. Hadn't she promised Drex Hamilton that she would trust him? Not easy to keep that promise when she hadn't seen him for two weeks.

Dilly-dallying again. If she had more to do she wouldn't be so spineless. She'd plunge into some sort of work pronto. Gordon had suggested she might help Hugh. She had qualified for a secretarial job in college, was an expert steno-typist. If he would take her on she'd promise that no important bits of information would leak out through her. If she became a secretary at the Consulate she would have a chance to carry out her plan to test Von Haas. What was that? Sounded like the breathing of a horse against cinches. The creak of saddle leather. Who would come—

She sprang to her feet. Was it a nightmare or was she really seeing that rangy body slouched with one leg thrown over the saddle horn, rifle across his lap, gallon hat tilted back on his rough hair, the piebald horse? She brushed her hand across her eyes. Looked again. She was awake. The face which appeared to be split by a grin, two burning black eyes and Joe, late Justice of the Peace, were real.

"Lost ag'in, Marm? Sure'd like to help if I kin."

"What are you doing here?"

"I'm hungry, Marm. Reckoned you might have some cash along you'd like to hand over." In spite of his grin she detected the threat in his voice.

"I haven't. Not even a centavo."

"O.K., Marm. You needn't get so mad about it. I hain't never robbed the poor. Just seen one fella who'll hand over later. Now I'm lookin' for another who'll be plumb tickled to death to shell out quick or else—say, why you arunnin' for?"

VIII

"Didn't you notice the blueness of Castello's chin at the Small garden party, Consul?" Drex Hamilton, perched on a corner of the flat desk in the softly-lighted library at Casa Blanca, paused to tamp out a cigarette. "If I had had a doubt that he was the guy at Casa Fresco who directed that epic wedding party, the evidence of the recent shave of a heavy beard would have wiped it out. He must have worn one for months."

Chesney tilted back and forth in a swivel chair which was as out of character among the carved Spanish furniture as a man in tweeds at a formal dinner.

"Got any views as to what the Governor of this state thinks about him? Does he believe the suave Señor will remain loyal?"

"It's a hope rather than a conviction."

"Then why reinstate him? He was taken into custody after the showdown at Casa Fresco. He's been playing round with that vicious Scorpion gang. I'd say he rated a stiff dose of discipline."

"Right—but, as I told you, he was released by Government order. Before I left for Washington I had a conference with the Governor about a job I was doing for him, a matter of adjustments. He asked my advice about Castello. I suggested that he be reinstated and argued that a man who came from a long line of fiery patriots *might* make a comeback and be of enormous help."

"I'll be darned! How long have you been carrying a torch for that hidalgo?"

"I'm not carrying a torch for him. It's just that I can't believe that a man with the tradition Castello has behind him can be an utter heel. His Excellency agreed with me about his pardon. The Government is adopting a policy of permitting free discussion and the democratic right of criticism, even when it is venomously opposed to existing conditions.

"That was two months ago. If the authorities hadn't been so infernally slow with their repatriation act the course of several lives wouldn't have been changed that night, at least not in the way they were." Drex crossed to the open window. The gravity of his voice brought Hugh Chesney up standing.

"What in thunder do you mean by that, Drex? Have you tracked down that no-good Texan, Joe?"

"Yes."

"Quit answering over your shoulder. Come here. Is the man a genuine Justice of the Peace?"

"Yes."

Back at the desk Hamilton picked up a silver-sword paper cutter and bent the slender blade back and forth between his fingers.

"As real as a renewed commission, signed, sealed and delivered can make him."

The chair into which Chesney sank received his weight with a protesting squeak.

"Are you telling me that you and my sister are really married? That by a crazy fluke you have lost your stepfather's enormous estate?"

"Looks like it, but forget the estate. I don't want it and I know now that if this hadn't happened I wouldn't have carried out the conditions which would have made it mine. Change 'really married' to legally married and it makes a whale of a lot of difference. There's another word, annulment, remember."

"Doesn't the old law still hold that a forced oath is not an oath? Have you been trailing that Texan during the last two weeks when we thought you were at the ranch, Drex?"

"Most of the time. After checking up with the bailiff of the hacienda and the *caporal* of the cattle ranch on conditions there, I slipped through the mountains and across the river into Texas where I proceeded to smoke out the bailiwick of Joe, alleged Justice of the Peace. It was hard going, believe me. I found it only to establish the fact that he is what he claims to be. I wouldn't trust the word of the slimy official who swore he was, but I couldn't doubt the record he showed me."

"Admitting that, there may be a law in the state requiring several days' notice before a ceremony can be legally performed."

"That's what I thought. I cross-examined a padre and a Protestant clergyman pretending I was a lawyer investigating for a client who had got himself in a jam. The two agreed that in a country where a couple might be married while an enraged parent held a rifle at the head of a balky groom—technically known as a gun marriage—the ceremony I described seemed as solid as the Constitution. It's up to us now to watch 'Air Waves.' If Castello is behind that column it will soon be time for him to twist the thumbscrews to force me out of the estate. Where's Kay?"

"Dining at a native cantina with Gordon Slade."

"Why do you let her go out with him?"

"What's the matter with Slade?"

"Nothing's the matter with him so far as I know. I don't like him. Perhaps I'm unfair; perhaps it's just that we're congenitally at odds. Isn't it time she was home?"

"It isn't late. Kay is getting to be a problem. She declares she has been feted to the saturation point and has begged me to find work for her. Slade suggested that I take her on as my private secretary. As I prefer to keep my correspondence under my hat, as it were, never got round to engaging one. I can trust her not to talk. I wish she trusted me enough to confide that Casa Fresco affair."

"Probably doesn't want to worry you till she finds out just how serious it proves. Does she know about that property clause in my stepfather's will?"

"If she does she hasn't mentioned it. That's an old story now; you've been in possession of the de la Cartina estate so long I'll bet the fact that your ownership is conditional is forgotten."

"Don't tell her. It would trouble her."

"O.K. Will you tell her what you've found out?"

"Not yet. First I'll—"

"What am I—I—not to be t—told yet?"

The breathless voice came from the open window. Kay stood there gripping the frame. She held up a protesting hand as the men started toward her.

"You two are staring as if you saw a g—ghost. I'm real. I'm perfectly all right. A bit weak in the kn—knees, that's all."

She sank into the chair Hamilton pushed behind her, rested her head against its tall back and closed her eyes.

"Kay! Kay, my dear! She's fainted, Drex. Come quick."

"Hold everything, Consul. She hasn't. Drink this, Kay."

She opened her eyes and pushed away the glass in Hamilton's hand.

"I don't need that, all I need is a chance to catch my breath and get my knees reconditioned. I raced up from the lake." She sat erect. "All right now." Her eyes seemed enormous in her white face. "It was that horrible Joe, Drex. Shouldn't we tell Hugh about—about—"

"He knows. Don't try to talk."

"I must. I'm all over the jitters. There may be danger for you."

She told of what happened after Slade left her at the house, of her horror when she realized that the horseman wasn't the figment of a nightmare.

"When he bragged, 'I'm lookin' for another who'll be plumb tickled to death to shell out quick or else—' I knew he meant you, Drex, and smashed all uphill records, expecting to be shot in the back at any minute, to tell Hugh you must be warned; and here you are. It's a break. Did he mean blackmail?"

"Possibly; if so we'll call his bluff. Perhaps he wasn't looking for me. A cutthroat like him must have a lot of victims for whose scalps he's gunning. Something tells me I'm not his meat, this time. Now that you are back to normal I'd like to have a heart-to-heart with you. Let me handle this alone, will you, Consul?"

"With the greatest of pleasure and I mean pleasure. I'll go on sentinel duty outside. Trust Drex, Kay. He's a grand guy."

Chesney stepped to the terrace and closed the long window behind him. Kay's perplexed eyes, which had followed her brother, returned to Hamilton, who was standing behind a high-back chair, his arms folded on its top. His jaw line was clean-cut and hard; his lips were set in a firm line.

"Apparently I frightened Hugh white with my dramatics. I'm sorry."

"Sister, he wasn't the only person you scared stiff. When I saw you, colorless, breathless, standing in that window my blood froze. The Consul had just told me that you had gone to one of the native cantinas with Slade."

"Why should the fact that I was dining with Gordon freeze your blood? If it had been the glamorous Señor Castello . . . There's a man who would set a starry night like this vibrating with heartthrobs. Just between you and me, Gordon is a bit—well, call it 'heavy'—on the romantic side."

He laughed.

"Back to normal, aren't you?"

"'Yes. 'Ol' Demon Jitters, he skulk down de back stairs, sure has.' Quoting Beeny, in case you're interested."

"I am. I presume you've been told time and again that you have what it takes to set a man's pulses quick-stepping."

"Is that the profound confidence you had to impart with which Hugh couldn't help?"

"You're jeering at me. You didn't wait for me to finish. I was about to add, even the pulses of an old married man—like me."

Her friendly eyes reflected the laughter in his.

"Humorous type. Where do you get that 'old married man . . . '" Her lips remained parted as understanding gave way to amazement, amazement to horror. She sprang to her feet.

"You don't mean that you—I—are—" She put her hand to her throat as if to loosen the tightness which had stopped her voice.

"Take it easy, Kay." His cool, friendly eyes released her tension.

"Married! Was—was *that* what you had to tell me? Is *that* why that hideous Joe was here? We can't be! We *can't*. Such a thing couldn't happen."

"Come here!" He caught her hands and drew her toward him. "Stop being jittery and listen. Ever heard of an annulment? Know what it implies?"

"Of course."

"All right. We'll put one through."

"Tomorrow?"

"If you say so, but I'm asking you to wait. When we start annulment proceedings it's going to mean a whale of a lot of publicity."

"*Publicity!* Not a fraction of what the announcement of my—your—"

"*Our* marriage, that's what you're trying to say, isn't it? You've got me wrong. At present no one knows about that ceremony but you, the Consul and I."

"And the outlaws."

"Right. They won't dare talk yet. They're basking in the shadow of jail if not in it. The Consul won't and it's the last thing in the world I want broadcast."

She sank back into the chair.

"There go my knees again, darn 'em. You may trust me not to tell. Of course it mustn't get on the air. You might lose that adorable Señorita Mansilla."

"That's my side of it. How about a man in your life named Hewins?"

"Bill! I'd forgotten him. It can't, can't be true. I married! I—who had dreamed of a wedding gown of silvered satin trailing clouds of malines—instead of glory—as I paced the church aisle to the strains of 'The Voice That Breathed o'er Eden.' I, married in a quick-lunch dive to the juke rendition of 'Marquita! Marquita!'" She brushed her fingers across her suddenly wet lashes. "You'll admit the contrast has its humorous side, if you see what I mean." The quiver in her valiant voice betrayed her.

Hamilton gravely admitted that he saw.

Color stole back to her face; sparks of laughter

glinted in her eyes. "We appear still to be in the same boat, Skipper."

"Good sport. Just to keep the record straight, I'll confide that Amelia Mansilla is not my reason for wanting the Casa Fresco episode kept dark for the present. I wonder if you are to be trusted with a secret."

"A secret!" She crossed her throat with a rosy-nailed finger. " 'An' hope to die.' "

He went to the window and looked out.

"Your brother is still on the job. Lucky for him it's a warm night. Take his chair and I'll sit on the desk. Don't be so tense."

"I'm not. I can't be tense when I'm fairly tingling with curiosity, can I? There's mystery in your voice. Looks as if this evening would provide all the thrills of a Crime Club special. First, I—I—" better not tell him about her burst of patriotism—"Gordon is dictatorially summoned while we were dining and—"

"What do you mean, 'summoned'?"

"One might think from your wide-eyed amazement that I had said 'dragged.' The word was 'summoned,' Mister."

"Charge it up to shocked surprise that Slade, who knows this town from A to Z, would leave you alone at a cantina. That sort of thing isn't done in this country."

"But I wasn't alone. I had a most glamorous companion."

"Quit fooling, Kay. Your voice is cool as glass but your eyes are warm with mischief. You may think it a joke for Slade to walk out on you. I don't. Don't go out with him again.

"Close your lips—by the way, have I told you your mouth is perfection? I know what you started to say—'Who are you to tell me what to do?' Just at present I happen to be the man to whom you're married. No fireworks. Relax and keep calm. Let's get back to cases. What did you mean when you said you weren't alone? Did a Mexican glamour boy try to pick you up? Tell the truth unless you want your Gordon's head punched hard."

"He isn't my Gordon."

"All right. All *right*. Will you *please* quit stalling and tell me what happened? I don't want to blame Slade for what may have been impossible for him to avoid."

"That's downright noble of you. Now that you've abandoned that 'Hands up, or I'll fire' attitude, I'll treat you to a cut-back. Shall I begin with the menu?"

"Skip it. Begin with the call for Slade."

That freed her conscience to omit all that had gone before. She told him what had happened, that Castello had joined her at the table, but omitted the fact that Von Haas had stepped into the picture.

"The American must have been in a tough spot; the piece of paper on which his message to Gordon was written was dirty enough to have rolled in the street with him. Now you know all. Nothing in that to keep me from going out again with my brother's senior clerk, was there?"

"No. We'll let him off easy. You said he had not met Castello before?"

"Not unless they were pretending they were strangers. If they were they are grand actors."

"That seems to wash up the situation nicely. Forgotten that I have something to tell you?"

"No, but I had begun to wonder if you had."

"I'm about to trust you with important information. Ready? Why are you looking at me without seeing me?"

"Because I was visualizing Señor Castello as he bent toward me and said:—

" 'Something tells me that romance was mixed with that adventure. Am I right, Miss Chesney?' I had the creepy feeling that he knew of that Casa Fresco nightmare and was impelling me to confess about it."

"Did you?"

"Now who's tense? No. When I think back I can't understand why I should have imagined that a man of the world like Señor Castello, with whom I've danced and played tennis almost daily for two weeks, would suddenly be interested in my motor trip here even if he does edit a gossip column. Never before has he shown the slightest curiosity. Sounds pretty silly when I put it into words, but it's only fair to tell you of his almost hypnotic effect on me before I let you confide that important information."

He stood at the window looking out while the clock in the corner solemnly ticked off the passing seconds. He came back to his seat on the desk and regarded her with grave eyes.

"I'll trust you. You're entitled to know why I can't go hell-bent after that annulment. I'm doing a bit of G-Man work for this Government, helping to stave off the threat of international interference between this country and the United States, trying to stamp out the spark which may set off an explosion. The powers that be on both sides appear to feel that my influence counts. I am not considered a gringo here; I'm thought of more as a Mexican with the Mexican point of view. All this is strictly off the record, understand? You and your brother are the only persons who know."

"Already I've dropped it into a locked box in my mind where I keep confidences. Could I possibly help?"

"Only by keeping that phoney marriage a secret."

"That's too easy. You'd be a public benefactor if you would give me something real to do. For a year I've been engaged in serious, vital Defense work. It sounds ungrateful but I'm terribly fed-up with the social round here. It was fun at first but day after day I meet the same people, say practically the same things. I enjoy a game of cards, but I don't want to make contract a lifework. I can't discuss the fascination and skill of the different matadors; that's a social requirement here, I've discovered, as I've not yet attended a bullfight. Much as I love it I can't read all the time or practise singing. I adore clothes—only the executor of Mother's estate knows how much—but I don't care to talk about them. At home every female between the ages of ten and one hundred is expected to do something to defend, strengthen and sustain the American way of life. It seemed to be my job to come to Hugh but most of the time I feel like a drone. What a tirade. I just had to get it out of my system. Forgive me for inflicting you."

"I can take it. Feel better now?"

"A whole lot better."

"You understand, don't you, why my personal life must be kept out of the spotlight? Why that annulment must wait, even though it seems infernally unfair to you? I'm up to my ears in this investigation."

"Of course I understand. Forget about the annulment. I will too. It will be a challenge to my strength of mind."

"Shake on our compact." He quickly released the hand she impulsively laid in his. "Now we'll call in the Consul and explain our agreement."

"Just a minute, Drex. You've forgotten Joe. Suppose he threatens to tell that we—that I—"

"That you are Mrs. Drexel Hamilton, *pro tem?* We'll gag his mouth with filthy lucre."

"I'm glad you can take blackmail as a joke."

"It wouldn't be blackmail. He would be telling the truth, wouldn't he?" He threw open the long window.

"Come in, Consul, and hear our plan."

IX

At a table in a shady corner of the patio outside the Consul's office Kay expertly copied a long list of figures. As she worked she was subconciously aware of the mixed scent of gardenias and orange blossoms, of the tinkle of the fountain, the breeze which fluttered the sleeve of her lettuce-green linen frock and the chatter of the gaily colored bird in the split-cane cage which accompanied the click of her typewriter keys.

"Stop work, Kay." Hugh Chesney spoke from the doorway.

"Can't I finish this page?"

"Nope. Remember our agreement? A week ago when you started to work for me you promised to call it a day at noon."

"O.K., boss."

"That promise was made the day after you sprang to the back of your charger and rode capapie at Von Haas in the Cantina, figuratively speaking."

"So you've heard about that? I had hoped you wouldn't, Hughie. After the Casa Fresco affair that seems minor-league stuff, but my face still burns when I remember my outburst. I suspect that I rushed in where angels fear to tread. I hope I haven't made matters difficult for you?"

"Not too difficult, but don't do it again. You're a grand person, Kay, but sometimes your swift comebacks make me slightly dizzy; but then, I'm a plodder."

"It isn't really me, it's that sprite in the watch tower of my mind who whispers advice, then gives my tongue the green light. Don't worry, I won't listen the next time. I'll smother his voice. I've had my lesson and have made up my mind that I'm a big girl now, old enough to look before I leap. I'm glad you know about the Cantina brainstorm. My conscience has been at war with my affections. I wanted to tell you and I didn't want to worry you."

She hooded the typewriter and brushed back a lock of shining hair. If only he realized how keeping busy helped push that Casa Fresco episode to the back of her mind, he wouldn't insist that she stop work. Living with that memory was like living with a time bomb in the cellar. One never knew when the tricky thing would go off. She picked up the pages she had typed.

"I'll leave these papers on your desk. You'll have to remind Pedro to set the table inside. He forgot it last night. Lucky we didn't have the usual late-afternoon shower."

"I'll tell him. Now go home for lunch and a siesta. Want you looking your best for Castello's dinner tonight."

"I don't need to rest. You should have seen me at home where I punched the time clock promptly at nine A.M. and picked up my tools, figuratively speaking, at six P.M.; then off again in the evening, perhaps to sing at a Relief Benefit."

"You may get away with that in New England but this is a different climate. You've been here a month. You're not getting bored with Mexico, are you?"

He asked the question as they entered his office. She was quite sure that that was not what he had intended to ask, that while speaking he was considering a tactful approach to what he really wanted to say.

"Bored! If it were anyone else I'd think your voice was panicky. I'm not in the least bored. I love it here. Love the pink-and-blue adobe houses in the cobble-stoned streets, the peons with their gay serapes and their laden burros, the purple shadows cast by the snow-topped mountains with their unpronounceable Aztec names, the blue water of our lake, the markets with their piles of red and green peppers, their ocher, clay, terra-cotta pottery and—"

"Period! You're tipsy with color."

She laughed and pulled on a milan-straw sombrero which matched to a tint the star sapphire on the little finger of her right hand.

"I was trying out on you my impressions of Mexico that I'm writing journalese style for home consumption. At times I even feel the pricking of fiction wings. Lucky you brought me down from the mountaintops to earth." She wrinkled her nose in disdain. "But such dirty, smelly earth in some places. Earth in this case meaning streets and houses. Why don't the authorities do something to better conditions, Hugh?"

"They are fighting for improvement every day of the year, prodded and urged on by the leaders of Mexican thought, one of whom is Chiquita de la Cartina who, with her high social and economic status, has tremendous influence. They are catching the native population young by building schools in which the kids are taught habits of cleanliness and are working out a common language to substitute for the fifty-odd now used. Oh, by the way, here's a letter for you." He drew an envelope from his coat pocket. "I was so fascinated by your monologue on Mexico I forgot to give it to you."

"Glad you enjoyed my rave or do I discern a hint of sarcasm in that last sentence?" She held out her hand. "Gimme! Gimme! Texas postmark! It's from Bill." She perched on the arm of a chair, tore open the envelope and smiled at her brother who was leaning an elbow on his desk, chin on his fist, watching her.

"Forgive this exhibition of excitement, Hughie. This is only the second letter he has written since we parted with declarations of mutual esteem. Want to hear it?"

"Sure, unless you think Bill would object to having his protestations of affection on the air."

"Protestations, nothing. Bill isn't that type. Now that I come to think of it, I wonder how it would seem to have a man go a little white, his voice husky when he spoke to one, as they do in novels."

"Do you mean to tell me that no man—has ever—"

"Made passionate love to me? I do, humiliating as the confession is. As I told you, I've been considered Bill's girl. Of course I've met any number of potential heartthrobs but as soon as they began to get a little warm, someone would tell them I was engaged and they would veer off as if I were a third rail. I presume that had I been really attractive they would have risked an electric shock."

"I haven't seen any lack of courage in the men here. You are surrounded by the male of the species wherever you go socially. The Mexicans like you. Von Haas hovers. By the way, I've been intending to speak to you about him."

He rubbed his chin thoughtfully. Was this the subject she had felt he was trying to approach tactfully?

"I haven't referred to his evident admiration of you before because you are quite old enough to form your own judgments. But he's a foreign agent, eternally on the scent of information. Watch your tongue when you are with him. Get it?"

"Yes."

"Good. I've been working up to that warning for some time. Now that's off my mind we'll return to your stag line. Slade's eyes and ears are in the back of his head the moment you get to work in the patio. Johnny Shaw is spending his cigarette money for gardenias—"

"I'm sorry about that. He shouldn't do it."

"Good for him. Obliges him to cut down smoking. There are others to say nothing of Señor Edouard Rafael Castello. Something tells me that there's a man who will defy the third rail."

"What do you mean? He doesn't know about Bill Hewins. *Does he?* You've gone red to your hair. You haven't told him, have you?"

"Certainly not. Why in heaven's name should I spoil your fun? Speaking of Bill, how about that letter in your hand?"

"Still there. Unread. That ought to prove something." She drew the closely written sheet from the envelope and scanned a page.

"Let's see—misses me like the dickens—camp life isn't what it's cracked up to be—glad though to be doing his share—snooty major in command of his battalion—swell gals at the canteen . . ." She laughed as she turned a page.

"Bill has an all-out eye for what Beeny calls 'good-lookers, sho has.' He's coming here!"

"Here! From that Texas camp? Is he going AWOL or has he been discharged from the army?"

"Neither. Furlough. Week-end leave. He's found that by flying we can have a whole day together. Wants me to meet him at the air field. Isn't it thrilling, Hugh?"

"It begins to have that appearance. When will he arrive?"

She consulted the letter. "Tomorrow! He hasn't given me much time. What am I doing tomorrow?"

"We accepted an invitation from Señorita Mansilla to have tea at her hacienda."

"You're right, but of course I can't go. I can't leave Bill."

"Take him along."

"He'd hate it. I'll telephone the Señorita as soon as I get home and explain."

"Better make it good. These Mexican *grandes dames* are sticklers for etiquette."

What had she better say? Kay's mind was still busy with the problem at luncheon in the patio at Casa Blanca at the same time that she attempted to keep afloat a conversation between Jill and herself, occasionally interrupted by Verbena who was serving.

Jill dropped her fork and leaned back in her chair. "I wish I didn't have to eat old chicken and vegetables! I wish I didn't have to go to school. I wish I was grown-up like you, Kay, and didn't have to know anything."

"Are you implying that *I* don't know anything?"

Kay was aware that the indignation she felt was absurd, aware too that if she hadn't had doubts as to her common sense in the conduct of her own affairs recently—first, allowing Bill Hewins to think she cared for him enough to marry him; second, her crazy scheme to appear friendly with Von Haas in the hope of sidetracking at least one of his schemes—she wouldn't have been so touchy.

"Beeny says you don't."

"Shush, now, honey child, I didn't say dat fo' yo' to go an' tell Miss Kay, sure didn't."

"I won't 'shush,' Beeny. You said Kay ought to know better than to run round to night places with that poisonous—only you didn't use that word—Gordon Slade, didn't you? An' you saw an eight of clubs in her fortune you were telling the day before she came and you said it meant something *terrible*, didn't you?"

"Terrible? In my fortune, Beeny?"

"Now, jes see w'at you done, Miss Jill. Yo' jes gone an' scared yo' aunt white, sure have."

"Who's been scaring who white?"

With a shriek of delight Jill flung herself on the man in the doorway; the Dalmatian clawed eagerly at his sleeve.

"Drexy! Drexy! Where've you been? I haven't seen you for weeks." She pulled him toward the table.

Kay looked and listened in amazement. Never before had she seen Jill express enthusiasm for anyone.

He nodded to Kay before he glanced at the child's plate. "How's she eating, Beeny?"

"Laws, Mr. Drex, she don't eat at noon 'nough to keep a teeny bird alive, dat honey child sure don't. She jest lak sof' food."

"I don't like to chew. It's a bother."

Hamilton lifted her into her chair and drew up another beside her.

"But you're going to keep me company. I'm ravenous. Can you hunt up a squab chicken for me, Beeny?"

"Sure, Mr. Drex. We's got plenty in the kitchen. I'll fetch one right along, sure will."

"You don't appear to have a voracious appetite, Kay. Anything the matter with this chicken that you two gals are giving it the cold eye?"

"No. It's delicious. It's just that I'm not hungry."

"I guess Kay's in love, Drexy. She hasn't heard half I said an' she's been looking at the door as if she hoped someone would come through it any minute. I guess she wants to see the man whose picture is in the silver frame beside her bed. Perhaps he doesn't want to see her."

"That would be just too bad. Here's Beeny with my chicken. Fall to, Jill. Eat every scrap on your plate. When you've finished, you'll find something on the terrace I promised you."

"A kitten? You said you'd bring me one from the ranch. Goody! Goody!"

Jill wasted no time talking. She gobbled. Showed her empty plate to Hamilton. "O.K.?"

"Double O.K. Scram." Girl and dog disappeared into the house.

"What's on your mind, Kay? Is it the gentleman in the silver frame?" Hamilton asked.

"In a way. He's flying here to spend the day with me tomorrow and I have accepted an invitation to tea with Señorita Mansilla."

"That's easy. Take him. She'd be pleased as punch to have him."

"There wouldn't be time. If there were, he

wouldn't go. After all, he's coming a long distance to see me and—"

"He wants you alone. Don't blame him. Just tell the Señorita the truth. She'll understand. She—"

"What was that? Sounded like something dropped among the flowers."

"Sit still. I'll look for it." Hamilton parted the plants in the border. "I have it." He held up a silver cigarette case as he returned to the table. "Yours?"

"No. I don't smoke. It's Gordon's. He lost it at the Cantina the night he was called away from the table. What a curious way to return it and why leave it here?"

"Perhaps the finder hadn't heard that Slade had moved to the Consulate. May have been a waiter who feared he would be accused of stealing it."

"Sounds plausible. I'll take it and give it to Gordon when I go to work tomorrow."

"I'll save you the trouble. I have an appointment with your brother this afternoon." He slipped the case into his pocket and rose.

"By the way, that case was left the night you sang at the Cantina, wasn't it?"

"Good heavens, have you heard of that?"

"Who hasn't? Just remember that a goldfish bowl is a dusky undersea cavern compared to the glare of publicity in which you are living now. Don't do it again."

"You're telling me. You bet I won't. From now on I'll be dumb as an oyster."

"Oysters contain pearls. I won't say that your defense wasn't a pearl of untold value, but we can't allow you to take risks. I'll make sure Jill has the kitten, then I'm off. Don't worry about Amelia's tea. Phone your explanation and I'll put in a word for you. Come to think of it, you won't have to phone. You're dining at Castello's tonight, aren't you? So is she. Make your excuse then."

"Will you be there?"

"Yes. I don't like the smooth *señor* and as a rule I don't accept the hospitality of a person I don't like."

"Then why go?"

"To look after you and do you require looking after! I'll say you do. Can't have him trying his hypnotic stuff on my wife. Good-by."

X

"Esta es su casa."

Castello had greeted Kay with the courtly Castilian phrase of Spanish-speaking countries as she entered his home. She had responded vaguely.

"This is your house" didn't mean much in comparison with the two words which had kept springing up like a jack-in-the-box in her memory since Drex Hamilton had left her in the patio—"my wife."

They had intruded at dinner as she sat at Señor Castello's left with Cynthia Small aglitter with gold sequins, iced with diamonds at his right, smugly complacent that she had been given the seat of honor. Once he had repeated a remark with a suave "Did I not make my meaning clear, Miss Chesney, or are you distrait?"

It was maddening to have her memory keep cutting back. She had intended to make mental notes of the table appointments that she might add the description to her journal, but she had only a confused impression of exquisite lace, the sparkle of crystal, the glint of heavy silver, the rich sheen of gold, flames of tall tapers; crimson roses, strange, highly-seasoned food that burned her mouth and soft Spanish voices superimposed on the crisp, decisive ones of the American guests.

Now that she was in the library where coffee and liqueurs were being served by two servants in tight-fitting, bolero, maroon livery perhaps she could hold those two words under water till she drowned them by her interest in this perfect room.

The dark marquetry floor had been burnished to a rich bronze; the hand-hewn beams in the ceiling toned to match by that tireless craftsman Time. Massive carved chairs glowed with the crimson and gold of Spanish leather; heavy tables were enriched with scarves of gorgeous embroidery.

Three long windows with a heraldic device in color in the middle of their leaded panes were thrown open on the flower-and-palm–bordered patio. Set into the mahogany paneling above the high mantel was the portrait, dark and sonorous as a Rembrandt, of a Castilian grandee, with thin haughty face, pointed Vandyke beard, a hard line of red lips and brilliant, demanding eyes. The master of the house might be the man in the portrait—minus the beard. His features and imperiousness had descended with the blood.

The great room had a dreamlike quality. She felt like *Alice,* in silver gauze instead of pinafore, gazing into the Looking-Glass House—as deep in her chair she observed its occupants. The white evening clothes of the men accentuated the richness of the stage-set. Señorita Mansilla fitted into it like a Goya. Her hair was piled high under an exquisitely fine white mantilla; her frock of stiff yellow brocade, the heavy necklace and bracelets of Spanish topaz set in intricately carved gold, were perfect complements to her gardenia-smooth skin with its undertone of pink and her dreamy eyes. Her face, usually cool and reserved, was alight with interest as she talked to Drex Hamilton, who sat at the other side of the small table between them.

Kay withdrew her eyes from him with the speed of a finger from a hot stove and studied his sister, "Chiquita." She was as modern as a simple turquoise-blue dinner frock, an up-to-the-minute hair-do—sleek as black satin—and one lustrous string of pearls could make her. Her brilliant eyes—dark as her hair—her delicate but firm lips, the cameo charm of her oval face, the olive skin touched with soft red at the high cheekbones, warmed into lovely animation as she laughed in reply to a remark of Hugh's. Cynthia Small and her host were standing in front of a rich tapestry which might have been hung there by Cortes himself.

Von Haas, stiff and undeniably bored, stood beside portly, bald, pink-cheeked Charles Small who was valiantly attempting conversation. The oil magnate was reputedly a giant of finance, but he appeared as discouraged and snubbed as a disqualified dog at a bench contest. She'd better snap out of her Looking-Glass House act pronto, and do her share toward entertaining him.

Hope flashed in his myopic eyes as she approached. She shook her head as Von Haas stepped forward.

"Not you. I feel a Robinson Crusoe urge coming on, Mr. Small. Will you be my man Friday while I explore the patio?"

His boredom gave way to cordial response to her gay voice. There was a gelatinous shake to his white waistcoat when he laughed.

"I'm all out for it, Miss Chesney." He followed her to the terrace. "Thanks for rescuing me from Von Haas. It's hard to remain a perfect gentleman when under the same roof with him. He's as dangerous as TNT. He thinks American women are easy marks for his vicious propaganda. I forgot—you like him. I hear he's very attentive?"

Kay hoped he couldn't see the color that burned in her cheeks. "Was that a question or a statement? Do you realize that I'm the only American girl in this town? I have to keep reminding myself of that repressive fact or my current popularity would go to my head."

"I'll bet you majored in diplomacy at college. That was a neat evasion." He rested an elbow on the sundial and, chin in hand, looked up. "Great night, isn't it? The heavens seem so near here in Mexico. Tragic that we can't see a gorgeous moon like that without the chilling thought 'a bombing moon.' "

Beside him Kay crossed her bare arms on the sundial. "It's hard to believe that 'God is in His heaven' while the tragedy and horror in the world go on and on." She steadied her voice. "Do you believe that the stars are hung up there that you and I and millions like us may chart our lives by their wheeling and swinging in space?"

"Not quite that, though I think they have an influence. Speaking of stars, ever heard the story of the Plumed Serpent of Mexico?"

"No. Tell me about him."

"He was a wise king, a lover of peace, honored by his people. He knew about the stars and how they moved in heaven. Enter Smoking Mirror, a wicked magician who loved war and violence. He enticed Plumed Serpent to drink pulque. It made him drunk after which he was despised by his subjects. Shamed and despairing, he burned his palaces and threw himself into the flames. His heart was seen to rise into the sky where it was transformed into the evening star."

"That's a grand story. After this, wherever I am, when I see the evening star I'll think of Mexico and the Plumed Serpent. What a beautiful fountain! In the moonlight it's like a cascade of diamonds. Look back at the lighted windows. The place doesn't seem real. I've felt as if I were in a dream since the moment I entered the house."

"These old estates have a way of getting you. Castello almost lost this one when he stood against the march of progress, progress in this case meaning better government. Von Haas has proved 'Smoking Mirror' to his 'Plumed Serpent,' for our host isn't naturally a bad sort. I've never believed that he is behind that scandalous 'Air Waves' column. He was respected and admired, by women at least. Now he is suspected and disliked."

Kay remembered the woman at the Cantina who had turned a disdainful shoulder.

"Doesn't he realize what is happening?"

"It happened the moment he began to pal with Von Haas. He suffered under the land reform and was encouraged by the foreign agent, and others, to think he could put back the hands of the clock. He can't. Social consciousness, social revolution are in the air and won't be blacked out. This is valuable property to chuck away for a hopeless cause."

"But men have sacrificed more than an estate like this for a cause in which they believed."

"Sure, they have. Take England. Take the U.S. Look at the young fellas flocking to volunteer for service in the army. Do it myself if they'd take me." He cleared his voice of emotion. "But this is different.

"Cynthia, my wife, has been crazy to own one of the old places here. Now that it looks as if we'd spend the rest of our lives in Mexico, I tried to buy Señorita Mansilla's hacienda, heard she was up against it financially. Nothing doing. Perhaps she'll change her mind when she marries Hamilton; she won't need it. He has houses to burn."

Kay traced the figure VIII in the bronze top of the sundial with the tip of her finger.

"Are they to marry? I hadn't heard."

"Why not? She's a beauty, old Castilian family, poor as a church mouse. Señor Gonzalez de la Cartina, Drex's stepfather, left his entire estate to him, except for a trust fund for his wife and daughter, but there was a catch in it. Rumor has it that the *hacendado* was bitterly disappointed that his American wife hadn't borne him a son to carry on the family. Unless Drex takes the name of de la Cartina and marries a Mexican woman of caste before he is thirty-five, he loses the whole shootin' match."

"What!"

"Hadn't you heard that? How'm I doin' as a gossip?" Small's chuckle indicated that he was immensely pleased with himself.

"You—you're doin' fine," Kay encouraged while an inner voice declared, "So that's why he wanted to keep the marriage secret. He would lose the estate. 'Up to my ears in an investigation,' he had said. Plain phooey."

"Curious how stories, or facts, get twisted isn't it? I had heard that Señorita Mansilla was engaged to our host."

"To Castello! Nothing to it, Miss Chesney. They say, that anonymous they, that he wants to marry Chiquita, and Hamilton won't stand for it. Almost came to a duel, I've heard."

"What is this, a conspiracy? What dark and desperate deeds are you two planning in whispers?"

Castello's voice was light but his eyes narrowed as they flashed from Small's face to Kay's when he joined them at the sundial.

"Talking of angels," she evaded gaily.

"Were you talking of me?"

"The conceit of the man. Shall we tell him what we were saying, Mr. Small?"

"Sure, it's all right with me. First, Miss Chesney and I discussed the influence of the stars on the life and loves of the male and female of the species. I told her the Plumed Serpent yarn. Then, I handed it to this estate and confided that I was in the market to buy one as near like it as I could."

"That sounds innocent enough." Even in the dim light, Kay could see the satiric twist of their host's lips. "Maybe this will be for sale someday."

"Look here, Castello, that doesn't mean that you're going to be darn fool enough to buck the Government and get kicked out again for doing it, does it?"

"I beg to remind you, Mr. Small, that the subject of politics is tabu. Your wife is already at the card table waiting for you, Señor."

"All right. All right. I wasn't trying to butt in on your affairs, Castello." Charles Small appeared to grow a few inches taller. "Sometimes outsiders see most of the game. A lot of you *señores,* who should know better, sit around at bars and listen to the enticing whispers of the stooges of foreign powers who are spending vast sums in your country. You're not fool enough to believe that it's a purely altruistic deal, I hope. It's to stir up animosity against the country to the north. You've taken Von Haas into your house. He's living on you. So what?"

"Well, *so what?*"

"Trouble later, trouble to burn, into which, no matter how innocent you are, you may be drawn because of the association. I repeat, it would be a crying shame to lose this place because you can't keep a cool —and loyal—head on your shoulders." He paused to light a cigar. "That doesn't mean that I won't snap it up quick when—or if—you're ready to sell. Coming in, Miss Chesney?"

"Miss Chesney will join the cardplayers later."

"Suit yourselves. Suit yourselves. I'll be seeing you." Smoke from Small's cigar rose like an Indian signal fire as he crossed the patio to the long windows.

"You might have been nicer to him, Señor Castello. He was only trying to save you—"

"From *what?* What does he know of my reasons for what I do and think? He is rich, rich beyond belief. He's made his money in this country. Herr Von Haas is not 'living on me.' He shares the expense of this establishment. He—"

"Please! Please don't slay me. I didn't mean to drop a bomb. What he said made sense to me but who am I to advise, Señor Edouard Rafael Castello?"

Her laughing voice acted like salt on fire. The flames in his eyes went out.

"Who are you? An entrancingly beautiful girl, Miss Chesney." She hadn't liked his anger; she hated his caressing voice. "If it were not imperative that I marry money, I would lay my heart and this estate at your feet."

"How exciting. That's what might be called a half proposal. Oh, dear, I can put only a half star in my journal. You see each real proposal rates a star. I've adapted the plan from the old hunter's custom of notching his gun for every scalp. That's me, adopt, adapt, become adept. I've got something there, don't you think?"

He caught her wrist. His grip brought tears to her eyes.

"You're mocking me. I do not permit—"

"Edouard, what is it you do not permit? How you dramatize life." Chiquita de la Cartina sent her voice ahead of her as she crossed the terrace beside Von Haas.

With a muttered execration Castello released Kay's wrist. She saw Chiquita's eyes flash to her hand and hid it in a fold of her filmy silver skirt hoping that the red mark made by steel-like fingers on her wrist had escaped notice.

"Oh! Chiquita *mia,* I am glad you have come. Miss Chesney was about to join the cardplayers and I do not permit my guests to leave the patio till they have made a wish at the magic stone. You can attest to its potency. You've made many there yourself."

"And they are always granted. Try it, Señorita. Is there not something you long for with all your heart?" There was mischief in the dark eyes and not a little understanding.

"Heaps of things." Kay fell into the Mexican girl's mood. She had a chilly feeling that she had been saved from an unpleasant experience. "Where is that magic stone? Lead me to it."

"While you are wishing those heaps of things, Miss Chesney, I will return to my guests."

"Edouard. Wait for me." Chiquita slipped her hand under his arm. "Herr Von Haas will explain to Kay the magic rites. I want to consult you about the fiesta we are planning at the hacienda. You are to be master of . . ."

Her voice died away. Kay looked up at the man looking down at her.

"Where is the magic stone, Herr Von Haas? I want to wish."

"That can wait. Since you made that speech at the Cantina have you considered my proposition to work with me?"

"Work with *you?* When did you make it?"

He readjusted his monocle and stared at her appraisingly.

"I think I like you even more when you're scornful, your eyes are so—so magnificent."

"Not interested in what you think of my eyes or in any proposition to work with you."

She had intended to encourage him to be friendly that she might block his plans in one direction at least and she had snubbed him. Mr. Small wouldn't think she had majored in diplomacy if he had heard that.

"Why talk of propositions and problems on a

night like this?" she inquired gaily. "Isn't that a waltz I hear?"

"It is. Radioed from Monterrey." He slipped his arm about her. "We'll dance."

She let the dictatorial command pass; she had more important matters to consider. Brazen of him to think he could persuade her to work against her own country. "Dangerous as TNT," Mr. Small had said.

"Like your job at the Consulate? I presume you have queer situations arising there which you have to report?" he asked as they drifted into a waltz. His voice was tuned to encourage confidence.

"Smoking Mirror, the wicked magician who loved war and violence," Kay reminded herself.

"Queer is too mild a word. The other day an American wanted to put through . . ." She stopped dancing, looked up in consternation and met his intent pale eyes.

"I shouldn't have referred to that! I'm on honor not to mention anything that happens between the two countries. The combination of music, moonlight and your perfect dancing must have cast a magic spell."

"You can trust me. I'm sure we can work together. You have what it takes—here's Hamilton! We'll talk of this later."

His whisper was that of a fellow conspirator, as if they two had combined for an unlawful purpose. Her plan to circumvent his scheme to get news of Consulate activities didn't look so good. What was she getting herself into?

"Did you wish on the magic stone, Kay? Chiquita reported that you were about to try your fortune." Drex Hamilton sent the question ahead of him as he crossed the patio. His keen eyes glanced from her to the man beside her.

"You're wanted at the card table, Von Haas."

"I go at once. *Auf Wiedersehen, Fräulein Chesney.*"

His quick footsteps rang on the stone flags of the patio and died away.

"What was Castello saying to you when Von

Haas and Chiquita interrupted a few minutes ago? She said he hurt your wrist."

"He was only proposing to me—perhaps I'd better say half proposing."

"Marriage?"

"Sounded like it. I haven't had a lot of experience, but—"

"Quit fooling. I'm serious. What did he say to you?"

"A number of things, but it wasn't he who gave me the shock of my life, it was Mr. Small."

"What did Charles Small say to make your eyes blaze with anger?"

"That unless you married a Mexican you would lose your stepfather's estate."

"Didn't *you* know that?"

"You *know* I didn't. You *know* I believed you when you told me that you couldn't start annulment proceedings because you were up to your ears in investigation for the Government. Investigation—my word—you deceived me and—"

"Kay, please—"

"Pardon, *gracias,* Señorita," the soft Spanish voice of a servant interrupted, "*el Señor Castello* would like your presence at the card table."

"I'll go at once." She looked up and met brilliant eyes in a pale-golden skin. "Aren't you Miguel, the waiter who served Mr. Slade and me at the Cantina the other night?"

"*Sí, Señorita.* I beg you not to mention it to *el Señor Castello* who hired me for service here. He would be much displeased if he knew I had one time waited at a cantina."

"Of course I won't speak of it, Miguel. Did you find Mr. Slade's silver cigarette case?"

"I do not understand your meaning, Señorita. You do not think I—"

"I don't think anything about it. I merely wondered if you were the person who returned it. Now I'll obey the royal summons."

The two men watched her as she ran across the

patio, the gauze of her frock glinting like quicksilver in the glow from the windows.

"A light, Señor?"

The servant held a flaming match to Hamilton's cigarette.

"Danger for the Señorita," he whispered.

"Drex, you're holding up the game," Castello called. "To whom were you talking?"

"Talking!" From the terrace Hamilton glanced back at the patio lying silent, motionless and fragrant in the moonlight. "Don't tell me you're hearing voices, Edouard. As you can see, there's no one there. Let's go in. Something tells me I can beat even your game tonight. That would be going some, what?"

XI

Drex Hamilton paced back and forth across the patio of his town house quite unaware of the sunlight which was bringing out the golds and yellows, iridescent greens, blues and pinks in the flower borders and the red and purple of the bougainvillea cascading down the high, white-tiled walls. Two bright-plumaged macaws, in gilt cages on each side of the lacy iron gates, squawked and fluttered in vain to attract his attention.

During the wakeful hours of the night that whispered warning—"Danger for the Señorita"—had flitted tormentingly through his mind. Each train of thought led up to it. Ended at the question, "Which Señorita?" There had been three at dinner. Who was the man who had warned him? Kay had recognized him as the waiter who had served Slade and herself at the Cantina. Would Edouard Rafael Castello hire him without knowing his history from the cradle? Not likely. . . .

Kay had been furiously angry last night and bitterly unjust when she had accused him of wanting to delay the annulment of that *opéra-bouffe* marriage because of the clause in his stepfather's will. He had resisted the temptation to tell her that long before he had met her he had begun to prepare the way to transfer the responsibility of the great estate, had been looking for a capable manager who would take over till Chiquita married a man who would be the *Patron*. Until recently Castello's exile had put him out of the running as an heir. Would his return restore his legal standing?

Would she believe that he had taken on the care of the de la Cartina estate to safeguard the fortunes of his mother and sister, that more and more he longed to return to a life in his own country, to the profession of law for which he had been trained, or to serve in the air force? That was where he belonged when the whole world was in the turmoil of systematic destruction, unbalanced economic systems, dislocated trade and huge debts. Perhaps when he had finished this present job for the country of his adoption, which was inextricably tied up with his own, he would find his way back.

That meant he must smother his conscience, which kept reminding him that there were hundreds and hundreds of lives in field and cottage on the de la Cartina estate for which the head was responsible. Through work and festival, joy and sorrow, birth and death. Men, women and children who would look to that same head for help during the critical years already in sight. He knew now that a gay, breathless voice saying, "What is this? A movie company on location?" had been like a burst of fire in a long-smoldering log. The spark of love for Kay Chesney must have been in his heart. The flame had burned higher and stronger since the moment he had seen the flesh-and-blood girl whose photograph had always held his eyes as steel to magnet. That love had strengthened his determination to break away, had changed the world for him. Even this home he had known for years, this patio were different.

For an instant the future opened before him rolling up its mists. Just ahead stretched a road . . . Rough. Pitted with peril. A road which in no way her life should touch.

"*Buenos días,* Drex! You are staring at this patio as if you'd never seen it before. Walking in your sleep?"

Smiling, debonair, his sister stood under a swaying spray of purple bougainvillea which brought out the rich olive tint of her skin, the satin smoothness of her black hair, the brilliance of her eyes. She was slim, soignée from the top of her head to the tip of her dusty-pink sandal which matched her slacks and shirt.

Her brother drew out a chair at the white table with its sparkling glass, shining, steaming silver coffee urn and centerpiece of fruits in all shades and tints of yellow and ocher.

"I'm sufficiently awake, Chiquita, to take in the absolute all-rightness of your perfectly tailored outfit. Why do girls and women without slim hips wear slacks?" he asked as he sat down opposite her.

"Page Cynthia Small for an answer. It's pretty lowdown of me to criticize a woman's clothes. She has a right to wear what she likes. I wonder why Edouard counted the Smalls in on his party last night. Her husband is a dear but she—there I go again scratching like a cat."

"Sometimes it is hard for me to realize that you're a Mexican *señorita* of high degree, Chiquita."

"I'm only half-Mexican. It's the mother in me that keeps me speaking Americanese and the father in me that keeps me in love with this country and both that make me passionately eager to see it so strongly bound by friendship and commerce to the United States that no propaganda *Blitz* can break the bonds. You love it too, don't you, Drex?"

"Sure, it's home to me."

"Love it enough to give up your plan to return to the United States to stay?" Her wistful question brought his startled eyes to hers.

"How did you know I was planning that?"

"There have been so many signs I couldn't help knowing. Padre Carlos was here yesterday. He suspects you, too. He made me promise that I would remind you of how greatly you are needed on our estate. He's right. Believe me when I say that though the bottom of my world would drop out if you went, I wouldn't try to hold you here if I didn't feel with the padre that you are desperately needed in Mexico.

"Now let's talk of something else. Do you believe that Von Haas is here to make trouble between us and the country above the Rio Grande? That vast sums are being spent by a foreign Government to achieve that result?"

"You took the words right out of my mouth. Undoubtedly he is an agent, and Mexico is still friendly with his country. No use shutting our eyes to it. The showdown is bound to come."

"On which side will we find Edouard, Drex?"

"Only time will tell. Much as I dislike and distrust him sometimes I think there's a smoldering spark somewhere deep within him that may one day flame to nobility; other times I think I'm cockeyed to imagine it."

"I didn't mean to refer to it again but, as long as we're on the subject, is one of your reasons for wanting to give up all this—" she waved a comprehensive hand —"the lovely Chesney girl?"

"The lovely Chesney girl, as you call her, is engaged to a boy at home. She isn't the reason of my determination to put on the return of the native act, but she is the reason I asked you to forego the luxury of breakfast in bed this morning and have it with me. I'd like to invite her with her brother and Jill to stay at the hacienda for the next two weeks."

"But we've just moved to town. My calendar is crowded with engagements."

He pushed back his chair and rose.

"I know. I know it's a lot to ask of you, but it's terribly important to me to have them there, Chiquita."

Beside him she slipped her hand under his arm. An enormous green-and-black swallowtail butterfly lighted on the top of her head and fanned its gorgeous wings.

"It must be to bring that strain into your voice and deepen those sharp lines between your eyes. Is it love, Drex?"

"Love? I wish it were that harmless." He looked about the patio before he said in a low voice, "Danger."

"To Kay! But she's an American citizen. No one would dare——"

He couldn't tell her that she, herself, might be the person in danger, that it could be Amelia Mansilla. Why alarm her?

"You've heard of Kay's reply to Von Haas' propaganda blast at the Cantina, of her singing of 'America the Beautiful,' haven't you?"

"For two days after I didn't hear of much else. She must have been magnificent."

"Von Haas and his gang won't take that sitting down if I know their kind, and I do. I'm afraid for her. That's why I want her at the hacienda. She can be guarded there. Do this for me, will you, Chiquita?"

"Of course, Drex. Then you do love her."

"Suppose I do? Where will it get me with one Bill Hewins in the offing. Plan a house party. Ask the Smalls, Amelia, Von Haas and Castello."

"Von Haas! Edouard! I thought you distrusted the first and detested the second, Drex."

"I do. That's why I want them where I can watch them. I'm going to the Consulate this morning. Write a note for me to give Kay, will you?"

"*Sí, Señor.* I'll send the invitations to the others. On second thought I like the idea. I should have gone back for the village *fiesta*. We'll make a party of it. Attend in costume."

"Thanks, Chiquita. When you give, you give with both hands, don't you?" He regarded her thoughtfully. "I'll have lunch with you on your balcony. I've just decided I'd better tell you an astonishing story. No! *No.*" He shook his head and laughed as she took an eager step toward him. "Not *now.* Send the note for Kay to my room; I'm going there to pick up a paper I want the Consul to examine."

What queer hunch had been behind his sudden decision to tell Chiquita about the Casa Fresco affair, he wondered, as he ran up the stairs. Had it been a premonition that he might need her help? She would give it unstintingly. He would repay but not to the extent of giving up his plan to make his home in the United States. No, *sir!*

It wasn't a paper but a silver cigarette case he took from the pocket of the coat in the wardrobe in his room. Slade had been absent from the Consulate yesterday. He had held on to it wanting to watch the senior clerk's face when he delivered it. He had a feeling there was something curious behind its return.

He turned it over and over in his hand as he unseeingly watched a vine sway outside the long, leaded window. Kay had questioned the servant at Castello's, who admitted he had been a waiter at the Cantina where this very cigarette case had been mislaid. That was the night she had defied Von Haas. The same man had warned him, "Danger for the Señorita." Was there a link between the two?

He opened the case . . . Full. That was queer. Unlikely that Slade hadn't smoked one before he had dropped it to the table for Kay. He removed the cigarettes and disclosed a thin paper. Writing!

The blood swept to his hair. A drawing of four wheels. The word *Roll.* The name of a city to the north. An arrow pointing south. The word *Dusk.* All of which translated might mean that trucks would roll at dusk—when? Suppose this was the night. They must be stopped. Not a minute to lose. He picked up the telephone on his desk and called long distance.

Trip hammers of excitement tapped at his veins as he drove through the city streets in his long, sleek black roadster. Would Don Pasquale act on the code message he had sent? Was he at last on the track of the gang which was shipping the metal?

Johnny Shaw looked up from his desk in the outer office.

"Gosh, I thought 'twas a cyclone busting in the door to disturb this cloistered calm. What's on your mind, Drex?"

"Where's Slade?"

"Gone to bail out one of our tourist countrymen who looked too long on the wine when it is red. I hear that Mexico expects fifty thousand of them—tourists, I mean, not drunks—here this season. Looks as if we might have to increase the glad-hand force. Need a job?"

"Not this minute, Johnny." Hamilton dropped the silver case back into his pocket. "May need one later. Where's the Chief?"

Shaw thumbed over his shoulder.

"In his den and I mean *den*. He's a roaring lion this morning. The Missus' lawyer has served notice that the divorce is final. He ought to be hugging himself that he's free. Thanks to 'Air Waves' I guess he's the only person in this city who didn't know that she and—"

"Skip it, Johnny."

"O.K. Better fasten your head down tight before you go in. If it comes flying through this door don't say I didn't warn you. Tread softly, brother, tread softly."

The smile Shaw's theatrical warning had brought to Hamilton's lips lingered as he entered Chesney's office.

"Good morning, Consul."

Chesney looked up from the papers on his desk and tipped back in his swivel chair. "What's so good about this morning to bring you in here grinning like the Cheshire Cat, Drex?"

"Take life by the smooth handle, boy, take life by the smooth handle. I can hear my maternal grandfather saying that to me when I got all het up over examinations."

A smile tugged reluctantly at Chesney's lips.

"You're a great guy, Drex, you and your 'smooth handle.' I'll be darned if I can find life's smooth handle this morning."

"That's because you've been under an emotional harrow so long." He dropped two envelopes to the desk. "There's the cure-all. Two weeks at the hacienda with ranch overtones. You and Jill and Kay."

"You're crazy. I can't take a vacation, now."

"Johnny says this office has been advised that tourists fifty thousand strong will safari this way during the next few months. That means extra headaches for you. Get a ready on. You've been saving up your leave, haven't you?"

"Yes. I intended—"

"Never mind what you intended. Beware, my boy, of the skiddy highway paved with good intentions. Take two weeks now and come back fresh to meet the problems and—" he tapped the papers on the desk —"to readjust your life to changed conditions." His eyes met the tired, disillusioned eyes across the desk. "The junket hasn't been planned entirely for you, Consul. I have a hunch Kay will be safer—"

Chesney was on his feet.

"Kay *again!* In danger! Good Lord, why did I ask her to come here? Danger from Texas Joe? Johnny Shaw has been trailing him. I warned him not to pounce until we had discovered the man's game."

"Not Texas Joe this time. It may be a backwash from her Cantina outburst, but I'm not sure." He explained the reason for his anxiety, concluded:—

"And confound it, I didn't have time to find out which Señorita the guy Miguel meant. Castello appeared and the servant did the vanishing act. One minute he was there and the next without a rustle or a sound he was gone."

"Sure he wasn't the ghost of the great Houdini trying out a disappearing act?"

"I'm glad you see a joke in it. I'll be hanged if I do. What would be his object in putting on a show for me? I believe he had something. I believe it so much that Chiquita is sending an invitation to the house party to Amelia Mansilla."

"Why should she be in danger? She's taken no part in the political turmoils of the country. I'll bet there isn't a resident of this city who isn't proud of her family's noble lineage, of her cosmopolitan education. When you come down to reasons why should your sister, my sister be threatened? It isn't likely that Kay's flare-up at the Cantina would be taken seriously. Sure you're not suffering from nightmare hangover, Drex? Can't be any other kind. You don't drink."

"It was a warning, Consul. You may remember that Casa Fresco wasn't an experience all sweetness and

light. Will you come to the ranch and help me take
care of those girls or will I have to carry on with Señor
Castello and Von Haas?"

"Von Haas! Castello! Have they been invited?"

"They will be. We need Edouard as *entrepreneur*
of the *fiesta* and Von Haas—call him window dressing.
He's decorative and worth watching. If he is a threat to
your sister's safety we'll get the lowdown on him there.
How about it? Will you come?"

Chesney folded the papers on his desk. "If I were
to object to meeting Von Haas, Drex, it would be an
acknowledgment that I believe those 'Air Waves' hints
about him and Blanche. You appear startled. Did you
think I didn't know? I knew that and a whole lot more.
The divorce has gone through. I no longer have a wife.
I'll get in touch with the Consul General and arrange
for leave. Jill will be in a seventh heaven at the prospect."

"Bring Beeny along. Now that you've signed on
the dotted line, I'll sell the idea to Kay."

"She isn't here. Gone to meet Bill Hewins."

"So she has. I've had this other thing stewing in
my mind and forgot that. Where do they intend to
spend the day?"

"At the nearest town north of the air field. We
came through it on our way here. Kay figured that its
charm and antiquity would interest the boy friend. I'll
bet he won't take much notice of it when he has her to
look at."

"Likes her a lot, does he?"

"I suspect that today will settle the amount each
cares for the other."

"Give her the note when she returns tonight, will
you? Just a minute. Will she be driving home alone
after dark?"

"Looks like it. I objected, but she argued, 'What
can happen to me on that highway with cars coming
and going continuously?' She was right. What are you
staring at, Drex?"

He was thinking, "Alone. After dark," seeing a
drawing of four wheels. The name of a city to the north.
The city from which certain trucks would roll at dusk.

They might roll this very night and Kay would be on that road alone. Oh, no she wouldn't. He tried twice to speak before his voice came from his tight throat.

"I'll be shoving along. Get in touch with your chief about that leave before you backslide, Consul."

As he entered the outer office the phone rang. Johnny Shaw looked up from a row of figures.

"Answer that call, will you, Drex? Pretend you're Slade. May be one of his heartthrobs and you'll get an idea of what it means to be a male menace. This report is giving me the heebie-jeebies."

"American Consulate. Slade speaking." Hamilton successfully imitated the senior clerk's voice, not because Johnny Shaw had suggested it but because an answer might help in the solution of that message in the cigarette case.

"Eet start thees night. Check as eet go through."

He heard the click at the other end of the line. Cradled the telephone. Slid the silver case under papers on Slade's desk. He didn't need now to watch the owner when he received it.

"Was that call for me?" Slade demanded breathlessly as he entered the office.

"It was a guy speaking broken English."

"Make out what he said?"

"Seemed all broken up because he had the wrong number. I've just proposed to the Consul that he take a vacation at our hacienda. I found him poring over those divorce papers. Back me up, will you boys?"

"You bet, we'll back you up. We'll get his nibs out there if we have to chloroform him, won't we, Slade?"

"Sure thing, Johnny."

"Eet start thees night. Check as eet go through."

The words went with Hamilton as the car shot ahead. He would be willing to swear on oath that it had been the voice of the bearded, black-spectacled Mexican at Casa Fresco. . . . Señor Edouard Rafael Castello speaking.

XII

The straight highway extending for miles ahead left Kay's mind free to wander as she drove her sedan toward the air field. She thought of Von Haas and his curious eyes, pale and expressionless as those of a dead fish; of his attempt last evening to gain her confidence, of his smug assurance that she would "work" with him, and she thought that it was curious that the waiter at the Cantina should have been serving at Señor Castello's dinner. Apparently he had been frightened when she recognized him, terrified for fear he would lose his job. Perhaps he wasn't honest enough to serve in a house full of priceless treasures. Even his shocked "The Señorita does not think that I . . ." hadn't convinced her that he knew nothing of the return of Gordon Slade's cigarette case. However, it wasn't up to her to regulate Castello's domestic economy.

What had Drex been about to say when the servant had interrupted? Lucky for her he had been interrupted before he had realized how bitterly she had been hurt by his deception. Why hadn't he told her at once that his real reason for keeping that forced marriage under cover was to prevent the transfer of his stepfather's estate? Had he really believed she had not heard of the condition in Señor de la Cartina's will? When you thought of it, why hadn't she? Apparently it was common knowledge.

Darn that road runner . . . She swung the car sharply to avoid hitting a speckled gray-and-white bird with long neck, long tail and even longer legs, which had streaked in half-running flight across the highway. Missed by a feather. Serve the stupid creature right if it had been knocked out flat.

She'd better park her reflections on the events of last evening in the back of her mind and pay attention to the country through which she was driving. She hadn't been over this road since the day she had motored from Nuevo Laredo with Hugh. She had been too excited then to pay much attention to the scenery.

Those spots of glistening white in the distance must be the adobe walls of village houses. Clouds floating across the sun threw tints and shades on low growing trees and shrubs, on acacias, cacti and desert palms. She had seen that same shifting effect produced on the stage by light projected through prisms of lovely colors. The breeze was laden with the smell of mesquite baking in the heat, the strong resinous scent of violent-yellow marigolds. Toward the west rose mountain after mountain like the rollers of a malachite sea.

In and through and out of a cloud of yellow butterflies . . . Passing automobiles in all stages of luxury and debility; a truckload of little brown soldiers; country peasants, mounted or walking, prodding with sharp sticks their burros overladen with firewood or pottery or charcoal . . . A black-shawled woman, dragging a pig by a string tied to one leg, called, "God be with you, Señorita!" A drunken cavalier insecurely seated on a saddle contrived from a folded piece of sacking jingled his spurs, whacked the nose of his dejected mount with one hand while with the other he swept off his straw sombrero and grinned at her.

"Buenos días, Señorita!"

These people in a strange country seemed millions of miles from home and a planet or two removed from the man she had come to meet.

"I know now, even before I see Bill, I can't tell just why, that the affection between us is not the stuff upon which a marriage which lasts is built and that's the only kind I want. Will separation bring him to that same conclusion?"

The hum of a plane vanished self-questioning. She reached the airport just as the great silver ship taxied to a stop. The door opened. Passenger after passenger walked down the ramp. Suppose he hasn't come. Why should that possibility make me breathless? There he is! Snappy in his khaki uniform, the sun shining on his bronzed face. Has he always been so straight, so tall, so blond? Has he always squared his shoulders as if he owned the universe? She asked herself.

"Bill! Bill! Here I am!"

His mouth widened in an engaging grin. He broke into a run, caught her in a bear hug as she stood beside the sedan and kissed her.

"Perhaps I really do love him." The thought raced through her mind as she kissed him warmly in return. She held him away with one hand on the double chevron on his sleeve.

"A corporal so soon! Bill! You're marvelous! I'd forgotten you are so good-looking."

"Oh yeah? You've fallen for a uniform. They do say the fancy wrapper sells the goods. You're not a pain-in-the-neck yourself. Wore that swell outfit because I like emerald-green, I hope. Wise kid to wear that big navy sombrero; the Mexican sun is piercingly hot. Let's get out of it. Hop in. Plane returns at six P.M. Eleven now. That gives us seven hours." He tossed a folded newspaper on the back seat.

"Where does it go from here, Bill?"

"South. Makes a stop nearer your town than this. Only got wise to it after I was on board. It would have made it a lot easier for you, I guess, if I'd found it out sooner."

"That's all right. I've loved the drive. How will we celebrate this great and glorious occasion?"

"Gosh, Kay, you're certainly a knockout when you smile. Let's go to the nearest town and do some decorating in red, rich, rosy red. I'm fed-up with wallowing through mud, snapping to attention and breaking my neck to answer bugle calls. Want me to drive?"

"No. You're the passenger. The city nearest the airport isn't far. I didn't see much of it the day I arrived but enough to know that you'll get Mexican atmosphere slightly denatured with U. S. publicity methods."

"Sounds O.K., though I don't give a continental

for atmosphere. I came to see you. How about eats? Money no object. I could toy with one de luxe meal."

"Isn't the camp food good?"

"Good, if slightly on the monotonous side. Don't get me wrong, I'm not crabbing. I'm glad we're going all-out to save Great Britain and darn glad to be able to help if it does put a cramp in my real-estate business that will set the date of my marriage a good many years ahead."

"My," not "ours." Did it mean that already he had seen the wisdom of their separation?

"It's grand to be with you, Kay." He drew a long breath of satisfaction, laid his arm across the back of the seat and gave her an impulsive hug.

"Haven't you met girls since you've been at camp, Bill?"

"Not many. Too busy. Believe it or not, at the end of the day my dogs are so tired I'd give my eyes if I could pull 'em off with my boots and stand 'em up someplace I wouldn't feel the ache. There's a cute trick at one of the hostess houses, reminds me of you, has your same lovely voice."

"I may be 'a popular little number'—end quote —but I hadn't supposed that by any stretch of the imagination I would be called 'cute,' Bill."

"I don't meant cute the way you think of it. I mean sort of gay and understanding and—and heart-warming, just a little bit of all right. Kind of responsive, you know."

Of course she knew. He had found a girl who would love him if he loved her . . . Silly to feel as if the bottom of her world had dropped out.

"What a sigh, Kay. Homesick? Aren't you happy? Don't you like it here?"

"Love it, Bill. Don't know why I sighed. Perhaps a sort of nostalgia goes with the country, an undercurrent that gets you, makes you long for something, you don't know just what, but for something you never had."

"Couldn't be a lad by name Bill Hewins, could it?"

"No, Bill. I feel more strongly than ever that you and I were wise to Stop! Look! Listen! We'll always be grand friends—"

"*Friends*. Smile when you say that, stranger. I don't like it, but I get your drift. Perhaps you're right," he added thoughtfully.

Was he thinking of the "cute trick" with the lovely voice? "I'm always right. I never make mistakes, I make corrections," she boasted gaily. "Have you noticed that this highway has been rising slowly through a broad corridor between those lofty mountain ranges?"

"You take a lot of telling, don't you? I'll remind you again I'm looking at you. I'm not interested in scenery. I came to see my girl."

"Your girl *pro tem* is terribly glad to see you, Bill. There's the hotel across the street. We'll leave the sedan in the garage. I can't carry that fur coat around even if it is short. It will be safe if I lock the car."

Pigeons feeding on the cobbles rose like a platinum cloud when they crossed it. From the plaza came the click of typewriter keys where a public letter writer was taking down letters for an Indian who could neither read nor write. On some of the benches men were humped in siesta. Three cowboys who were entertaining each other with stories stopped their shoulder slapping and bursts of laughter as Kay and Hewins passed.

"What shall we do first, Bill?"

"Eat, then we'll paint the town. Here's your handbag. Heavy as lead. For Pete's sake what do you carry in it? A wardrobe trunk? The blue matches your hat, sapphire ring and bracelet, doesn't it? Remembered I'm nuts about blue and green together, didn't you? Your get-up is a little bit of all right. Those guys leaning against the wall apparently thought so; they were staring as if they'd seen you somewhere before. Looked like Texas cowhands we've seen hundreds of times at the movies."

"Where are they?"

"Drifted off now."

Texas cowhands. Kay's heart broke into quick-

step. Were they members of that Casa Fresco gang?
Bill had said they stared as if they had seen her somewhere before.

"Gardenias, Señor?"

A black-eyed girl held out the board laden with
waxy blossoms she had taken from her head. She
rubbed one dirty foot against another, kept her brilliant, wild eyes on the man as he selected the flowers.

"That's enough, Bill. Don't buy any more," Kay
protested. "How many pesos?" The girl held up two
fingers.

"Holy smoke, cheap as that? Let's go into the
business of importing them to our hamlet in New
England, Kay."

"You are now in a cup of the Sierra Madre Oriental," she droned in the best guide fashion, as she fastened the corsage at her shoulder. "This city was
founded by the Spanish Conquerors—"

"Skip it. I read all that flying over, that and a
whole lot more. Picked up an American-Mexican paper published on our side of the border. It's got all it
takes. Even had a gossip column 'Air Waves.' There
was a yarn about a rich Mexican hacienda owner who
slipped across the border and married an American girl
without benefit of clergy."

"Bill! What do you *mean?*"

"Nothing crooked. No minister would marry them
so they hooked a Justice of the Peace. Why so scared?
No one you know, is it?"

She shook her head. For one horrible breath-
snatching moment she had thought it referred to Drex
and herself, but the paper had said *Mexican* hacienda
owner. That let him out.

"Is this the local Ritz, Kay? Let's eat. Come in."

They stepped from the hot noisy street through a
too modern lounge into a patio fragrant with the scent
of flowers, cool with the spray of fountains. From the
ornate iron-railed gallery on the second story hung
cages, with canaries and blue, green and scarlet birds
which kept up an incessant chirp and chatter. At a
small table they ordered luncheon.

"Lovely here, isn't it, Bill? It would be fun to sit

behind that lacy-iron railing on the gallery in the evening and look down on this patio. I've heard it's the smart night spot for dancing in the city."

"Maybe, but I'd feel as out of place here as a comic strip in the *Atlantic Monthly*. I wish those musical-comedy guys walking from table to table would cut out that strumming. It gets me down. At long last. Food."

They talked of home, of the different branches of Defense work friends were doing, of the army, of Hugh's divorce, of Kay's job. As they rounded off the meal with an exotic fruit and black coffee a clock struck the hour.

"Two! I'll hand it to the chef, the eats have been superb, but he sure has taken his time," Bill Hewins protested.

"Perfection takes time. Come on. I've been told that the market here is something to see."

"How about a picture?"

"Oh, Bill, *no. Not* a movie. I can't let you go back to Texas without seeing something of Mexican life."

"You might remember that I came to see you, not Mexico. We could hold hands in a movie. However, you're the doctor. Let's go."

In his interest and enthusiasm as they explored the city, she stopped feeling apologetic because she had substituted sightseeing for a picture, but through it all the memory of the Mexican *hacendado* who had married an American pricked like a splinter run deep under the cuticle of her mind.

"Quite a country, quite a country," he admitted. "Something about it kind of gets you."

"It's a fabulous land of romance and colorful adventure, a troubled land of perpetually conflicting, often sanguinary, political aims. I've learned that much since I've been here."

He liked the colorful market with its Indian merchants, inscrutable, passive, completely indifferent as to whether he bought or not; liked the way people stood about the streets talking and laughing; admired the handsome women in white-cotton blouses, thick, many-colored strings of beads, red-woolen skirts and black *rebosas*. Insisted upon buying a serape for her, a carved swizzle stick for himself; invested in a lottery ticket. Stopped at every oil-can brazier at the curb to sample the titbits, the black coffee, sold by the chattering Indians, and topped off with a cup of foamy hot chocolate, cakes and honey.

"Bill, don't eat anything more," Kay protested. "You'll be sick going back in the plane."

"Darned lucky if I'm not before. Come on, we've done the market—if the market hasn't done me."

They dodged into a baroque cathedral with a pink façade and tower to escape a sudden downpour that blew and swayed like wraiths of malines, and wandered into a chapel of exquisite design, where the walls were covered with rich carving and the air was heavy with incense.

"Why all the candles?" Hewins whispered.

"Perhaps it is *El Día de Candelaria,* the Day of the Candles," Kay whispered back.

"Are they forced to do this?" He indicated the many kneeling figures.

"No. Religion is now considered a private affair in this country. See how the lights set the gold leaf on the exquisite carvings shimmering. The beauty of the blue gown of the Virgin against it fairly takes my breath. If—if you don't mind, Bill—I'd like to say a little prayer myself."

"If the shades of your Puritan forebears can stand it, I can. Of course I don't mind." He cleared the gruffness from his voice and turned away.

"Feel happier now?" he asked as she rejoined him.

"Stronger. Church, any church atmosphere, does that to me and prayer helps me meet my problems with an I-can-take-it tilt to my chin. Try it sometime."

"I do." His reply was curt. "Why are you looking over your shoulder? What did you see to take the color from your face?

Of course it had been pure imagination, set on edge by Bill's reference to Texas cowhands and that across-the-border marriage, which had made her think for one hectic second that she saw the black-bearded Mexican major whispering to a companion whose face she couldn't see but whose outline seemed familiar. They were not only whispering; she had seen a slip of paper change hands. Silly; there must be more than one bearded man in this country.

"Thought I saw someone I knew. Just a flight of fancy. This would be the last place in which that person would appear. As for being colorless, must be the reflection of this blue hat on my skin that makes me look ghastly. The rain has stopped. Let's go."

"What did you mean by problems?" he asked when they were again on the street. "Is Jill cutting up rough? You wrote you couldn't seem to reach her heart."

"I have now. I'm teaching her to sing. She loves music and I'm reading *Alice in Wonderland* to her. She gets more friendly every day."

"Any lads giving you trouble? How about those clerks at the Consulate?"

"No time for sentiment, Bill. I really work. Hugh's a slave driver."

"I presume he doesn't keep your nose to the grindstone after dark. You're not a convincing evader, Kay. Now I know there's a man in your life." A clock struck. "We'd better get a move on or I'll miss the bus. Guard house for me if I don't report to camp a minute before my leave is up."

They were in the sedan speeding toward the airport when he asked: "Will you be warm enough going back? Getting colder every minute."

"Cast your eye on that swank mink jacket on the back seat. I know by your scowl what you're thinking. Extravagant gal! Relax. It is Mother's coat made over."

She chattered to break the emotionally strained silence. He mustn't have time to make a declaration which he would regret when he returned to the "cute trick" at the hostess house. He interrupted as if his thoughts had wandered from what she had been saying.

"How long are you planning to stay here, Kay?"

"Until Hugh's sister Sally reaches Washington and

takes over my job with Jill. It may be a short time. It may be months. No can tell."

"Stop at the camp on your way home. There's a dandy inn where the relatives of officers and men stay. I'll show you round. We're training a lot of Mexican pilots there. I may be really flying by that time. You'd be crazy about it. Will you come?"

"I will. I'd love it."

The plane was waiting when they reached the airport. Kay parked the car and went to the gate with him. She held out both hands.

"It's been a grand day, Bill. I'll never forget it."

"That goes for me, too. Happy together every minute, weren't we? Don't fall so much in love with this country that you'll forget a little piece of U. S. A. called Massachusetts."

"As if I could. Nothing would tempt me to live here permanently, though there's a saying, 'Once the dust of Mexico settles on your heart you can find peace in no other land.' "

"Then for Pete's sake wear a gas mask over your heart when you meet these guitar-strumming *caballeros* —they'd drive me haywire—and don't forget you're a dyed-in-the-wool New Englander. I hate to say good-by, but here goes." He caught her in his arms and kissed her twice. The huskiness of his voice tightened her throat.

"Let's not say it, Bill. Let's say 'until we meet again.' You'll have to go. Quick!"

He was through the gate. He turned before he entered the plane, waved and shouted, "Good-by, darling." Why did he seem so young, so boyish to her now? Her heart stumbled. Already he belonged to a life that was over. She waited till the propeller swung.

"Bad luck to watch it out of sight," declared a voice behind her.

She dashed tears from her eyes and turned. Stared incredulously.

"Drex Hamilton, where did you come from?"

"Off that plane. Thought perhaps you'd let me drive home with you. It will give us a chance to finish that talk which was interrupted last night."

XIII

"Haven't forgotten that the law declares a man innocent until proved guilty, have you? Hop in. I'll drive."

Kay was in the sedan and he was at the wheel before she emerged from the coma of surprise.

"You're taking a great deal for granted. Perhaps I prefer to drive home alone."

His eyes, smiling a little, disconcertingly cool, met hers. "You may prefer to but you've done all of the driving alone at night you'll do while in this country."

"Driving alone would appear to be among the prerogatives of free, white and over twenty-one."

"Still have it in for me for what you consider my deception, haven't you?"

She was a bit disturbed to find that the resentful memory of that conversation in the patio, which she would have sworn was indelibly impressed on her mind, was slightly blurred by the events of the day like a snapshot when the subject has moved. He mustn't suspect it, though.

"You did ask me to postpone the annulment because you were up to your ears in an investigation, didn't you?"

"Right."

"And you will lose your stepfather's estate if it becomes known that—that—you are—"

"Married's the word."

"Married to an American, even if absurdly, illegally—"

"Happily."

"What do you mean—*happily*—"

"I thought you were reaching for another word and that popped into my head."

"I don't consider this a subject for joking."

"Neither do I. It's getting to be serious. You don't trust me."

The memory of his rush to her rescue at Casa Fresco flashed through her mind. He must have known then that he was taking a chance at losing a fortune. She'd been horribly unfair. She'd better tell him the "Air Waves" story about that across-the-border marriage. Bill had left the paper. Why tell him? He could read it himself later.

"I do trust you. Suppose we agree that you have two reasons for postponing the annulment and forget it."

He sent the car ahead in a burst of speed.

"You're right. I have two, but not the two—What did Hewins think of Mexico?"

Why had he so abruptly switched the subject? Was her sudden let-down feeling disappointment that he was so ready to fall in with her suggestions that they forget it? He was frowning at the road ahead, his lips set in a hard line beneath the slight mustache.

"Bill balked at sightseeing at first but after luncheon at the hotel—that reminds me. He said three Texan cowhands near the door when we went in stopped talking and stared as if they'd seen me before. Could they have been those horri—"

"The memory of that night still has power to choke off your voice, hasn't it?" The strong pressure of his hand over hers checked the slither of icy splinters through her veins. "Snap out of it, Kay. I doubt if they were the same men. For one reason, those cut-throats know they are wanted by the authorities here; they wouldn't be likely to attract attention in a plaza. They looked at you because you are so good to look at probably. Hard for me to keep my eyes on the road this minute."

"Emotional crisis. Would it perhaps be safer if I drove?"

"Thank the Lord for that laugh. I feel as if we were on firm ground again. Now I can tell you my plan."

As she listened adventure beckoned alluringly,

conscience held her back like a child tugging at its mother's skirt.

"Two weeks at a hacienda. On a ranch! It sounds heavenly, but I've taken a job. I can't walk out on Hugh. He needs me."

"You haven't been paying attention. He's coming; so are Jill and Beeny."

"In that case I accept the invitation with pleasure. I'll write to your sister the moment I get home. Why are you stopping? Is that mix-up ahead an accident? Is that a truck beside the road—"

"It is. *Camiónes,* they are called here." He cut the engine. What was he thinking as he scowled at the black mass ahead? Whatever the thought, it had drained his face of color, carved deep lines at the corners of his eyes. The truck motor came to with a roar and died down.

"Can you see? Was it a collision?"

"Seems to be nothing there but the truck. Accidents and breakdowns are a daily routine to those modern dinosaurs. Cars behind us?"

"No. Not one in sight."

"We're in luck. Fold the seat and crawl over. Sit on the floor. *Don't* ask *questions.* Cover your shoulders with that fur jacket. Be quick. No matter what happens, don't yip. Get me?"

"I get you. Here we go again, Skipper. Not a dull moment when we are together." A hysterical giggle bubbled up behind him. "Scorpion gang?" she whispered.

"Maybe. I'm not taking any chances. Hide!"

"At least they can't marry us again." Her low voice was so close it tickled his ear. "Perhaps they'll insist on a divorce this time. Man jumped into a bramble-bush stuff. That's a thought."

"Kay, *please.*"

"I'm sorry. I can't believe it's real. Hand me my bag. Quick. I'll be good."

"What's in it? Been collecting scrap metal?"

"Souvenirs from Bill—the dear. Here's where I do the Cheshire Cat act. Going—going—gone."

The last word was a mere sigh. Had she really been

as unconcerned at the situation as she sounded or was she the best sport in the world? Past experience should answer that question. She was.

He started the car. The truck ahead might be on perfectly legitimate business, but he wouldn't take a chance with that message in Slade's cigarette case burning in his mind like a neon sign. Wheels were to roll at dusk and "Eet start thees night; check as eet go through" echoed in his ears. Had his warning to Don Pasquale been sidetracked? He would attempt to pass. If he wasn't hailed he would know that he'd had an attack of hectic imagination.

"Here we go," he said to himself and stepped on the gas. . . . Not too fast. Just enough speed for a man who knew where he was going and was on his way.

Past two enormous red eyes. A black bulk with light from electric torches flashing over it like fireflies. So far so good. A figure in the road. Two upraised arms. Not so good. He slowed to a stop with his foot on the accelerator.

"Hiah, buddy!" American voice, not Mexican. The man leaned on the door of the sedan. Two ferret-bright eyes peered from under the brim of a straw sombrero. The open shirt collar revealed spirals of matted red hair, like a sprinkling of fine-curled copper springs, on a fat chest. He'd never seen this guy before. That was a break.

"What's the trouble?" he asked.

"Broken connecting rod."

"That's a mean one. Can't help you. Sorry, I'm all out of connecting rods."

"Oh, yeah! Fresh guy. Well, I'm tellin' you, 'taint nothin' to grin about. Hey fellers—" The three men working on the truck turned at his shout—"I'll go back and send someone to pull us out."

He swung open the car door and wedged himself into the seat beside the driver.

"Now what?"

"Turn around and take me back where I come from, buddy."

Hamilton glanced at the motionless men by the truck . . . Something sinister in their quiet. Watching his next move? If he protested now there would be four against one. With Kay in the car he couldn't risk it. He'd get this tough egg up the road a way and throw him out.

"How do I know where you came from?"

"Turn around and be quick. I ain't got no time to argue." Something hard pressed against Hamilton's ribs. "Get my meanin', buddy?"

"Sure. Sure, I get it. I wasn't born yesterday and I go to the movies." He backed and turned with an ear-splitting grinding of gears. If another car came along and found the road blocked he might signal the driver for help.

"Cut out the racket unless you want to be chucked out an' me take the wheel."

"That wouldn't add up right. You see, this isn't my car."

"Snitched it, did you?"

"I like the word 'borrowed' better. Something in my bones tells me that on the way back we'll run into the owner looking for it. All right with me. They'll catch you with a gun; that'll clear me and it sure will be one on you."

Hamilton wondered that he could laugh when his throat was tight with fear of what Kay might do if she had heard that word "gun."

"Here we go. Back to the city, yo ho!"

"Shut up, you." A pressure against his ribs. "If we're stopped I'll shoot first and explain to the other fella later. Step on the gas."

Hamilton stepped on it. The light from a crimson afterglow was in his eyes; the scent of mesquite in his nostrils; the heavy breathing of the man beside him in his ears. A car *whoosh*ed by; the pressure on his ribs increased. The speedometer clicked off the kilometers. Ten more to the city. He'd better get to work, quick. A crash of glass. The back-seat window?

"Now what in hell was that?" The pressure on Hamilton's side was removed as the trucker peered behind him.

"Sounded like a shot. Got any pals hidden in those bushes at the side of the road?"

"Pals! Say, what you stoppin'—"

Hamilton choked off the man's voice with one hand and opened the sedan door with the other. "Out you go, Big Boy."

"Then—you—come with—me, smart . . ." The last word was a gurgle.

He fell backward to the road dragging Hamilton with him, helpless in his iron grip. "This—is—where you—go out cold—buddy. You—"

"Smile when you say that, stranger," ordered a girl's crisp voice.

The trucker looked up with a curse, raised the gun in his hand. Something smashed in his face. He fell back without a sound.

"Kay! Kay!" Hamilton had her in his arms. "Did he hurt you?"

"He didn't touch me. I—I—" She shivered uncontrollably. "Did I k—kill him?"

"No. Stunned him, that's all. Quick! He'll come out of it in a minute. Get in the car while I drag our late passenger into the bushes and get his gun."

When he dashed back to the sedan her foot was on the running board. She glanced over her shoulder.

"Shouldn't we do something for . . ."

He lifted her in. In an instant he was behind the wheel. She drew a long, ragged breath as the car leaped forward.

"Life's just one thrill after another in Mexico, isn't it, Drex? Our late adventure fits into the hectic design of the present-day world like a missing piece of a picture puzzle. Forgive me for being practical but how are we to go back home with that road fairly crawling with thugs?"

"Take it easy, Kay. You don't have to be a sport every minute. Your voice is strained to breaking point. We can't go over that road tonight. I'll get in touch with the Consul. He has friends here with whom you can stay. I must report what happened to an official in the town in which you spent the day. We'll go to the hotel. Where in thunder did you get the automatic you smashed in the thug's face?"

"From my bag. It was given to me as a joke before I left home. I've carried it all the way. Gave me a feeling of security. Never thought that the handle, not the business end would save us. I—I—couldn't stay covered up, Drex. I knew you were in danger. I heard the word 'gun' and then I smashed the window—you know the rest."

"Stop shivering. You're safe now. Rest against my shoulder and watch the lights of the city ahead prance toward us."

"Thanks, I'm quite steady enough to sit up straight. Those shivers are merely excitement signing off. I've been training in Defense work too long to be a shoulder addict. Before we make our dramatic entrance at the hotel, you'd better straighten your tie and readjust the collar of your shirt. You look as if you'd been in a street brawl."

She met his grin in the mirror. After they reached the hotel she would tell him about the story in "Air Waves," but it might worry him at first as it had her and she hated to wipe that smile from his lips.

"You look a trifle messy yourself, sister. I've got to check up on a phone call. After that we'll stop and repair damages. How about dropping those gardenias overboard? They're beige around the edges."

"That's a masterpiece of understatement. They are done to a scorched brown." She started to drop the flowers into the road, regarded them thoughtfully, laid them in her bag instead.

"Bill gave them to me. I'll keep them as a souvenir of a perfect day. Perfect until we saw that truck."

"Hewins is terribly in love with you, isn't he? I heard him call you 'darling.' "

"What does that prove? Doesn't everybody call everybody 'darling,' in these days?"

"I don't. That word is reserved in my vocabulary for a very special person—if and when I find her."

"Ah, romantic as well as humorous type."

His silence made her slightly ashamed of her laughing jibe.

Conversation languished after that until they reached the city.

"Here's where I get busy." He stopped the car in

a narrow street before what appeared to be a wine shop. "I won't be gone but a short time. Don't mind being left alone while I phone, do you?"

"Certainly not. It will give me a chance to repair those damages to which you so unchivalrously referred a moment ago."

As she powdered her nose and retouched her lips a bell tolled above the lighted door of a church at the end of the street. Men wrapped to the eyes in serapes, women shrouded in *rebosas* pattered by in their sandals to worship.

She saw his black shadow before she saw him, then the softly closed door of the shop shut off the light. As he slid behind the wheel, she whispered:—

"Did you make the connection, Drex?"

"Yes."

"I've read somewhere that an authoritative statement is death to conversation. I'm dumb till I am again addressed."

"Wise gal."

There was a laugh in his voice but the two lines between his eyes deepened as bending slightly forward he drove through narrow streets, up one, down another.

"Don't worry. I'm not lost." He took a quick turn and retraced his way. "I'm trying to lose anyone who may have seen me stop and decided to tail me."

To Kay the next quarter-hour moved with the speed and color of a pantomime behind a gauze screen, the gauze being her unbelief in its actuality. . . . Narrow streets and the highway. Lights. The patter of hurrying feet. People. A military band playing in the plaza. Locking the car in the garage. Drex at the entrance to the hotel saying:—

"Wait in the patio. I—"

A man stepping from the shadow of a palm, his face distorted with anger. A man with a newspaper in his hand, his smooth voice insinuating:—

"Miss *Chesney*! It is possible? Drex! Together. A thousand apologies for my surprise. I have intruded on a rendezvous—or perhaps—"

Catching Hamilton's upraised fist, leaning against

him to hold him back. Remembering Bill saying, "A rich hacienda owner who slipped across the border." Hearing her own laughing voice.

"Drex! Now everyone will know we've eloped. Oh, dear, and we wanted our marriage to be a surprise. Come on. Under the circumstances I'm sure Señor Castello will excuse us."

Hearing Castello's smothered Spanish curse. Feeling Drex push her before him into the hotel. Realizing that the time bomb had gone off and burned her bridges behind her.

XIV

"This way, Kay."

Drex Hamilton gripped her arm with a force that stopped the circulation and hurried her into the table-filled patio. The maître d'hôtel beamed welcome. This was not the head man she had seen at noon. She had time only to wonder why his face seemed familiar before he drew out two chairs at a table in a corner almost hidden under a palm.

"Welcome, Señor Hamilton. Thees ees all I have to give you. Sorry; eef you had phoned the best would have been yours."

"This is all right. I prefer to be on the side line tonight. Dinner for two. I've just realized that I'm ravenously hungry, Kay. You know what I like, Amando. I'll leave it to you. Make it the best the house affords and make it fast."

"*Sí, Señor.* I weel tell the chef eet ees you who order. He weel be happy to serve you, but he ees an arteest." Hands and shoulders shrugged apology. "He weel not make the haste even for a *grande magnífico* like yourself, Señor."

"*Grande magnífico.*" The words echoed through Kay's mind. Drex was known, well-known in this very hotel. What would be the result of her impulsive announcement to Castello? Had he read the story of the marriage in the paper he held? Even had he suspected it referred to Drex Hamilton there was no possible reason why he would think she was the girl. She had turned on the floodlight of publicity. Now what would happen to Drex's plans and the plans of those whom he was helping?

"Do Amando's suggestions sound good to you, Kay?"

"Sorry, Drex. I didn't recognize a single dish with its Spanish name. When I go to strange places I always order the speciality of the house, so whatever you've planned will suit me to a T."

The maître d'hôtel bowed. "Then if the Señorita is—"

"*Señora* Hamilton."

"A thousand pardons, Señor. I had forgotten—now I remember." He beamed and shrugged in a veritable agony of pleasurable embarrassment. "I am happy for you. Pedro!"

The swarthy-skinned waiter answered his summons, nodded in response to the rapid Spanish instructions and vanished with the written order.

"I go now to speak to the chef, Señor. He weel do himself what the *americanos* call proud." With another beam, another bow, he hurried away.

"Why, why, did you do it, Kay?" Hamilton's low voice was harsh.

"I don't know why I was such a dumbbell," she flayed herself with savage intensity. "Remember how cocky I was when I assured you *I* wouldn't broadcast the Casa Fresco episode. I should have let you handle it." She told him of the newspaper story Bill had read.

"When Castello, with that folded paper in his hand, spoke to us I had a chilly certainty that he was about to comment on the 'Air Waves' reference to the marriage of a rich *hacendado* across the border, that he suspected you were the man. He glared at you with deadly hatred and I remembered that you stood between him and a great estate. You doubled your fists, looked as if you were getting ready to kill him and I thought 'Better for Drex to lose an estate because he has married an American, that marriage being only temporary, than because he has murdered a man.' Something compelled me to stop you. Did you have to add to my blunder by correcting the maître d'hôtel when he called me Señorita? Do you think that the 'Air Waves' gossip referred to us?"

"Yes. I haven't really believed that Castello had a finger in that scandalous column; now I'm sure he has."

"Why? How could he know of that Casa Fresco affair?"

"You're right, he couldn't. One of the cutthroats has talked. I'll bet Edouard has called the attention of the estate lawyers to that paragraph already. They are located in this city. Though no matter what I do the income from and the management of the de la Cartina estate remain mine until I am thirty-five—always supposing I want to retain them—my marriage to an American cuts me out of the property eventually, and eventually it will go to him, the bulk of it, unless Chiquita marries before my birthday or he is exiled again. I thought for one horrible second you had gone screwy. Sorry I crabbed, but for a minute I didn't know what move to make."

"Do you now?"

"Sure. Have it all doped out. Fast worker, Drex. Here's the story. You and I met in the States. I was already in love with your picture which I had seen at your brother's home. I moved into the boy-friend spot previously held by one Bill Hewins."

"One would think you were announcing a change in a radio program. How can you smile about it?"

"Steady, that was a sob you swallowed. Remember we're in a crowded night spot. To proceed with the romance of the *hacendado* and the lady. We decided to marry, then for fear your brother, if he knew, wouldn't allow you to stay with him and help with Jill, we concluded to keep the ceremony secret for a while. I heard today that I must be at the hacienda and ranch for the next two weeks. On the way here for dinner and dance we read 'Air Waves.' Decided that as the cat was out of the bag we might as well face the music and have a honeymoon together."

"That explanation will baffle your friends. It couldn't be much more incredible. You in love with me! You've hardly looked at me since I arrived at Hugh's. Do you think for a minute that anyone will believe you fell in love with my picture?"

"Why not? I could mention several historic cases where it happened. Anyway it will take time to prove it isn't true and what I am fighting for is time. Smile, Kay. Try to look happy. Remember you are a bride. Stars in your eyes, sister."

"Bride. It's too serious to joke about. How can I smile when by my impulsiveness I've messed up your life? Perhaps that gossip tidbit wasn't about us. You're not even a near Mexican. Perhaps the paper in Castello's hand wasn't the one I imagined it was. I'm sorry; I'm terribly sorry. What demon prompted me to tell him?"

"You instinctively react to the dramatic, don't you?"

"It wasn't drama this time; it was panic. You looked as if you were making ready to pummel him to pulp. I felt I must stop you."

"You were right. I was seeing red. His voice was an insult. You doubtless saved me from a night, perhaps longer, much longer, in jail. A Mexican of Castello's rank, even if he has been a rebel, could get anything he wanted in a court here against an American. That's what I am in spite of my stepfather's attempt to make me a citizen of his country. You tried to save me. How about yourself? Looks as if you'd messed up your own life. I saw Hewins kiss you good-by. Don't worry. We'll work it out. We are married. No sense in trying to keep it secret."

"But you said you must remain out of the spotlight of publicity."

"The next edition of 'Air Waves' would have named names, doubtless. So we're only a week ahead of the news break. Someone who was at Casa Fresco that night sold the story to the paper. I'll bet the editor paid by the nose for it. I'm glad it's out. I hate underground situations. I'll get in touch with your brother at once. He'll go haywire if you're late getting back, but before I go, put your left hand under the table."

Her hand met his. A ring was slipped on the third finger. "No, Drex. No. It—it isn't honest."

His eyes, black with intensity, met hers. "Are you, strictly?"

She let that go and laid her hand on the table. The diamonds in a circlet blinked at her knowingly. He answered the quick question in her eyes.

"I've been carrying it round since you returned mine. I'm all for preparedness. Don't look so terrified. That ring changes nothing between you and me. I shall have to leave you for about half an hour. I'll engage rooms. Amando will serve dinner there."

"No, Drex. No. I'll wait here. *Please.*"

His eyes glowed with laughter. "For a gal who laid a thug out cold you're showing signs of panic. If I leave you alone here I'm doing what I threatened to break Slade's neck for doing."

"This is different. No one will see me under the palm."

"All right, but promise you won't leave this table till I come back?"

"Where would I go? Strange as it may seem at the moment I've lost the urge for adventure."

"Getting your smile back aren't you? Don't speak to anyone. If a foreign propagandist orates here in the patio—it may happen—*don't* rush to the defense of your country."

"I won't. I promise. This time I'll keep the promise. From now on I'll do exactly as you tell me."

"Mean that?" Before she could answer he rose. "Of one thing I may be sure all the rest of our—my— life: you didn't marry me for my money." His boyish grin eased the unendurable smart of regret for what she had done. "Our suave *señor* will be so busy watching you he won't have me on his mind. That will be a help. Chin up. Remember, no walkee, no talkee, no singee."

At the entrance to the patio he spoke to the

maître d'hôtel. Curious the impression she had that she had seen the man before. . . . He was glancing toward her. Now he was speaking to Drex. They had gone into the lounge together.

She tried to forget the ring burning on her finger, the events of the last half hour, by observing the men and women at the near-by tables. They seemed gay, lighthearted. No one of them appeared as if he had changed, dangerously perhaps, the pattern of his own or another's life as she had. Incredible, the swiftness with which humans who were confident of the control of their destinies could be brought together, dragged apart like two-dimensional figures on a screen, at the will of an invisible director. Was Fate the name of that same director?

Apparently about half the diners were tourists. Sleek, well-groomed men and gorgeously gowned women. They made a kaleidoscope of color, high-lighted by the flash of jewels, which continuously shifted its pattern. The Mexican women wore black. Their heavily powdered patrician faces were beautiful.

The musicians strolled toward her strumming their guitars. The maître d'hôtel furtively waved them on. Had he instructions from Drex not to allow anyone to approach her table?

A girl in white blouse, full skirt striped in orange, white and green—a red rose in her hair to match the broad ribbon from which hung her flower tray—laid a spray of white orchids and a card on the table and walked away.

Wear these. They'll help you feel in character.

D. H.

Drex had sent them. She pinned them to the shoulder of her green frock wishing that he himself had come instead of sending flowers. She glanced at her wrist watch. Already he had been gone a half hour. Could anything have happened . . .

"Of all people! What are you doing in this town alone, Kay?"

She looked up. Closed her eyes and looked again

at the tall, exquisitely blond woman in a gauzy-black frock and a sensational corsage of purple orchids who had stopped at the table. She was really seeing her. It wasn't another dream. She dropped her hands to her lap and slipped the circlet from her finger. Of all the events of a supereventful day this was the most amazing.

"Blanche! I thought you were—were—"

"In Reno. Oh, no. That's behind me. Von, it's my sister-in-law, Kay Chesney. Imagine finding her here."

She had been so amazed at the presence of her brother's ex-wife in Mexico that she had not noticed the man. Gordon Slade's story of their intimacy recurred to her as she glanced at his expressionless face, at his smooth, blond hair. She hadn't really believed the gossip about the two but their presence together here gave the story substance. Did he know what she was thinking? He half raised his hand as if by habit to adjust an eyeglass, dropped it quickly, bowed, clicked his heels. His full lips widened in a smile that did not touch his pale eyes.

"We are old friends, are we not, or—perhaps it is old enemies, Miss Chesney."

"I hope not the last, Herr Von Haas." Kay had recovered from surprise not only at his presence with Blanche but from the absence of the ever-present monocle. "I haven't yet forgotten our dance in the patio at Señor Castello's last evening. It had everything. Moonlight, stars and a perfect setting for a perfect waltz."

"Don't come now, Drex, don't," she pleaded in her mind even as she noticed her sister-in-law's quick, annoyed glance at Von Haas . . . How explain his presence if he did come?

"You haven't told me yet why you are hiding under this palm, alone, Kay," Blanche reminded in a tone of virtuous disapproval.

"I'm *not* hiding. I—"

"A thousand pardons." The maître d'hôtel laid his hand on the back of her chair. "The long-distance call for you has come. Would you make haste, please?"

For a split-second she looked up at him. Drex had told her not to leave the table, but he had not thought of Blanche's appearance to complicate matters. She rose quickly.

"Sorry to break away like this, but I promised Hugh that if I were delayed I would phone him. It seems hours since I put in the call. Came here to have a day with Bill Hewins who flew over from a Texas camp, then my car went blooey and I had to wait for repairs. Good night."

In the lounge she slipped the ring into her bag. As she glanced up at the maître d'hôtel, she suddenly remembered where she had seen him before tonight. No wonder he had looked familiar. No wonder he had stammered, "I had forgotten—now I remember," when Drex had corrected him for calling her "Señorita." He was the bartender at Casa Fresco who had put the spare on her sedan. She could trust him.

"Where do I go from here, Amando? Mr. Hamilton told me to wait at the table until he returned."

"He told me that also, Señora, and that eef he were delayed I was to serve the dinner een the room he has engaged."

"Room! Oh, no—"

"Please! The blond Señora and her escort are coming thees way verra fast."

"Quick. Tell me where to go!"

Now what? she wondered as she entered the sitting room into which an Indian bell-hop piloted her. The windows were open on the gallery. Beyond a doorway she glimpsed the corner of a bedspread. From the patio below rose the strum of guitars, the click of castanets, soft laughter, the tinkle of silver on china, the fragrance of heavy perfumes and of flowers. Was it only a few hours ago she had said to Bill, "It would be fun to sit on one of those galleries in the evening and look down on the patio"? *Fun . . . A few hours* . . . It seemed like years. If only she were miles away. It wouldn't surprise her when next she looked in a mirror to discover that her hair had turned white.

Her body tensed. A knock? She stared at the door.

Would Castello dare—of course he wouldn't. "Brace up, my girl, scoop up your courage and grab it tight," she prodded herself.

"Who is it?"

"Room service, Señora."

The dinner. She threw open the door. Somewhere in the corridor a radio was broadcasting the music of woods and strings and brasses, blending into melody heartbreakingly sweet. Pedro, the waiter who had taken Drex's order, wheeled in a table set for two; an Indian boy in native white clothes followed with another. The first man placed chairs, closed the door and shut the music out.

"Shall I serve, Señora?"

"No. I will wait for Señor Hamilton. He will be here soon."

"*Bueno*. If you need me, ring here." He indicated a push button in the wall, followed the boy from the room and closed the door.

"That seems to be that," she said aloud. She lifted a silver cover and then another from the dishes on the serving table. If the food tasted as well as it looked and smelled the chef was indeed an artist.

She pulled off her hat before a mirror; shook her head at her reflection. The short coppery waves of hair stood out like a glinting halo.

"You think you're real, but you're not. You're as much in a dream world as—"

Footsteps on the marble-floored gallery. Drex? No. They were cautious footsteps. Breathlessly she watched the progress of a shadow toward the window. Who could it be?

"Dinner for two and only one to eat it. Won't you accept me as a substitute for the absent bridegroom?" Señor Edouard Rafael Castello asked and stepped into the room.

XV

Drex Hamilton looked back at Kay as he left the patio. Was he taking a chance, leaving her alone? He must go. When he had phoned from the wine shop he had promised Don Pasquale he would report at his home in person. Even Kay's sensational announcement to Castello didn't cancel that appointment.

"Amando, keep your eye on the Señora, understand?"

"*Sí, sí, Señor.*"

"If anyone speaks to her get her away."

"*Sí, Señor.* But to where?"

"I'll engage rooms. Serve dinner there."

"*Sí, Señor.*"

Amando was a good scout and loyal—he had proved that before—but would he be a quick thinker in an emergency? If he wasn't, Kay was; he would have to trust to them and finish this evening's business. Little he had suspected, when he flew to the airport to meet her determined that she should not drive home alone after dark, that his intention to secure her safety would result in this mix-up.

Kay. . . . The thought of her kept him company as he walked along the street. He lived over the breathless moment at the door of the hotel; Castello's white, anger-distorted face, his smooth insinuating voice; his own mounting fury, the warmth of her body holding him back, her gay announcement, "Drex. Now everyone will know we've eloped. Oh, dear, and we wanted our marriage to be a surprise."

Surprise! It was a mild word for the gossip and chatter the news would cause. If that story in "Air Waves" had referred to the Casa Fresco episode of course Edouard Rafael Castello was responsible. It had seemed wiser to agree with Kay that he couldn't know about it, better for all concerned that she did not suspect the identity of the bearded major. The smooth Edouard must be jubilant. The news was out of a marriage that turned over to him the handling of a huge fortune, a large part of which would be his—if Chiquita did not marry—*if* he remained loyal. But why should he have been white with fury if he were behind the publication? Something queer about that.

Perhaps Don Pasquale would help concoct a story of the time and place of the ceremony that would pass muster. If only the news hadn't broken just now. This very errand he was on might drag Kay into danger. Why let that thought turn his blood to ice? If the servant Miguel were to be believed, her safety already was threatened—but was it she or Chiquita or Amelia about whom the warning was intended? Whichever it was, the developments of the last hour had given him the right to protect Kay. The moment he returned to the hotel he would talk the situation out with her, would tell her his plan and if she agreed to it he would phone the Consul.

He stepped into the shadow of a *portal* in a white wall. His personal problems must be shelved for the present. Apparently his phone call to Don Pasquale from home had been too late to stop the contraband-loaded *camiónes* from "rolling." He glanced at the il-luminated dial of his wrist watch. Kay had been alone only ten minutes. With luck it would take him five to complete his call, ten to return. Nothing could hap-pen to her in so short a time.

The gate swung open in answer to his soft, im-perative knock. His shadow followed him as he hur-ried along a paved walk beside the house. Once he thought it something more than his shadow. He left it behind as he softly lifted the latch and slipped into the house. The furnishings of the hall hadn't been changed since the last time he was here. It was the atmosphere which was different; it was as if the house were hold-ing its breath. The air was acreep with warning . . . Cockeyed thought. The experience of the last two hours must be getting him down. Don Pasquale had assured him the coast was clear when he had phoned from the wine shop.

The library at last. His feet felt as if they were dragging ball and chain. He pushed open the door. Listened. No sound save the ghostly *tap, tap* of a vine against a window. Silent as a tomb. That eerie thought helped. He crossed the threshold into the softly lighted room.

"Here I am, Don Pasquale. I . . ."

His body turned to ice. The man was bound to his chair. His bushy gray head lolled to one side. Dead? Murdered?

Shocked, incredulous, he stood motionless. Did everyone up against a situation like this feel a mad desire to run? The thought flashed through his mind as he dashed forward.

"Don Pasquale! Don Pasquale!" he whispered as he listened to the man's faintly beating heart. He tried vainly to unknot the rope. Whipped a knife from his pocket and sawed at the cord about the lax shoulders. Hang it, it took forever with such a small blade. He looked over the desk for something larger. Brandy! Two glasses. A carafe of water.

He drenched his handkerchief and sopped head and face. Hacked again at the bonds. Freed the muscular arms and rubbed them vigorously to restore circulation. Now if he could get the cords off his legs and—He looked up and met wide-open, staring eyes.

"Don Pasquale! Don Pasquale! It's Hamilton. You're safe!" In the exuberance of his relief he shook the bulky shoulder. "Did you hear? You're safe."

The open mouth closed. The lines of the jaw tightened. The glazed eyes cleared. The blue lips made two attempts before words came:—

"Received—first—warning. Acted on your—advice, *mi amigo,* let—one—*camión* go—through—for—bait."

Hamilton bent his head to hear the faint voice.

"My—men—they—work—queeck. Stopped—one—minute—" His eyes closed. "I get—my breath!"

"Take your time. I understand. They stopped the other *camiónes*. How many?"

"Four. Loaded—with you—know—Seized. Drivers taken."

"Go on, Don Pasquale." Hamilton hacked at the rope that bound the fat legs. "Why were you alone here? Where are the servants?"

"It ees—Church *fiesta*. I feel—so safe, lately, I let them go." Two double chins sagged forward on the broad chest. "Drivers. *Camiónes*. What good—unless we get the—men behind? We—must get—them."

"We will."

Even as he answered, Drex was thinking that the highway would be safe. He could take Kay back tonight and get her out of the net which might be closing him in. Not a doubt but that the thug whom he had left beside the road had recognized him and even if in jail would manage to report to the "cover-up" man.

"We'll get 'em, Don Pasquale. Don't lose your nerve. Seizing those *camiónes* will put a crimp in the plans of the men behind the scheme. Go on. What happened to *you?*"

"I—return here. Message comes that—*camiónes* are taken. I listen in my dark closet. So much done. I feel fine. I step to hall. Something soft drop over my head. I know notheeng—more teel I open my eyes— and see you, Señor."

"Did the person who knocked you out hear the phone message?"

"Imposseeble. After the first whispered word I did not speak. He was too late to stop my warning. Already I had set my men to work."

"Was there no sound, no movement by which you could identify him?"

The man in the chair thrust his arms high above his head, stretched his legs forward with a long sigh of relief.

"He deed a good job. They were very tight, those ropes. That is better. They preeck alive, my veins. I heard only one sound, Señor. A soft '*Ach.*'"

The eyes of the two men met.

"That's how it is."

"That's how eet is, Señor. Foreign agents again. Go. You have done your part well. I am what you call O.K. Thees house weel be watched. You are not safe on the street thees night, *mi amigo.* Help me up."

Steadied by Hamilton's arm he hobbled to a sofa.

"Turn back the rug een front of the desk. Each moment count. Queeck!"

Hamilton needed no prodding. Now that the excitement of finding Don Pasquale bound and unconscious had subsided all he could think of was Kay sitting alone in the patio with Castello in the same hotel. All he could hear was Miguel's whispered warning last night, "Danger for the Señorita." He worked quickly. . . . Threw back the rug. Jerked at a trap door. Up through the opening shot a blast of cold, dank air; beneath it were steps.

"Where to?" he whispered.

"Under thees house to wall. Find door there. Be quiet. Very quiet. Under next house to patio." A faint, fat chuckle. "He ees *mi amigo, mi paisano,* the owner. He does not know; he is very stupeed; he cares only for what he eats. He speaks English much of the time. He weel not hear; he ees very deaf, but—the servants may. Move queeck. Pull door down after you. Find electric flash at side of first step. Think not of me. They won't come again tonight. Go, *mi amigo.*"

Hamilton heard the last word as he closed the trap door above his head. . . . Down the stairs. Across a cellar illumined by a spot of light which served only to increase the darkness outside its orbit. The wall at last.

He flashed his light along the rough whitewashed surface. Softly raised a heavy iron latch. A sound in the dark. He held his breath. Listened. Only the thudding of his heart. The door responded to his gentle pull. Came as easily as if on greased hinges. Another cellar. Colder, darker than the one he had left. Splinters of light at the farther end. Must be the opening on a moonlit patio. He stole forward. A grilled gate. The scent of fine tobacco.

"Señor, it is the telephone." The loud announcement in English apparently to a deaf person was so near he could touch the speaker if he tried.

"Why did you not take the message, Emilio?" The voice was querulous, old. "You know I like to sit here after dinner."

With difficulty Hamilton restrained an urge to make a dash for liberty. Kay was alone in a city honeycombed with danger, where a man who hated him was at large. He must get to her. Even with the trucks stopped he wouldn't take her home over the road tonight; his other plan was better. Why didn't *el señor* go in and take his darn message . . . *Why?* Steady. Steady. Take this situation by the smooth handle. Smooth handle! Good Lord, was there one?

"He would not give it to me, Señor. It is you, yourself, he must speak to and at once."

"Stupid! Don't shout. Anyone would think I could not hear. Bring in my books, Emilio; I will not come out again." Footsteps crossing the flagging. A door closing. The servant moving about.

Why in thunder didn't Emilio get out? He was whistling now, coming toward the gate.

"Across the patio. The gate swings," a voice directed softly. "Then to the right. Wait for the house door to close."

Hamilton's tense muscles relaxed with a suddenness which sent him against the wall for support. Emilio was one of Don Pasquale's agents, conveniently in service on the adjoining estate.

That bang must be the house door. He slipped through the narrow opening. The patio was bright with moonlight, fragrant with the scent of gardenias and jasmine. Palm fronds clattered in the light breeze. Flowers in the border were faint blurs. Running water tinkled. It was light enough to see the gate, which seemed miles away. Light enough also to see the man at the telephone at the open window above, to hear him say softly, "My part is done. Carry on, but watch . . ." The whispered word was inaudible.

Was that man speaking the neighbor whom Don Pasquale had called *"mi amigo, mi paisano,"* my friend, my countryman, whom he believed was deaf? How and where did he fit into the picture?

A chair fell with a metallic clatter as he tiptoed toward the gate. Immediately through the open window came the click of a cradled phone, an irritable roar:—

"Emilio! Emilio! Where are you? What was that sound?"

"Pardon, Señor." The answer was shouted. "I did not take in the chairs; the breeze must have blown one over. Time for your favorite broadcast, Señor."

Under cover of trumpets, brasses and strings playing the triumphal march from *Aïda* Hamilton stole across the patio. . . . Softly, cautiously, opened a gate. Turned right. Kept in the shadow of vine-covered walls. From behind him came faintly the exquisite loveliness and exaltation of *Celeste Aïda*. Forced himself to a leisurely walk along a street. Puzzled over the phone conversation by the open window. Had Don Pasquale been fooled by a neighbor who pretended to be stupid, a neighbor who spoke fluent English? Didn't the servant Emilio know that his employer was not deaf or was he in turn fooling Don Pasquale? The plaza. The hotel at last.

Amando hurried toward, whispered:—

"I deed as you say, Señor Hamilton. When the blond lady and Herr Von Haas—"

"Von Haas! Who was the woman?"

"Your *señora* call her 'Blanche.' "

The Consul's onetime wife here— With her late admirer . . . Why?

"I tell your *señora* that long distance call. She trust me. I send her to room you engage. You weel find her there."

Safe. . . . The relief. . . . The incredible relief. . . . Now he would phone her brother.

In a fever of impatience he waited for the connection, told the amazed Consul what had happened, outlined his plan, heard his answer. He waited only for Chesney's slow: "O.K., Drex. Whatever you think right *is* right with me."

Until he knocked at the door of the room where Kay was waiting he had not realized the inferno of anxiety through which he had passed since leaving Don Pasquale.

Why didn't she answer? The door wasn't closed. He pushed it open. A table set for two. The appointments unused. He lifted a silver cover. The food untouched. No sign in bedroom or bath that she had been there. Hat and bag gone.

He stood in the middle of the sitting room trying to control the terror which was rising like a tide. Amando had said a man and woman had spoken to her—Von Haas and Blanche. Von Haas, whose tirade she had challenged at the Cantina. Would Kay have gone without leaving a note? A note! Why hadn't he thought of that before?

A wave of thanksgiving submerged terror when he reached the desk. Of course. Here it was. He picked up the sheet of paper in the middle of the green blotter. For an instant the words on it blurred, then stood out as if printed in neon.

> *Your* bride *is with me.*
> CASTELLO

XVI

Kay had read of horror turning a person to stone and had thought it the hectic invention of a fictioneer. Now she knew it to be fact as she stared unbelievingly at the smiling man leaning against the frame of the long window. Her feet were rooted to the floor. The door was but a few steps away but she couldn't move. The silence of fear, her fear, brooded in the room.

Why had she hurled that marriage announcement at Castello because he had a newspaper in his hand? There was more than one sold in Mexico. Why had she assumed that he had read the story to which Bill had referred? Why hadn't she thought then of the excuse of a broken-down car to explain her presence at the hotel —which had tripped from her tongue so glibly in answer to her sister-in-law's surprised greeting? The human mind certainly moved in a cockeyed way its wonders to perform. Better face the cold, undeniable fact that she had messed up another life and her own and check and double-check every word she uttered from now on.

"Don't look so startled, Señora Hamilton. I was strolling on the balcony, saw you here and couldn't resist offering my best wishes. You didn't give me a chance at the door. Why not sit down? It's a pity to allow the chef's masterpieces to spoil while you wait for —your husband."

Anger at the assurance in his voice and eyes, the suggestive pause before the word "husband," sent blood in a hot tide through veins she had thought ossified. The sudden return from the Stone Age lifted the weight from her spirit, released her inventiveness. Through her mind echoed Drex's voice:

"What I am fighting for is time. Our suave *señor* will be so busy watching you that he won't have me on his mind. That will help."

An idea there if she could put it across. She could help that much. She glanced at the table, then appealingly at the man who had drawn out a chair.

"Just between you and me, Señor, I don't like waiting." Gaiety and impatience were delicately blended in her voice. "Drex went to phone Hugh and his sister our startling news. He said it might take ages to make the connection. Listen to that divine waltz rising from the patio and I'm here with no man to ask me to dance."

Her smile and the invitation in her voice were nothing short of brazen. Would he fall for it? He did.

"There's one right here. You won't mind if I still think of you as Miss Chesney?"

"No." She regarded him gravely. "I like it. Do— do you ever wonder, after you've done a crazy thing, why you did it?" That was a true statement of her reaction if nothing else had been.

"Do you regret so soon the step you have taken this day, Señorita?"

If she obeyed that impulse she would shout "Yes!" If only she had allowed Drex to handle the situation at the door. Jail would have been better for him than this bottleneck. She hated the look in the man's eyes but having started to get him away before Drex returned she'd have to finish the job.

"I—I—oh, it isn't fair to ask me such a question, Señor Castello. How about that dance?"

"We go at once, but not here. There is a charming club not far away, where the music is perfect and —forgive me—there will be no Americans."

"But this green linen and my blue sombrero are not suitable."

"The place is quite informal. You may leave your hat in the powder room. Shall we go?"

Kay glanced at the table and back to him. He couldn't know that she was saying to herself, "The farther away from this hotel I get him the better for Drex."

"I ought to leave word—"

"I will do it; then Señor Hamilton will know you are quite safe. He also is a member of the club."

"Tell him where to find me." She powdered her nose at the mirror and adjusted her hat while he wrote at the desk.

As they waited at the hotel door for a horse-drawn cab a voice exclaimed:—

"Now what?" It was Blanche with Von Haas. "Isn't that car repaired yet, Kay? Don't tell me you are driving her home, Señor Castello!"

"*Buenas noches, mi amigo,*" Von Haas greeted.

"The car isn't ready and Señor Castello is not driving me home, Blanche. He is taking me dancing while I wait."

"Dancing! Where? I feel a certain responsibility about you, Kay, even if—"

"If you are no longer in our family? Señor Castello, tell her where we are going. It would be a pity to have her worry about me on top of her anxiety about the welfare of her child." That drew blood, Kay knew by the color that rose to the woman's face. Von Haas' pale, inscrutable eyes were fixed on Castello, who had ignored his greeting, with an intentness which gave her a creepy sense of danger.

"You're impertinent, Kay. I have engaged rooms at the hotel near Casa Blanca that I may be with Jill for a while. I insist upon knowing where you are going."

"A charming place; do you think I would take Miss Chesney anywhere else?" Castello named a club. "We are wasting a lot of beautiful music, Señorita. Come."

She could see Blanche and her escort standing in the hotel doorway as Castello helped her into the *pulpitos,* gave directions to the driver and followed. What information did Von Haas expect to get from Blanche now that she was no longer the wife of the American Consul? She, returning to be near her child! Phooey. What was her real reason? Whatever it was, it would prove to be an unbearable situation for Hugh.

"Don't you recognize your best boy friend when you meet in public, Señor Castello? Why didn't you speak to him?" Kay inquired not because she cared, but to break the strained silence as the wheels bumped over the cobblestoned street.

"I uncovered a fact a while ago which has broken my friendship with Herr Von Haas." His usually smooth voice was sharp with anger. "However, we will forget it. You did not tell your sister-in-law the real reason of your presence here?"

"No. I had learned my lesson. I shouldn't have told you. Drex and I had agreed to keep it a secret but when I saw you—I don't know why—it just exploded like a bomb."

For a person who prided herself on being honest she was developing into a facile liar. Better not think of that, but concentrate on her companion and whither they were bound. Of course she was in no danger. Blanche had made no protest when he had named the club. If this was just one more crazy thing she was doing, it was a crazy world in which she was living, wasn't it? Besides, Drex would know where to find her, when he read Castello's note.

The chilly sense of guilt vanished as she entered the clubhouse and noted the consideration with which

her escort was welcomed. Why should she feel guilty?
She wasn't really married to Drex. She had come here
to help him, hadn't she?

"How beautiful!" she exclaimed, as she entered a
large room decorated in the red, green and white of
the national colors. "I wish I had my camera and a
color film."

"I am happy that you are pleased, Señorita. Shall
we dance?"

He was the perfect host. She liked the personality
of the men and women who greeted him with a nod
and smile and a furtive glance at her. . . . Charming
persons of cosmopolitan type. The covered-up frocks
of the women kept her from feeling conspicuous in the
emerald-green linen.

"You were right, Señor," she agreed as he seated
her at a small table on the balcony. "The club is perfect, the music divine and your compatriots charming. I wished as I watched and listened to their soft
voices that I spoke Spanish fluently."

"If you intend to live here you must learn. Dif-
ficulties between United States Americans and Span-
ish-Americans are primarily due to inadequate knowledge of the language."

"But I don't intend to live . . ." She caught herself in time. "If you don't mind, I'd like not to spoil
this perfect evening thinking of the future *or* the mistakes of the past."

He was all Latin as he leaned toward her, flames
in his dark eyes, color mounting to his cheekbones.

"Has it been perfect? I would like to make every
day and night perfect for you, Señorita."

She snatched her hand from under the fingers laid
over hers. She had felt secure in his apparent friendliness. Now he was turning on the old mesmeric charm.

"I love you. If I—"

"Here they are," Blanche announced over her
shoulder as she stepped to the balcony. Drex Hamilton and Von Haas loomed behind her.

For the first time since she had known her, Kay
was glad to hear her sister-in-law's exultant voice.
"Don't act as if you'd been caught stealing, *don't,*"

she warned herself furiously. "You did this to help, didn't you?"

"Sorry to break up the party, Kay, but the car is ready. Shall we go?" Hamilton suggested in a voice which showed no trace of annoyance. After all, why should he care with whom she stepped out?

"What a yarn you told me, Kay, about the broken-down car." The former Mrs. Hugh Chesney's voice was iced with amusement, tinged with malice. "There have been elopements before."

"Who told you I'd eloped?" Kay demanded and then would have cheerfully bitten out her tongue.

"Told me? Your husband, of course. I met him in the hotel lounge, ghastly with anxiety because you had flown. I'll say you haven't done too badly for yourself, *chérie*. You've caught a man who has been as elusive as a trap-shy tiger. I presume wedding presents are indicated—and will they be spectacular! Pretty mean of you, I should say, to run off on your wedding night with a seasoned charmer like Señor Castello."

"Señora Chesney!" Castello's voice was sharp with warning; if his eyes had been blades they would have slashed her to ribbons. "I am not—"

"Thanks a million for entertaining my wife, Edouard." Hamilton's cool voice interrupted the angry protest. "I was held up trying to broadcast our news to her brother. You know what it means in this town to put through a long-distance call. I thought I'd never get back. How about one dance, Kay, before we leave? No hard feelings if I snitch your partner, Edouard?"

"I am sure it will be the perfect climax to what she had just told me has been a perfect evening. May I have the pleasure, Señora Chesney? It is Señora Chesney? Or have you already changed your name?" Castello asked with a suave intonation which sent an angry wave of color over the woman's small-featured, fine-boned face and set her ice-blue eyes aglitter with hate.

As they danced Hamilton asked: "Was it a perfect evening, Kay?"

"Perfect! It's been hideous. Let's get away, quick."

It seemed years to her excited fancy before side-by-side in the sedan they were driving along the highway.

She snuggled deeper into the mink jacket, slipped low in her seat and leaned her head wearily against the back.

"What a day! It seems a century since I left Hugh's house this morning and years since Señor Castello spoke to you and me in the doorway."

"Why did you go with him?"

She told the story from the moment she had been left alone in the patio.

"I tried to help by getting him out of your way, but by your stony glare when you and Von Haas stepped on the club balcony I realized I had blundered. Did you notice how he—I'm talking about Von Haas now—kept fumbling for a monocle which wasn't there? I wonder what had happened to it. He and his pal Castello have had what is technically known as a falling out."

"Those two! Fallen out! They're close as a banana and its skin. You have a hectic imagination, haven't you?"

"The idea may be amusing to you but Señor Castello's voice crackled with ice when he told me he had uncovered a fact which had broken his friendship with his *Fidus Achates,* only he didn't call him that."

"Edouard and Von Haas no longer hand-in-glove? It's unbelievable."

"What's queer about that? I've been living in an unbelievable world since a tire burst on a certain road marked DETOUR. I thought we were having complications in the good old U. S. with the constant arguments pro and against helping England but looking back from the moment I approached the Rio Grande I begin to think that, I quote:—

" 'All our ways were ways of pleasantness and all our paths were peace,' unquote."

She sat up suddenly.

"Drex! Remember that horrible suggestion of Blanche's about wedding presents? There won't be any, will there?"

"Several hundred, perhaps a thousand."

"Don't be wooden! We must do something to stop them."

"Let them come. We can return them with thanks and regrets later. Wonderful night, isn't it? Too fine to spend worrying about tomorrow. The highway looks as if it had been silver-plated."

"It's lovely and so heavenly peaceful that it doesn't seem to belong with this day. This isn't the way home. I remember now, you said we couldn't go back over that road tonight. Where are we going?"

"We could, but I've worked out a better plan. The more I thought of the explanation that I had persuaded you to marry me and go to the hacienda the more plausible it seemed. We're on our way. Relax. We have over a hundred kilometers of mountain road to cover."

"The hacienda! *Your* hacienda?"

"Mine for the present. I phoned your brother of the dramatic denouement and he agreed that you and I would better sidestep town at present. Señor Castello will lose no time broadcasting the news. What difference does it make if you go tonight? Tomorrow will be Sunday. He, Jill and Beeny will be along on Monday. So will Chiquita and Amelia Mansilla."

"But alone there with you! Think of the gossip."

"You've forgotten something, haven't you, Señora Hamilton?"

She knew from his voice that his eyes were warm with laughter. It was light enough to see their reflection in the mirror above the windshield.

"Why do you look at me like that? Don't tell me I am being psyched," he protested in mock dismay.

If he were not making a tragedy of her break at the door of the hotel why should she? She shook her head and smiled back at his mirrored eyes.

"I was deciding it was a crime that your lashes are wasted on a man. Think what devastation a girl could do with them. Do you curl the tips with an iron?"

"I know of one pair of eyes that do not need my lashes to do their stuff." He cleared his husky voice. "Suppose we cut personalities? It will be a lot easier for me. What has brought the ex-Mrs. Chesney back to Mexico?"

"She says it is to be near her che-ild. Fancy that, and she with a heart as shriveled as a dried-nut kernel. I hope she doesn't try to see Hugh and upset his life. If only he would fall in love with a woman who would love him and make him happy."

"Then you do believe in marriage?"

"For him. Not for myself—like this."

There were long stretches of silence between them after that. The world was almost as bright as day. They drove for hours over a perfect road in air crystal-clear. . . . Through sleeping villages from which came the distant, lonely sound of a dog barking. Passed a ghost town white as the snowy peaks behind it. The moonlight pitilessly exposed leaning walls, the jungle growth hungrily creeping nearer and nearer to smother and devour the crumbling adobe houses.

"These mountains remind me of Wordsworth's 'Perfect Woman.' " Kay's dreamy voice switched Hamilton's thoughts which had been heading back to Don Pasquale and his successful move to block the attempt to send away goods being unlawfully exported. "Remember it? 'A creature not too bright or good for human nature's daily food.' They might so easily be grand and overpowering. Instead, even with their white caps they are lovable, friendly and picturesque. Do I really see lights twinkling in the canyon?"

"Yes. Little fires where bandits are supposed to hide out. Rumor has it that the chief has a large hacienda back in the hills from which he sends out forays to collect ransom."

"Bandits! To be captured by bandits is all that's needed to make this the perfect end of a perfect day."

"Steady. I said 'supposed.' This Government has put the highwaymen out of business. I'm glad you like our mountains. The hacienda property spreads over thousands of hectares—acres to you—at their base. The ranch is higher up on the slopes. The capital of the state through which we are now driving was settled about sixty years after Columbus reached the West Indies. You're an unpredictable person, Kay. I thought after the day and night you put in, you would drop off to sleep."

"Sleep! I'll never sleep again. I've been asking myself why I, who had sworn to be independent, am in this car, on this road? Why I allowed you and Hugh to decide my life for me and what in your profound wisdom you two men plan to do about my clothes? One might easily get fed-up on emerald-green linen after twenty-four hours of it at a stretch."

She bit her lips hard to steady them. If she didn't watch out her emotions, already strained to the breaking point, would betray her and she had no intention of turning sob-sister.

"Take it easy, Kay. Chiquita has dozens of frocks and other duds at the house you can wear till Benny brings yours. Her old Spanish nurse, Rosa, will fit you out. She'll try to mother you as if you were still in rompers; she'll call you *niña,* which means 'little girl,' and she'll try to boss you, but she's a good old soul. The Consul and I did think of your clothes and we are *not* deciding your life. We've just taken over the next two weeks."

"Do you mean that after that you'll start the annulment?"

"If you still want it."

"*Want it!* Where do you get that 'if'? I want it more than I ever wanted anything in my life. The mere prospect has sent my spirit soaring. I'm so happy I—I—mind if I express my appreciation by a chaste kiss upon your manly brow?" She swallowed an hysterical laugh.

"Goodness, don't glare at me like that. I didn't mean it, I went a little haywire at the prospect of getting out of this mess—and is it a mess—that's all." His look still burned and smarted in her heart. "I wouldn't kiss you if you were the last man on earth," she added for full measure.

"That suits me fine. See those two white pillars glistening in the moonlight? We've arrived. Welcome home, Mrs. Hamilton-for-two-weeks. Get-acquainted weeks, we'll call them."

That ended all give-and-take of conversation. It

seemed to Kay that they drove miles along a road flanked by hedges, where the air smelled strong of sage, till they reached a great low-spreading house with windows that were slits of light in the thick adobe walls. Intricately carved iron gates at the entrance were held back by two menservants in native costume of dark green and scarlet. A pompous major domo with silver braid on his livery instead of color opened the car door to the accompaniment of an excited flow of Spanish greetings.

For a breath-taking instant before the heavy-timbered, brass-studded doors of the house, Kay had the feeling that Drex intended to carry her across the threshold in the time-honored custom. She hesitated and looked at him. He shook his head and smiled.

"Not this time," he said as if he had read her mind. "I'm reserving that ceremony for the real thing."

He gave an excellent imitation of Edouard Rafael Castello's courtly Castilian manner, reproduced his voice to an inflection:—

"Your house, Señora. Enter."

She colored furiously and, head high, preceded him between the massive doors.

XVII

Hot morning sun in a cloudless, deep-blue sky beat down on Kay's head as she stood near the stone fountain, in the middle of the central patio, and looked at the low-spreading Spanish house with its adobe walls shrouded in vines and the bright-green leaves and red berries of pepper trees. It appeared to be older than any building she had seen since she came to Mexico. The walls were out of plumb. Opposite corners did not have the same angle. Heavy-timbered doors, studded with brass, a spatter of bullet holes near a window, suggested danger, tragedy. There had been blood, sweat and death here—one felt it—even in this dazzling sunlight. Through a window slit in the four-foot wall she could see the flicker of an open fire.

There had been a fire in the large room in which she had awakened this morning. Last night she had been so atingle with excitement that she was sure she would not close her eyes. Rosa, the old nurse, in a loose, billowy dress of scarlet and green, with a face for all the world like a crinkled English-walnut shell dotted with shrewd black eyes, puckered with a withered mouth, had led her up a broad dark stairway and installed her in a huge bedroom furnished in beautiful, heavy Spanish pieces.

The woman had kept up a steady chatter of English-spattered Spanish as she had drawn a bath in a sunken tub in a room walled with tiles, had provided pajamas of pale-blue satin and had finally tucked her in the massive carved bed with a crooned *"Buenas noches, niña."*

Lying wide-eyed in the dark she had lived over the moment of hesitation at the great entrance door.

"I'm reserving that ceremony for the real thing," Drex had said. Would Amelia Mansilla be carried across that threshold? Why think of it? If she herself were free why care? Why *care*—

It must have been at that point that her sound, vigorously healthy body had betrayed her mind, blurred the continuity of her thoughts and submerged them in deep, unconscious sleep.

She had been awakened by bells summoning the faithful to Mass and had suddenly remembered where she was and why. She pulled an old-fashioned bell-rope and immediately a pretty, dark-haired Indian girl, in a gay red-and-green dress, had appeared. She fluttered spectacularly long lashes as she smilingly announced that she was Carlotta, set a tray of hot chocolate on a bedside table and delivered a note which read:—

> *Care to ride over the place before the sun gets too hot? Ask Rosa for riding togs. Breakfast with me in the patio at nine. Please!*
> DREX

She had shivered under an icy shower, hurried to dress in rancher's pants of a warm ocher, white-silk shirt and sleeveless jacket of hand-stitched green doe-skin and *vaquero* boots, provided by chattering Rosa . . . Had stepped to the iron-railed balcony outside the window for a glimpse of the mountains, had raced down the broad stairs to the patio, and here she was attired as for a fancy-dress party. Where was he?

As if in answer Hamilton appeared between open iron gates as intricate in design as those at the main entrance of the house. Even an exceptionally fine-looking man acquired an extra touch of all-rightness in riding clothes, she decided. His eyes, clear, deeply blue, met hers.

"Good morning, Kay. Sleep well?"

"Like a log. Why a log? Ever thought of that?" The queer tremor which the sight of him had set quivering along her nerves quieted when he smiled.

"Just as I had decided that after the events of the day, and the unsolvable problems ahead, I would never sleep again I opened my eyes in a room patched with sunlight filtered through Venetian blinds, fragrant with scent from the flowers in the patio, spicy with the aroma of hot chocolate and with the aforementioned problems nicely pigeonholed."

"It would be a tough mind that this mountain air wouldn't anesthetize."

He drew out a chair for her at a small table in a pool of green shadow. Tomás, the tall Yaqui butler, hovered solicitously till Hamilton dismissed him.

"Mighty nice of you to breakfast with me, Kay. Didn't know but what you had the tray-in-bed habit."

"Not I. I'm one of those annoying persons—that occur even in the best-regulated families—who prefers to be up before she breakfasts. What a delicious grape-fruit. Home product?"

"Yes. A moment ago you spoke of problems, Kay. Let's make a compact to forget all the yesterdays and agree not to look forward to the tomorrows for the next two weeks."

"Does that go for both of us?"

"Of course. Chiquita and her padre have put up

a problem for me that I swear I won't give in to—and yet—it pricks incessantly at my mind. That, besides yours and mine, I'd like to ignore while we are here. How about it?"

"I'll do my best not to look back or forward."

"Shake. Double shake."

He frowned at the two hands she had placed in his extended across the table.

"Where's the ring? I don't mean your own star sapphire you're indicating, I can see that. I mean the one that belongs on your left hand. Haven't forgotten, have you, that certain conventions must be observed?"

She hurriedly withdrew her fingers from his. "Who's breaking the compact and going back to yesterday, now?"

"That isn't the past; it's the present. Where's the ring?"

She unbuttoned the pocket on the breast of the white-silk blouse and produced a diamond circlet.

"Ever-ready Kay."

"Give it to me."

"Yes, Your Highness."

"That's too English for this country. *Jefe del Hogar,* Chief of the House, that's *me.* Glad you appreciate the fact that I'm boss. Hold out your finger. I'll wish it on."

"For the duration—in this case, two weeks," she reminded gravely.

"For the duration," he repeated and pressed his lips to the ring.

She snatched back her hand as if from fire. "That's not in the compact."

"Isn't it?" His eyes were keen with mischief; the shocked surprise in his voice was denatured with laughter. "Sorry, you see I'm inexperienced. I was sure I had seen it done—on the screen. My mistake."

"Don't make it again. How about that ride?"

"Nothing more to eat?"

"Nothing. There must have been a million calories, more or less, in the chocolate I drank before breakfast. Let's go."

A servant in green and scarlet was waiting with

two horses whose sleek bay coats shone like satin in the sun.

"Juan. This is Señora Hamilton."

"*Sí, Patrón*. We hear that *la señora* ees very beautiful. Now, we know." The man's smile revealed perfect white teeth. Before he bowed low, his great dark eyes met Kay's.

"That's all, Juan." Hamilton's dismissal was curt.

"What a handsome man," Kay exclaimed when the servant was out of hearing. "But what hot, wicked eyes. Just what is he here?"

"Second houseman, a matador on the side and a thorn-in-the-flesh, if you ask me. Chiquita keeps him because he is the son of Tomás and she loves that tall Yaqui Indian who held her on her first pony. Let's start."

He helped her mount, showed her how to brace the high-heeled boot in the stirrup and handed her a gay-yellow bandana.

"Tie this round your neck under the collar of your shirt or your throat will burn to a crisp. Pull that flat green felt down hard on your head and draw the strap tight under your chin. Never could understand why Chiquita doesn't wear a sombrero when she rides; those darn things blow off. Let's go."

They rode between grassy knolls, among big timber and eucalyptus, cedars, pines and oaks. Came out on the side of a mountain green with ferns and mosses and low-growing cacti.

"You can get a good idea of the hacienda from here."

"Until I came to Mexico I thought a hacienda was merely a house. Live and learn."

"It is a self-contained community. We have dynamos for electricity. We even have a police-constabulary of our own and a jail. This estate was thousands of acres larger before the agrarian policy cut down the immense ones and handed some of the land back to the Indians, but it's plenty big now. It keeps me on the jump to cover and superintend its many activities. I'll be glad to drop it."

"Do you intend to drop it?"

"That's one of the problems tabu for the next two weeks. Dismount and rest."

"I'm not tired. I could ride for hours."

"Perhaps you could but you won't in this altitude. We're 6700 feet above sea level. Hop off."

He steadied her as she slipped from the saddle. . . . Caught her shoulders and turned her around.

"Now look. The de la Cartina holdings are bounded only by the horizon."

Hills and valleys, running streams and heavy timber. Patches of brown-and-white grazing cattle. Barns and corrals. Cottages by the dozens. A cobble-flagged plaza—on one side of it two one-story adobe houses, with blurs of color in the large patios; on the other three low buildings, palms and trees. An enclosure that looked like the Harvard Stadium with rows upon rows of seats. A blaze of garden color near the sprawling main house, a tennis court, two swimming pools like blue mirrors, golf links, an airplane landing field.

"It's incredibly beautiful. All this for one person," Kay reflected aloud.

"One person—in a way—but one person with tremendous responsibilities. A host of retainers to be looked after, supported, cared for in sickness, old age and death."

"What are you called by these people?"

"*El Patrón*. The Master."

"That accounts for it."

"For what?"

"When Gordon Slade first told me about you, he said you were a man who took what he wanted. You're a sort of dictator here, aren't you?"

"The gentleman has me wrong. I don't always take what I want." His eyes on hers started that curious quiver along her nerves.

"How would you like to make your home in a place like this?" he asked quickly. "Would you say with Ruth of Biblical fame, 'Whither thou goest, I will go and whither thou lodgest I will lodge: thy people shall be my people and thy God my God'?"

"Fancy your being able to quote the Bible like

that! You have the words right but the meaning wrong. Ruth made that declaration to her mother-in-law after she had been widowed, not to a prospective husband."

"Fancy your knowing that." He mimicked her voice to an inflection. "You've evaded the question. Would you say that to a man?"

"Do you mean would I make my home in Mexico for *life?*"

"That's the idea."

"And leave my own country? I couldn't. I wouldn't."

"Then that tears it." He turned her by a hand on her shoulder. "See the pink church? The original bells in that tower were melted into bullets one hundred years ago. My stepfather replaced them. Its gates were handmade by Jesuit monks. How'm I doin' as a guide?"

"Fine. I can't get used to the immensity of the place. One could set up a Defense Production Organization on this estate and get somewhere. And you took a chance at losing all this when you came to my rescue at Casa Fresco. It's—too tragic."

"That belongs to yesterday. Remember our compact. As you have decided that the words mumbled by Texas Joe are not to hold, why worry about them? When they are crossed off the books I can still marry a Mexican and assume the title and estate; I'm not yet thirty-five—so stars in your eyes, sister. We'd better get back to the house or the sun may do you up."

"Just a minute. Listen to the bells. Can't we ride by the chapel? I'd love to see the people going to church."

"Sure can. Up you go."

Kay was too engrossed with thought to talk on their way to the plaza. Would he marry a Mexican woman and give up his American citizenship? The United States needed men like him.

"A centavo for your thoughts, Señora," he offered lightly. "Or must I raise the bid to pesos?"

She had to think quickly; she couldn't admit that he and his possible marriage had been in her mind.

"I—I was wondering about the people of Mexico—" Color warmed her face as she sensed his quick look, as if he knew she was evading the true explanation. "Are they mostly Spanish?"

"They are a blend of three peoples—Indian, Spanish and North American—but the most important for the future is the Indian. Does that answer your question? Any others?"

"Not a question, a request. *Please* don't call me Señora when—when we are alone. It—it isn't honest —and I don't like it."

"What shall I call you? Darling?"

"You told me that word was reserved for a very special person when and if you found her."

"I did. What does that prove?"

"Drex, please don't joke about it. Has anyone ever told you that you have a curious sense of humor?"

"Can't remember. I shall have to think about it. Here we are at the plaza. The business of the estate is transacted in that adobe building which stands by itself. I have an office in the house where I handle affairs of a more personal nature."

Peons and Indians made a gay pattern of color with their broad sombreros strapped under their chins, their white jackets and blue trousers, sandaled feet and serapes thrown over their shoulders. Many of the women had a baby tied to their backs with a *rebosa*. Hamilton smilingly responded to their respectful, friendly greetings.

"When you get to know your Mexico, Kay, you will be able to tell from which region an Indian hails by the shape of his sombrero, or the coloring and designs of conventionalized sunsets or Aztec gods on his serape."

They stopped at the house entrance. He caught her in his arms as she slid from the saddle.

"Now I'll introduce you to Chiquita's pet room. Modern to the last inch."

A groom appeared to lead away the horses. Tomás swung open the lacy-iron gates. In the wide hall Kay pulled off the yellow bandana around her throat and the flat hat.

"This place reminds me of *A Thousand and One Nights*. The servants appear as if by magic, without even the clap of a hand."

"Your dramatic, extra-size eyes remind me just now of the brown eyes of a deer in the moonlight."

"Pity we haven't a movie moon to really get the sensational effect." Laughing nonsense but somehow rather sweet and breath-catching.

As they entered the great room Juan was setting down a tray on which stood a crystal decanter of pineapple juice and tall glasses clinking with ice cubes. Kay's eyes were attracted to his as by a magnet. She thought as he left the room, "Unless I'm mistaken you're a very bad boy, Juan."

"Here you have Spanish Colonial with a Hollywood influence. Chiquita's pride and joy," Hamilton announced with a comprehensive wave of his hand.

"I don't wonder she loves it. It's perfect."

Color only in the green japonica leaves printed on the cushions of the broad couch and in the red-lacquer cabinet. . . . White Venetian blinds and off-white adobe walls. . . . Gold-and-white hangings, a huge Kermanshah rug in ivory and the same dull gold. Applewood furniture covered in shades of ivory, pale beige and old white.

"I've never been in a room so absolutely soul-satisfying," Kay declared rapturously as she sank into a deep chair near the great curved window which had been inserted in the four-foot–thick wall. On the other side lay a garden gay with climbing pink geraniums; single dahlias high as young trees, roses, fuchsias, heliotrope, Madonna lilies and for colorful accents, in just the right places, red-hot poker plants, gladioli and snapdragons. Above the blaze of color mountaintops pricked a robin's-egg blue sky.

"I love this house. I love the sense of permanence. One just can't think of its being razed to make room for an apartment building or that it can possibly be touched by the savage forces let loose in the world."

"It has been touched, has been in the path of two revolutions, has been riddled with bullets, may be again. There is no real political truce in this country;

subterranean fires are always smoldering. Struggle between progress and conservatism is becoming more intense."

He placed a tinkling glass on the low stand beside her chair.

"Forget the savagery of the world, Kay. We've agreed to a two-weeks respite from problems. Let's make it a gala two weeks we'll never forget. This day is all ours and such a lot to do in it. Bullfight this afternoon."

"Bullfight! Here? Not *really?*"

"Not really bulls; they'll put on a show with cows today and nothing more dangerous for weapons than heavy sticks and red capes. But cows can be nasty in case you crave blood. Drink this; then upstairs you go to rest before lunch. You're tired. I let you ride too far."

"Nonsense. Bill and I ride for hours on holidays at home."

"But this isn't home and I'm not Bill. I beg to remind you that I am *Jefe del Hogar*. Drink and then scram."

Her eyes laughed up at him over the rim of the glass.

"Chief of the House—I scram."

"Don't look at me like that—unless you want to be kissed."

She set the glass down with a little crash and sprang to her feet.

"*I!* Kissed! You've lost your mind!"

"Better, a whole lot better, than to lose my heart, isn't it?" Unwillingly her mouth responded to his boyish grin. "Much more fun and a whole lot less painful."

"Señor."

"What is it, Juan?"

The servant responded in rapid Spanish. The message cut two deep lines, to which Kay was rapidly becoming accustomed, between Hamilton's brows.

"I'll see him at once." He waited till Juan left the room before he said:—

"Rest for two hours, Kay, otherwise nix on the bull—rather cow—fight. *Don't* protest. I know this altitude better than you do. Rosa will serve lunch on the balcony of your room. You'll find plenty of books and American magazines to read. We'll have tea in the patio at four, then on to the fight. Until then—" He waited for her to precede him into the hall.

"You're not acquiring a Mother-knows-best complex, are you, Drex?" she paused on the threshold to ask with exaggerated concern. "Next you'll be leading me about by the hand as my dad did when I wore Shirley Temple curls and a white sunbonnet."

"That's an idea. Next time we walk we'll try it."

What could one do with a man who laughed at one's delicately barbed sarcasm? At the foot of the stairs she looked over her shoulder. Was Drex impressed by her dignified exit? He wasn't even seeing it. He was talking to a man—a mere ghost of a shiver ran along her veins and for some inexplicable reason her heart stopped, raced on. He was talking to Miguel, the waiter at the Cantina, the servant at Señor Castello's. She had seen him since then . . . where? Why was he here?

XVIII

Hamilton waited until the sound of Kay's running feet on the bare boards had diminished to silence before he spoke again to the man beside him.

"Who sent you?"

"Don Pasquale, Señor. I have a message from him."

"You speak and understand English?"

"Yes, Mr. Hamilton. I spent years in *los Estados Unidos.*"

"Good. Come to my office."

They crossed the broad hall to a door near the main entrance of the house. Hamilton opened and closed it behind them. He motioned to a severe monastic chair and seated himself at a table which once had held a monk's tools used to illuminate parchment scrolls.

A ray of strong midday sunlight which had defied the grills at a narrow window set the faded gold of Spanish bindings on the wall shelves glowing, baked out the musty smell of old leather and did its best to set aglimmer the dim, tall suit of armor in the corner —made in the romantic past for a hidalgo of de la Cartina blood. But that was nothing to the revelatory trick it played on the face of the man whose head was tipped back against the carved chair. It brought out the waxen pallor of his skin, the fan-spread of fine lines at the corners of his grim eyes, the shadows under them, the deep creases between nose and lips, the hard-set mouth.

"You're the servant who, at Señor Castello's, warned me that a *señorita* was in danger?" The question shattered the cloistered quiet. "To whom did you refer?"

"Señorita Chesney."

"Explain. How do you know?"

"You have heard, perhaps, of her defiance of Herr Von Haas at the Cantina one night?"

"Heard! I'll say I have. It was a *crazy,* reckless thing for her to do."

"Magnificent, if you will pardon my disagreement, Señor. I was there. I heard her. The man was eloquent but the woman was irresistible. Her spirit, her passion and patriotic fervor were like a lovely light that spreads and glows till it illumines everything it touches. She had them all with her long before the last ringing note of her song 'America the Beautiful.' She made them realize that North, Central and South America are one country. They'll not forget."

The man was a poet. "And she is in danger because of that?"

"There is an element here which will fight an influence like hers. There is a rumor that you, pardon me, Señor, if I seem intrusive, are in love with Señorita Chesney."

"I'm married to her."

"Married! Of a certainty, that is worse, much worse."

"What do you mean? Why should that turn your face chalky?"

"Be seated, Señor, your face is whiter than mine." Hamilton dropped back into his chair. "It is the old story, hurt a man through the one he loves most. There are those who are against the American political ideas and theories being tried out in this country, who have lost heavily under the present regime, who would be glad to cause trouble between the United States and her neighbors. Add to them the venomous and unscrupulous criticism of the country to the north by the horde of foreign agents at large here. They are sly, those agents. Someday they will hurt an American, make it appear that Mexicans did it, to inflame the United States Government against this country. That is what they are working for. They hate you. They know and fear your influence and brains. Of a certainty, you interfered with their plans yesterday."

"They know that already? Who put you wise to it?"

"I am in the confidence of both sides, Señor, but Don Pasquale is my Chief."

"A spy. You are playing a dangerous game, Miguel."

"You are not playing the game as they call it safe, yourself, Señor."

"You've got something there. Why are you, a man who sees and knows all this, masquerading as a servant? Who are you?"

"Never mind my name, Señor. I am *el licendiado*, educated at Harvard University."

"A lawyer!"

"*Sí*, Señor, a follower of the present Government and the progress for which it stands, and a firm believer in the friendship of the country to the north, but, except to a few, Miguel, a waiter at the Cantina. It appears I can help more that way. I hear much at the tables. I speak and understand four languages."

"Why were you at the home of Señor Castello?"

"He needed an extra servant for the dinner. I was highly recommended."

"By whom?"

"The *cantinero*."

"The proprietor of the Cantina? He's one too? This country is as thick with intrigue as a spider's web with threads. The realization kind of gets you by the throat, doesn't it?"

"*Sí, Señor*. Those threads are strong. Don Pasquale sent me here with this message." He drew an envelope from the lining of his sombrero.

Hamilton read the card enclosed . . . reread it. Tore it into fragments, dropped them into a tray, touched the scraps with the flame of his cigarette lighter and watched them crumble to gray ashes.

"I saw Don Pasquale last night. How did you get here so quickly?"

"He sent for me after you left, Señor. I drove all night. He found this near the dark closet. He thought you should have it."

As Hamilton picked up the piece of broken lens Kay's voice echoed through his memory: "I'm talking about Von Haas now. Did you notice how he kept fumbling for a monocle that wasn't there?"

"Part of an eyeglass?"

"*Sí*, Señor, of a certainty."

"I'll follow it up. Anything else?"

"Your friend instructed me to ask for a position here. You are to entertain a house party. It may be you need an extra houseman, *sí* Señor?"

"You're hired. Will you stay now?"

"I will make a report and return tomorrow." He rose. "That is all, Señor?"

"Just a minute. Tell Don Pasquale that his next-door neighbor is not so deaf as he appears to be."

"He will be interested to learn that." He bowed before he jerked open the timbered, brass-studded door. Juan almost tumbled into the room.

"I—I—the—the telephone, Señor," the servant muttered.

"I'll take it here." A headlong entrance might have been Juan's usual method for all the notice Hamilton took of it. He lifted the phone from its cradle, nodded dismissal to Miguel over the top of it and waited for the door to close behind him before he spoke.

"You, Consul. Coming tomorrow? All of you? Chiquita? Amelia? Perfect. Castello and Von Haas are due in the evening. Can your office spare Slade for two days? Need him here. But I don't want to lose you. Can't you both come and leave Johnny Shaw to hold the fort? I get you. Hate like thunder to let you off,— only for two days, remember,—but it's all right if that's the best you can do—Fine. Glad it will fit in with your plans. Yes. I know that Blanche is in this country. Saw her yesterday with Von Haas. Knew that too, did you? Your scouts are certainly on the job, Consul. Kay? Fine. Resting now—"

"Your mistake, mister." Kay took the instrument from his hand. "Hugh, be sure that Beeny—"

Hamilton paced the floor thinking while she gave directions about her clothes. He went back to Miguel's statement that Kay was in danger because of the effect of her fervid declaration of the friendship of her country for its neighbor below the Rio Grande. Von Haas was behind the threat, of course. Was it true that he and Castello had fallen out or was it a yarn the cagey Edouard had told Kay to avert suspicion from himself when, or if, some attempt was made to injure her? If that were true, this house party was nothing short of an inspiration. The conspirators—if they were conspirators—would be where they could be watched for a short time at least. He touched the broken fragment of glass in his pocket. Had Von Haas dropped it? He thought of the words on the card Miguel had delivered:—

Locate the cover-up man in your town at once. Danger.

Locate him at once. . . . Not so easy. . . . He had a fairly clever conviction as to the identity of the person but could he prove it? Could he prove that Edouard Rafael Castello was the man who had phoned Slade that the *camiónes* would roll? There were others in the town who could speak broken English if occasion required. The smooth *señor* had dozens, probably hundreds, of followers who would shield him, who thought themselves as justifiably right as Don Pasquale and the men whom he represented thought themselves. Juan was spying. He had suspected it but his presence outside the door so suddenly opened tied it. Miguel was right. The threads of the web were strong. Could he break them before Kay was caught? The click of the cradled telephone recalled his thoughts and eyes to her.

"Hugh isn't coming for two days, Drex. He's sending Gordon Slade that the house party won't be a man shy. Why?"

"Didn't he tell you that Blanche is coming to town?"

"I knew that. One would think it would be an extra inducement for him to leave."

"She asked him to be there while she packs her personal treasures."

"Item one, her collection of those wax figurines by Luis Hidalgo, I presume. I don't wonder she wants them, they're precious. Speaking of figurines, who is the dumb gentleman in the corner?"

Perched on the table, Hamilton's eyes followed hers to the suit of armor.

"That was worn by a de la Cartina hidalgo in the seventeenth century."

"Just what does hidalgo mean?"

"Pure Spanish descent on both sides. Poor old fella has no back. He lost it in one of the revolutions. It was used to make ammunition."

"Beautiful, isn't it?" Kay traced the engraved design on the embossed, damascened surface of the breastplate. "It gives me a creepy feeling when I think of the tragic stories it could tell."

"Step behind it and in. There you are. Tuck in those pants and put your hands into the gauntlets. If it weren't for the glint of your eyes between the slits in the basinet—helmet to you—I wouldn't know you were there."

"It's a tight fit in this regalia." She wriggled out of

the armor. "The hidalgo for whom it was made originally must have been sliver-slim. Fancy having to fight in that steel shell."

"In the era in which it was worn it was considered the last word in protection. How about the rest you were ordered to take, or don't you care about the bullfight?"

"You have a one-track mind, haven't you? Of course I care. Just as I was about to slip out of these riding clothes and obey orders to settle down I remembered something and raced here to tell you. Heard you phoning Hugh and was diverted. Wasn't that the waiter, Miguel, to whom you were talking in the hall?"

"Yes. After a job. He thought I might need extra help at the house party."

"Here, where servants are so thick you're likely to step on one if you turn suddenly? Something wrong in that picture. Did you engage him?"

"Yes, poor guy. He's been out of work since the night at Castello's. He was engaged for the evening only."

"Mystery man." She thoughtfully traced the outline of a leaf carved in the table. "I'm glad he's coming. Unless I'm mistaken, he will bear a heap of watching. I've been suspicious of him since Gordon's cigarette case so mysteriously disappeared at the Cantina and reappeared in the patio of Casa Blanca."

"I think you're wrong."

"I wonder if you'll think so when you hear what I came to tell you. I saw him in a church kneeling beside—I'm sure it was the bearded, black-spectacled brute at Casa Fresco."

"Ca—that rebel with this man *Miguel? Impossible*. Are you sure?"

"Yes. I didn't believe my eyes then, about the bearded horror, I mean. I was shocked white. Bill noticed it. Something about the man with him seemed familiar but as he kept his head down I couldn't make out why. A hazy memory has been flitting through my mind since I saw the Cantina waiter in the hall. In my room I concentrated and caught it. He was the man kneeling beside the black-spectacled major. They were not saying their prayers—unless they write them—they were exchanging slips of paper."

"Why didn't you tell me this before?"

"I saw them while I was in church with Bill— was it only yesterday—it seems like a century ago. You may remember that much has happened since."

"I'll say. You've acquired a wedding ring and a husband. Come here." He caught her hands and drew her toward him.

"Drex, please. You promised we wouldn't look back. It's all so like a fantastic nightmare. I still don't really believe it happened. At any minute I'm likely to wake up and find myself directing a Red Cross or Defense class at home. Let's just enjoy this day."

"Think you can enjoy it with *me?* After that perfect day with 'Bill'?"

"Of course. When I forget what happened to us you're really great fun, Drex."

"O.K. Stars in your eyes, sister."

"What does that mean? You've said it before."

"When at Casa Fresco you looked up at me, I thought, 'An unconquerable soul. One with such stars of valor in her eyes will refuse to accept defeat. She has a winner's heart.' You—" He abruptly opened the door. "How about that rest? Our cowfight may not be the greatest show on earth but it would be a pity to miss it."

"On my way. I'm practically sound-asleep now. Until four."

He followed her with his eyes as she ran across the hall. Could she be right? Had Castello and Don Pasquale's man been together? Miguel had admitted that he was in the confidence of both sides. Was there a chance that he was fooling Don Pasquale? The next few days ought to answer that question—and many others—if his plans jelled.

"It may not have been the greatest show on earth, but that cowfight was thrilling if it wasn't gory," Kay attested as after dinner at a table in the patio she poured coffee. Moonlight overlaid with silver sheen the mint-green frock Rosa had supplied. "I liked the young braves with nothing more deadly than red capes and sticks, the audience in its gay colors, the hacienda police in their green-and-scarlet uniforms at the gates."

"Wait till you see the real thing. We'll put on a better fight at the *fiesta* with our own bulls and a famous matador. Juan may get a chance to show his skill. Enthusiastic followers and experts of bullfights will flock here to judge of the ranch's production. The Governor of the state has indicated his intention to be present. There will be plenty of bloodshed."

"Thanks. I'll wait. I hate to see creatures hurt."

"So do I. Animals or humans. In spite of the many years I've lived here I still dread a bullfight. Another reason why I will never make a real Mexican."

"Do you want to? Forget the question. I shouldn't have asked it. How fragrant the air is. How clear and still. One can almost hear the stars wheeling in space. What a moon! It spreads a lovely light."

"That was said recently of you, of your spirit. 'It spreads a lovely light.' "

"Of me? What have I done since I came to Mexico to warrant that? Nothing but try to keep Hugh and Jill well and happy. At home I really accomplish something."

Elbows on the table, hands clasped under her chin, she looked up at the sky. "When I think of myself as being of importance I remember those lines of Tom Moore's:—

> "The moon looks on many brooks,
> The brook can see no moon but this.

I'm just one little brook among millions of them."

"It's all in the point of view. You're tremendously important to—to your brother to say nothing of Bill Hewins. As for me—what's the hurry?" He stood up as she rose. "Not going in this early! A night like this? Where's your sense of romance?"

"Perhaps I haven't any. I'll call it a—day—a gorgeous day; thanks to you and at the risk of your 'I told you so,' I'll confess I didn't rest after lunch, got interested in a story and read till we had tea. I'm dead with sleep. You understand, don't you?"

"Sure, I understand, more than you think, but you needn't be afraid of me. I'm—well, if not satisfied, I'm ready to maintain the *status quo* for the present. *Buenas noches, Señora.*"

As later she slipped a matching coat over the blue-satin pajamas she wondered why he had repressed a grin when he had agreed that he understood. Why he had assured her that she need not be afraid of him? He had been maddeningly certain of his control of the moment.

She was wide-awake now. She stepped to the balcony and leaned against the window frame. . . . What a night. Air fresh and crisp. Fragrance rising from jasmine, mimosa, gardenias, dozens of other blossoms in the patio below. Strong moonlight turning mountaintops to silver, trees and shrubs to deep purple-amethyst —laying a path of diamonds across the surface of a distant swimming pool.

Drex was ready to maintain the *status quo*. Why not? Their present relations were as impermanent as that star reflection in the patio pool or the glint of dew on the vine leaf beside her. He intended to marry Amelia Mansilla as soon as he was free, didn't he?

She was suddenly, violently, unbearably homesick, homesick for the city in which her roots went down and down into its beginning; for her friends, for her work. She could see Bill coming into the living room at home. She could feel his tight grip of her hand. She could remember their walks along the river front. She blinked away a rush of tears, tipped back her head till she could see the moonlit mountaintops and sang:—

> " 'Mid pleasures and palaces though we may
>   roam,
>   Be it ever so humble there's no place like
>   home.
>   A charm from the skies seems to hallow
>   us there,
>   Which sought through the world is ne'er
>   met with elsewhere."

Her voice broke on the last word. Impatiently she brushed her hand across her wet lashes. . . . Silly! Sheer sentimentality. Homesick? Wild horses couldn't drag her back to staid New England—at present. If that was what moonlight did to her, she'd better cut it out, pronto.

She flung the quilted coat across the bed. Kicked off one mule. Stared at the door in the side wall as if hypnotized. Had she heard a knock or—

"Kay! Kay!" It was Drex's voice. Real, not in a nightmare. Did his room adjoin hers? Her heart pounded like an Indian tom-tom. "Open the door."

"What—wha-what do you want?"

"I don't want anything except to speak to you. I'm coming in."

"You—you can't. I'm—" Her voice died in her throat as a key grated in the lock. She clutched the lapels of the blue-satin pajama coat together as she sat on the edge of the bed. Drex Hamilton appeared in the doorway. He laughed.

"Don't stare at me as if I were the Big Bad Wolf come to eat up a little girl, Kay. I came to warn you not to stand on the balcony and sing in a flood of moonlight. It isn't safe. Never mind why. Understand?"

She nodded because for a second her voice wouldn't come. "I—I won't do it again. Now if you will kindly close the—"

"I'm going. Are you as homesick as that song sounded?"

"No. It was my instinct for the dramatic, acting up. The stage setting was irresistible. Balcony. Moonlight. I felt like a grand-opera star and turned on full force the 'heartbreak' my singing teacher has assured me is in my voice."

"I prefer the present laugh in it." He changed the huge key to her side of the door. "That may make you feel safer. There really was no need for you to be panicky. Good night."

He closed the door. She waited a second before she cautiously turned the key. Snuggled deep in the great bed she pressed her hands hard against her hot cheeks. . . . Thought:—

"You really should do something about that imag-

ination of yours, Kay Chesney; it certainly bolted with
you a minute ago. He looked so—tall. So—so darn
handsome, so like a dictator come to lay down terms,
for one panicky instant you thought—never mind
what you thought—forget it. Go to sleep."

Surprisingly enough she did.

XIX

The tennis court was set in brilliant-green lawns, bordered with benches under gay canopies. Kay was seated
beside Gordon Slade; her brown eyes switched back
and forth as they eagerly followed the four players.

"They're good, aren't they, Gordon?"

"Aha, Hamilton's an ace. Considering her weight
and siren complex, Mrs. Small isn't doing too badly as
his partner. She showed more sense than I thought she
had, not wearing a little-girl skirt like your white
pleated one. They sure made Chiquita and Von Haas
work for that last set. Look here, Kay, this is the first
chance I've had to talk with you alone since I arrived
forty-eight hours ago. What happened? One day you
barely spoke to Hamilton; the next you're married to
him. It doesn't add up."

"Charge it to—to instantaneous attraction—you
know, something about opposite poles—I'm not very
clear as to what it's all about. I haven't a scientific cell
in my brain." She applauded with enthusiasm even as
she wondered if she ever could free herself from the
snarl of untruth in which she was tangled. "Did you
see that lob, Gordon? It was a beauty."

"No. I was looking at you and wondering. Sure it
was attraction, Kay? Hamilton never paid you any
special attention. Sure he didn't have to marry you?"
Red flooded his face in answer to the color which
flamed in hers. "For Pete's sake, don't get me wrong. I
meant that you might have found out some of his plans
and—and the marriage was to keep you quiet."

"In other words you think I forced him to marry me by threatening blackmail? Mighty complimentary of you."

"Don't get sore. I'm just trying to work out a reason for this sudden marriage."

"A reason! How often does reason enter into a marriage contract? If it did, divorce wouldn't be Society's second largest industry, would it? If you must have a reason consider this colossal estate. Wouldn't any girl be thrilled to marry it?"

"You're not a mercenary person, Kay. Besides, if Hamilton doesn't marry a Mexican he loses it."

"But not the money his mother and stepfather left him."

"You've got something there. I understand it's invested in the good old U. S. He inherited his mother's jewels, too. I've heard they're sensational. But I can't believe you would marry for anything but love."

"Perhaps you're getting warm. Perhaps I was caught in a romantic brainstorm."

"Perhaps *you* were, but not Hamilton. When he falls in love—"

"Now who's in love with whom?" Mrs. Small inquired as slightly breathless she sank to the bench beside Kay, whose eyes were following Chiquita and Von Haas as they strolled toward the house. He had flung a sports coat of blinding black-and-white checks across his shoulders.

"Drex, if you prove as good a partner in marriage as you are in tennis, you'll come out with a perfect score." Mrs. Small glanced archly up at Hamilton with eyes as blue as her turquoise-linen frock.

"Thanks. You're pretty hot yourself at both games —but to get back to your quiz, Lady Small, who's in love with whom? What's the answer?"

She followed his lead like a donkey nosing after a carrot.

"Go on, children, tell us. I fairly dote on romance. Are you another suitor upset by Kay's marriage, Gordon? Señor Castello is putting on a masterly heartbroken act and Herr Von Haas watches her as if she were the Promised Land from which he had been forever barred, but don't let him fool you, my dear girl, his specialty is making love to married women."

The insinuation brought quick color to Kay's cheeks. Of course Mrs. Small was referring to the man's devotion to Blanche, equally of course she had observed and heard of his marked attention to herself.

"I don't know why you should butt in on a conversation which was not intended for you, Mrs. Small." Slade's voice bristled with resentment. "I was asking—"

"Don't be mysterious, Gordon." Kay flattered herself that her amused voice was indifference at its best. "Why not admit that you were cross-examining me as to the reason of my—our—hasty marriage, that, when you turned down money and a romantic brainstorm as explanations, you suggested love. It might possibly be that last, mightn't it, Drex?"

She looked up at Hamilton with gay daring, hoping to goad him out of the indifference he had shown toward her the last two days. Since the night he had opened the door to her room something had gone wrong between them; they were hopelessly out of tune. What might have been an inspiring, warm friendship had become an unendurable relationship.

"You're not listening to my answer, Kay." His cool voice scattered her reflections to unrelated fragments. "It not only might be love, it is. If the cross-examination is finished suppose we adjourn to the patio for tea and drinks. Come on, partner."

Kay's mind was in a tumult as she slipped a coral-colored waistcoat over her white shirt and followed. Drex was playing his part up to the handle. It behooved her to add a few convincing touches to hers. After all, it was a play they were putting on for a two-weeks engagement only. Why not get some fun out of this visit instead of going stiff with apprehension each time the marriage was mentioned?

"Hold on, Kay, you're running." Slade caught her arm. "Wait just a minute. So it's love with Hamilton. You could have knocked me over with a feather when he admitted it. I'm sorry I let you in for the Small woman's quiz. After all, was it my fault? I didn't suppose she would stick her nose into a private conversation."

"Didn't you? I did. Whenever I think of her I'm reminded of those gods and goddesses who were everlastingly running up and down Olympus, butting in and upsetting the private affairs of mortals."

"You should worry. She didn't upset yours. She jimmied an admission of love from your husband."

"My what? Oh yes, yes, my husband. You mean Drex?"

"For Pete's sake, who else would I mean? You haven't another, have you?"

"Another! Dozens, my lad, *dozens*. Like the sailor of song and story, one in every port. My mistake, his were wives. It adds up to the same thing."

"Gosh, Kay, you're a knockout when you sparkle. Glad you've got your gay spirits back. Since I arrived you've acted as if you were 'a dream walking.' When it comes to Castello she had something. There was a lot of talk about him and Chiquita de la Cartina. Now he eats you up with his eyes. If I were your husband I'd knock his block off. I may, if he gets too fresh."

"Thanks a million, Gordon, but wait till I yell for help, will you? I'm not exactly a leaner."

"You've said it, gal. She hit the bull's-eye about Von Haas too. You are, my mistake, were, the first unmarried woman to whom I've ever seen him pay attention. I'll bet you made him sit up and take notice that night you defied him at the Cantina. His sort are used to yes-yes females. Have you noticed the daggers in Castello's eyes when he glances at his pal? Wonder what's happened to turn that twosome sour. When I looked up and saw Hamilton and Mrs. Small standing there listening I was afraid I'd made it kind of unpleasant for you."

It was a struggle to keep her voice from exasperation. "Gordon, nothing you or anyone else may say or do can make the situation I'm in *more* unpleasant than it is."

"Do you mean you're not *happy*?"

Oh, dear, her part of radiant bride all to be done over. "Of course I'm happy in one way but, if you must have the hectic details, I'm worried about Hugh. I thought it would do him a heap of good to come here, that it would switch his thoughts from that hideous divorce into an entirely different groove, then he'd go back refreshed and ready to start all over, instead—"

"Here I am. I haven't yet figured out why he sent me in his place. When I think of it I feel a wriggling icy snake ascending my spine. Old Man Intrigue coming up? Did you plan my invitation or do I see Hamilton's Machiavellian hand in it?"

A hint of steel in eyes between narrowed lids reminded her of her first impression that he was cold, calculating.

"Machiavelli was a schemer. Drex is as straightforward a person as I've ever met."

"Oh yeah? He may be but I don't get this marriage stuff at all. What's he doing married to you when he had given Señorita Mansilla every reason to believe he intended to marry her? He's so tied up in Government intrigue and plots that he's been warned he'll be put on the spot. Straightforward, my hat!"

"You're speaking of your host."

"I know it. I know you think I'm a meanie to blow up like that; perhaps I am, but another thing I know, I'm here to serve some purpose of his."

"Good heavens, Gordon, you haven't gone Hollywood and picked up the scenario bug, have you? Why try to make a mystery of your being here? Hugh's exwife notifies him she will return to his home to collect her property. With a fairness I didn't suppose she had in her she asked him to be there to make sure there are no mistakes. This house party needs a man, a crack-a-jack at contract, one who plays tennis like a fiend, a nice fiend, has what it takes to put glamour into a moonlit stroll and who can dance the best gigolo in captivity out of the picture. You're invited. The explanation of the invitation is as simple as A B C, I'd say."

"As you put it, it makes me out pretty good."

"You know you're good, that self-conscious smirk betrays you. You know you're the answer to a hostess's prayer so forget all that mystery stuff."

When they reached the gates of the patio she whispered, "Look as settled as if they'd lived here always, don't they? As a piece of stage direction for an up-to-the-minute comedy that grouping has what it takes."

On a velvet lawn in the shadow of the house wall, a tea table was set with gleaming silver. Castello sprawled in a low chair beside Chiquita, whose white-sharkskin tennis costume was turned to a pastel green by light reflected from the vines. Von Haas sat stiffly in a garden chair on the other side, staring at space, tapping his monocle against the lapel of his checked sports coat. Amelia Mansilla in a pale-yellow-linen frock was talking earnestly with Hamilton, who was twisting a racquet between his hands.

Mrs. Small, stretched in a wheel chaise, was trying desperately to keep her heavy lids from drooping, her head from nodding. Her husband was working at a picture puzzle with Jill, who in a frock of rosy pink, sat opposite him at a small table. Squatted on his haunches, Mr. Pickwick, the Dalmatian, watched each move of the child's fingers. The radioed music of violins and guitars playing a sparkling bolero drifted from a window. The birds were at vespers in their green cathedrals.

Drex Hamilton looked up, flung down his racquet and rose.

"Here you are at last, Kay. Began to think you and Slade were lost in the mountains." He indicated the bench on which he had been seated. "Sit here. What'll you have?" Castello immediately drew his chair beside her.

"Tea with lemon and a honey cake. I didn't eat much lunch. My mouth hadn't become reconditioned after that delectable turkey we had last night. I didn't realize while I was eating the accompanying red sauce that it would burn the roof off my mouth."

"Was that the reason you had been crying when you came to bid me good night, Kay?" asked Jill.

Von Haas, who was passing a tray of cakes, re-adjusted his monocle and scowled at the child. Kay was flamingly aware that Jill's question had sent seven pairs of eyes to her face straight as arrows to the bull's-eye. Her laugh wasn't over-convincing but it passed.

"Crying and then some, honey. I thought my

tongue and mouth had become acclimatized to hot Mexican dishes—I had my first real experience at your house,—Señor Castello—but last night I knew I hadn't made the grade. In spite of the fact that I tried to be a perfect lady and control my emotion every swallow pumped up tears behind my lids." In an effort to turn attention from herself, she added: "Jill, you'd better borrow Herr Von Haas' coat when you go out with Mr. Pickwick. You two would be a symphony in black and white."

Chiquita followed her lead. "It would be a symphony never to be forgotten; even a Dictaphone would record those checks."

"You do not like this jacket, Señorita Chiquita?" Von Haas tapped a lapel with his monocle.

"Like it! I think it's the last word in smartness. Pass this tea to Kay, Drex."

"When I asked Beeny why Kay cried she said she married in haste an' she'll repent at leisure, sure will. What's repenting at leisure mean, Mr. Small?"

Kay and Chiquita exchanged despairing glances; their attempt at switching Jill's train of thought, so ably abetted by Von Haas, had failed to switch. Charles Small's shiny bald head as well as his rotund face had taken on the color of a bright-pink rose.

"Why—why—repenting is being sorry for what you've done. Don't you ever feel sorry when you've been a bad girl, Jill?"

"But I never know I've been bad till someone tells me, Mr. Small. Repenting's a nice long word. Was that what you were doing when you cried, Kay?"

"I was not crying—"

Castello laid his hand on her arm. "Were you crying, *carissima?*" he whispered.

Juan spoke to Hamilton in Spanish.

"*Està bueno,* Juan. Phone for you, Kay."

"It must be Hugh. Which phone, Drex?"

"Take it in my office."

"If that kid, Nettles, belonged to me, she'd be drawn and quartered," Slade observed in a low voice as she passed him.

Was there a phone call or had Drex suggested it to

provide an excuse for her to break away from that *Blitzkreig* of curious eyes? she wondered as she crossed the hall. Just why had she sneaked a side glance at Castello only to discover a mocking twist to his mouth? Why did he have the power to make her feel that he knew more than she did about the forces which had twisted her life out of its normal pattern? Did he believe that the poisonous paragraph in 'Air Waves' had referred to Drex and herself? Suppose it had. Why should he suspect it?

"Hello! Hello!"

No answer. Apparently Drex had translated Juan's message into a call to give her an out. Now that she had escaped she wouldn't return to the patio. She was fed-up with Edouard Rafael Castello and his love-making. Sometimes his ardor amused her, sometimes she encouraged it in the hope Drex would notice that she was admired; at other times it became so impassioned it frightened her. Von Häas wasn't a problem because she knew that every attention he paid her was motivated by the intention to find out what he could of Consulate business. Verbal fencing with him had taken on the thrill of an exciting game, he attempting to trip her into disclosures, she as determined that he should learn nothing which was true.

Why let a child's silly remark drag at her spirit? She hadn't cried before for years. The storm had been rising since that episode at Casa Fresco . . . Last night the deluge. What had touched off the cloudburst? Why worry? She had a right to let off surplus emotion hadn't she? The evening frock with the broad green-and-white-striped skirt and the green jacket, which she had reserved for a very special occasion, would do a lot toward helping her look the world and his wife straight in the eye at dinner. She raced up the stairs and pulled open the door of her room.

"Is it the custom in your New England to enter like a human whirlwind?" Chiquita smiled at her from the chaise longue, the only modern piece of furniture in the great room. "I didn't even wait to get out of my tennis clothes I was so eager to know if your brother will be here in time for the *fiesta* tomorrow. I like him very much, Kay."

"It wasn't Hugh." Kay shed her tennis frock and slipped on a pale-pink lounge coat. She snuggled into a deep chair and wondered just how much the girl opposite her knew. "Drex must have made up the message to give me a chance to escape Jill and her maddening chatter."

"Had you been crying?" The question was tenderly affectionate.

"I had for the first time in years. I can't explain the phenomenon. It might be the altitude. They say that sometimes it affects stomachs. Apparently it took a crack at my tear ducts. While I was at it I decided to do a thorough job. I cried till it was a miracle that like *Alice in Wonderland* I wasn't splashing about in a pool of tears. Pretty silly of me."

"I don't think it silly, Kay. You needn't bluff with me. Drex has told me all that happened at Casa Fresco and the sequel the other night at the hotel when you suspected that 'Air Waves' had printed a denatured version of the episode."

Kay sprang to her feet.

"He has! The relief! The incredible relief to realize that a girl like you, Chiquita—I fell for you hard the first time we met—knows the truth, that I needn't pretend to be happily married before you."

"Aren't you happy?"

"Happy! What do you mean, *happy?* Would you be happy married at gun-point to a man you'd never seen before, who never had seen you? *Happy,* when later you hurled the secret at Señor Castello as I did and messed up another person's life? You're crazy even to ask the question."

Chiquita pressed her lovely hands over her shell-like ears. Her eyes and voice brimmed with laughter.

"What an outburst!"

"I'm sorry. But, you see, it isn't a joke to me. It's too close to tragedy."

"Because you want to marry Bill Hewins?"

"Did Drex tell you about him? Good heavens, no.

I'm not even sure I love him. I don't want to marry *anyone*. Don't you see, can't you understand, that if it hadn't been for my brainstorm the other night Drex and I might have slipped out of the mix-up with no publicity? Perhaps you can explain what happened to that organ I had to date proudly called my mind. I can't. Now he stands a hundred-to-one chance of losing this estate and the woman he wants."

She dropped back to the chair. With elbows propped on her knees ran her fingers through her hair. Chiquita rose and laid her hand tenderly on the tousled head.

"Why not let him worry about that? I am sure that never, *never*, has he been sorry he came to your rescue. He was born a knight-errant. I know him, heart and soul. He is the dearest thing in my life. He will find a way out without hurting you or anyone else. I'm glad we've had this heart-to-heart, it has clarified the situation for me."

She tapped the diamond circlet on Kay's finger. "See that Señor Edouard Rafael Castello doesn't forget what that stands for," she reminded gravely. "Drex can be rather terrible when his rights are threatened."

Castello. . . . Rights. . . . Kay gazed unseeingly at the door Chiquita had closed behind her. Had she meant to imply that her brother's wife—*pro tem*—was encouraging his love-making? . . . Too silly to think of for a minute. Better to think of an absurdity than of the tragic past. Speaking of that hideous marriage ceremony had filled her mind with skulking little ghosts of memory. She'd freeze them out with a prickling, cold shower.

Refreshed, radiant, she smiled at her reflection in the mirror. Curious what dressing for dinner did for her spirit. She would prescribe it as an unfailing pick-me-up for a woman low in her mind. She felt on the crest of a wave. The act she and Drex were putting on was to have had a fourteen-days run. Four down and only ten to go. Speaking of waves, the green of her frock was the tint of the sea with the sun on it. Add the clip and earrings she had had designed from her mother's diamonds and she was ready to descend and make a dramatic entrance.

She opened her jewel box. How had that twisted paper come there? Was it a memorandum she had tucked in and forgotten? No. It was soiled as if it had been through many dirty hands. She smoothed it flat with reluctant finger tips. Her heart stumbled. Her breath stopped. She read and reread:—

> *Be at the chaple early Mass tomorrer mornin'. Somethin' you'll like to here, I bet. I see you with the guy in khaki. Come alone or you won't git it.*
>
> JOE

> *It will cost you 100 pesos. Bring 'em.*

XX

She clapped her hand over her mouth too late to stifle entirely a frightened cry. . . . Joe! The man on the horse! The Justice of the Peace! The—

"Kay! Kay!"

Drex! Knocking on the door between their rooms. Had he heard her shocked outburst? It must have been louder than she realized. What should she say to him? How explain it? Tell about the note? Not yet. It had warned *Come alone or you won't git it*. He would prevent her going to the church if he knew and she must find out what the man had to tell her. It might be only a hold-up for money. It might be a threat of blackmail. It might possibly be that he wanted to sell assurance that he wasn't really a Justice of the Peace. That last would be worth ten times one hundred pesos. He had seen her with Bill. Had he been one of the three Texans—

"Kay! Kay! Why don't you answer? Can't you hear me?"

Hear him . . . It was a wonder the last knock hadn't brought the house staff on the run. She tucked the note deep into the V-neck of her green frock, cringed as the soiled paper touched her flesh. Unlocked the door before she had decided what to say.

"You're here. Dressed. Why didn't you answer me?"

"Drex can be rather terrible when his rights are threatened," Chiquita's words flashed through her memory. He followed as she retreated to the dressing table. The blood was drained from his face. His eyes burned. In white dinner clothes he looked a little taller, a little leaner, more imperiously handsome even than in riding outfit, she admitted on one track of her mind, while the other was concerned with what or how much she would tell him.

"Haven't lost your tongue, I hope." He was close now. It seemed as if his keen eyes might penetrate the green stuff that covered that scrap of paper. "I'm not apologizing for being in this room—that's what your eyes are demanding—I thought you screamed."

"I accept your *handsome* apology." This was a situation where the light touch might avert explanations. "Why should I scream? This house is safe as a ch—church, isn't it?" Had he noticed the break in the word *church?* The sudden reminder of the note had done that.

"Why didn't you answer my knock at once?"

"Something told me you intended to inquire if Jill was right when she said I had been crying."

"You're a mind-reader. Did you cry last night?"

"Suppose I did. Isn't an occasional weep fest a girl's inalienable right? Like the best seat in the theater box or having a wheel changed for—" Memory cut off her voice.

"Take it easy, Kay. Flippancy won't get you anywhere with me. That last reference was unfortunate. Brought back Casa Fresco, didn't it? Sit down again."

He folded his arms on the tall back of a chair and faced her as she looked up at him from the bench before the dressing table.

"You and I are getting altogether too edgy with each other, Kay. Let's thresh out the cause now. Are you unhappy here?"

"No."

"Why did you cry?"

" 'I'll be judge, I'll be jury,' said cunning old fury. 'I'll try the whole case and condemn you to death.' " She was not too indignant to admit that his infectious laugh had what it took to make one like him.

"*Alice in Wonderland* always on the tip of your tongue ready for a comeback, isn't it?"

"It just happens that I'm reading the classic to Jill."

"You needn't explain. I apologize for my judicial manner. Let's begin over. Please tell me why you cried. Homesick for Bill Hewins?"

"*No.*"

"I wish I were sure that that *No* were as genuine as it sounded. I want you to be happy. I would have given my head, if it would have done any good, to keep the story of the Casa Fresco melodrama from breaking as it did."

"Wrong head. Mine should be lopped off. I broke the story and I'm ready to take the consequences."

"All of them?"

"I'm here. I answer to *Señora* Hamilton—when I don't forget. When we are together I give you back smile for sugared smile. My word, what more can I do to prove I'm sorry?"

He opened the gold cigarette case, regarded it thoughtfully, snapped it shut and dropped it back into his pocket.

"I agree, you're doing your part nobly. Hear the dinner chime? All set? Haven't been crying again, have you? Let's have a look." He tilted up her chin and laughed.

" 'Fraid to let me see your eyes or do you wish me to get the full effect of your exotic lashes? That brought them up. O.K., no sign of tears. Let's go." He opened the door to the corridor. Followed her across the threshold. "Don't let this situation get you down, Kay. Come on, give the 'all-clear signal.' Smile."

At the foot of the stairs he stopped her with a light touch on her arm. "Just a minute. Ready to tell me now why you screamed?"

"You get the queerest ideas, Drex. You ought to be doing scenarios in Hollywood."

"In other words you're putting it up to me to find out. All right. I've taken on harder assignments."

"Drex—please don't start any superdetective . . ."

He left her in the middle of her protest and crossed the hall to speak to Amelia Mansilla who drifted toward him in clouds of snowy chiffon trellised with sequin-spangled black lace. With it she wore a diamond-and-emerald necklace and a matching ring of incredible size and brilliancy.

Did Drex really mean that he intended to discover why she had screamed? The question kept bobbing up in her mind during dinner. Persisted in getting between her and Señor Castello's thinly disguised love-making as they waltzed in the moonlit patio to the radioed strains of dreamy "Esmeralda," being played by an orchestra in Mexico City hundreds of miles south.

"You appear distrait." His arm tightened. "Will you not confide your trouble to me? I might help."

There it was again in his voice. The quality of hypnosis that almost drew a confession of her present problem. She stopped dancing and slipped from his arms.

"Good gracious, or words to that effect. I was thinking that static could ruin even that beautiful music. The air witches are riding their broomsticks tonight. Why does everybody insist that I have trouble to confide? Do I look like a sob-sister?" The laughing challenge in her eyes kindled flames in his.

"You look like what you are. Adorable. I love you. I want you—for my wife."

"Have you lost your mind, Señor Castello? Or have you forgotten that I'm married?"

"Where and when? I have heard neither place nor date mentioned. The story is a build-up to further some scheme of Hamilton's, isn't it? *Es muy chango!*"

"What does that mean?"

"It's Mexican slang for 'He is very clever.' "

She hated his smug smile, his confident eyes.

"Clever. Build-up! You're not very complimentary

to me, Señor. You've just asked me to be your wife, why shouldn't Drex want me?"

"He doesn't. I happen to know he has other plans. Unless what you call your marriage is speedily terminated, your *bridegroom* will be missing."

"What do you mean? I—"

"Kay." Drex spoke as he crossed the patio. "Mr. Small will burst into tears if you don't come in soon. He claims you promised to be his partner at contract."

He was close beside her now, his hand slipped under her arm. "Sorry to break up the dance fest, Edouard, but a promise is a promise. Come on, darling."

As she walked beside him protest surged in a passion of fury. Hadn't Castello said he knew Hamilton had other plans for marriage?

"Don't ever call me 'darling' again."

"Why not? Isn't it customary between husband and wife? You see, I've never been married before—"

"You're not married now and you know it."

"No? There are times, sister, when I feel an irresistible desire to shake you, so watch your step. What was Castello saying to upset you? Did he refer to that yarn in 'Air Waves' about the marriage of a certain *hacendado* and an American girl?"

"Nothing about that, but he said that our—our marriage was a build-up to further some scheme of yours, that you had other plans for matrimony and that if that same marriage were not speedily terminated *you* would be missing."

What did his silence mean? It seemed ages before he answered:—

"Hmm. *Build-up.* You know better than that, Kay. You know it was a bolt from the blue. Wants you himself, does he? Hoist on his own petard."

"What do you mean, Drex? You're chuckling. What are you going to do?"

"Seat you at the card table, pronto, Señora. Come on."

An hour later her partner protested, "You're not playing with your accustomed brilliancy, Kay." It was an unusual reprimand for genial Charles Small. Lucky he wasn't a mind-reader. She couldn't rid herself of the memory that Drex had not denied Castello's statement that he had other plans for matrimony.

"Which fact is giving Amelia and me the chance of our young lives to win against you two invincibles," Drex Hamilton cut in quickly. "I bid four spades, partner."

It seemed hours to Kay before she could reasonably excuse herself and go upstairs. In between the give-and-take of conversation she had figured out a method of getting to the early Church service. The little Indian maid was puttering around her room when she entered. Had she tucked the note into the jewel box?

"Did I have a message this afternoon, Carlotta?" As she stripped off glittering clip and earrings at the dressing table she watched the girl's face in the mirror. Her eyes were big and liquid-brown.

"Not one was given to me, Señora."

If she wasn't answering honestly no one in the world was to be trusted.

"Are you going to early Mass tomorrow?"

"For why you ask, Señora? I go always."

"I'd like to go with you."

"You, Señora! With me?" Carlotta fluttered her lashes. *"Bueno.* Eet ees great honor."

"I like to go to church. Have been intending to ever since I came here." True in a way, if not this way. "But I'd rather no one in the house knows I'm going. Will you loan me a dress and *rebosa?"*

"A secret, Señora?" The little maid's eyes sparkled. *"Bueno,* I love the secret. I weel bring the clothes tonight. I bring chocolate very early and then—"

Kay checked the thrilled enthusiasm. "Bring the clothes tonight but no chocolate in the morning. Meet me near the side door. If we're seen it will be like two maids slipping out together."

"Sí, sí, Señora, I weel be there."

It seemed years instead of hours before the illuminated dial on the clock beside Kay's bed told her it was time to dress. She hadn't closed her eyes. How could she with that sentence, *Somethin' you'll like to here, I bet* swishing round and round in her mind like paddles in a churn.

Her heart thumped with excitement as, dressed in green and scarlet, with a black *rebosa* drawn over her head, she slipped out of the house and joined Carlotta. Soon they were lost in the humming activity of the cobblestoned plaza bordered by century-old ash and eucalyptus treees. Dim lights burned where little stalls had been set up and charcoal furnaces smoked. Grizzled old women cooked native delicacies or pounded maize for tortillas. A dozen tempting odors of food floated in the fresh air.

"Thees way, Señora," Carlotta whispered and led her among sombreroed men and *rebosa*-shrouded women, until she was lost in the anonymity of a crowd. She caught English words as well as Aztec and Spanish.

The chapel at last. Its front gleamed ghostly-white in the gray dawn. Stone figures of headless or armless monks stood in niches, as they had stood for centuries; tufts of green and blossoms flourished on their shoulders where bird or breeze had dropped the seed. Bulletholes spattered the walls. Somewhere Indian tomtoms beat monotonously.

The interior was surpassingly beautiful. All signs of devastation had been wiped out by its late owner. Intricately carved walls and ceilings, pricked out in gold, hung with ecclesiastical pictures painted in the soft colors of an illuminated missal, shimmered in the glow from countless candles behind a faint haze of incense.

Her heart transferred from its original location to her throat as she knelt beside Carlotta. All about worshipers were on their knees, their arms outspread, like Christ on the Cross, praying in low fervent tones which rose like the rhythm of the tide in the cool stillness to the accompaniment of the patter of sandals, the chant of red-cassocked boys.

Kay offered a fervent little prayer before she peered furtively from under a fold of the *rebosa*. Her eyes skimmed the chapel several times before she saw the rangy figure leaning against a wall in a dim corner —Joe the Texan! No mistaking him. Who was the man beside him in a black *charro* costume, with silver edgings and buttons? A serape hid his chin; black goggles covered his eyes. *Black goggles*. Her breath stopped. The Mexican major?

XXI

Long after the others had gone to their rooms Drex Hamilton paced the patio. The illimitable spangled-indigo dome above, the clear, cool, blossom-scented air helped him think. He had watched Kay's window till the light went out. She was safe for the present. Little she knew that when he had seen her standing on the balcony the night after her arrival the memory of the man Miguel's warning had sent him on the run to her door to tell her not to stand in the moon light. She had been so adorable, so desirable in her indignation at his intrusion that he had had to fight the temptation to catch her in his arms. Of course she had thought him crazy. Perhaps he had been in the instant he had realized what a target her slim figure offered. Why had she cried last night? Was she unhappy? Why had she denied that stifled scream?

He stopped walking to light a fresh cigarette. He had told Tomás to inquire if a note had been sent to her room. No servant had seen one. Either a member of the household staff was lying or the note was a figment of his imagination. Note or not, she had choked off a startled cry. Was Castello behind it? He had dared suggest that her marriage was a build-up to further a scheme. It was becoming more and more difficult to keep from letting the smooth hidalgo know that he had been recognized behind those black glasses and beard at Casa Fresco. What had he meant when he had told Kay that if her marriage were not speedily terminated her bridegroom would be missing?

Missing . . . These threats against his life were getting under his skin. Because of his American background and Mexican family ties he had been asked by the Government to make one of the commission to be sent to Washington in the interest of hemisphere solidarity. Much to his personal inconvenience he had gone. He had helped negotiate a mutual-aid pact which undoubtedly would be the forerunner of a series linking American republics in a far-reaching program for defense of the Western Hemisphere.

As a reward for his efforts to promote unanimity he was warned that his number was up. There was gratitude for you. Why crab about lack of appreciation? He wanted neither gratitude nor money. His reward for what he had done came from the glow of achievement, added to the fact that if he hadn't gone to Washington he wouldn't have been at Casa Fresco at the very moment Kay needed him. She couldn't believe Castello's yarn that the marriage had been a build-up; if anyone knew it wasn't true, she did.

As he looked back on it, his life before that night seemed colorless. Work, heavy responsibility, the social merry-go-round, endless conferences with politicians of both parties had at times become almost unendurable. His friendship with Amelia Mansilla had been that and nothing more in spite of the fact that Mrs. Small and other hostesses had paired them determinedly.

"Señor. A note for you."

He turned with a start. The soft voice had been an alert that set his nerves twanging. Castello with his phoney threat had done that to him.

"A note. Who sent it, Miguel?"

"Mr. Gordon Slade, Señor."

There was no trace of accent in that English "Mr." Who was this man Miguel, really? He slit open the envelope and read the short note.

> *Have just received a hurry-up call to the city. The Consul is ready to join the house party. Wants me at the office before he leaves. As your sister has gone to her room I am sending to her, through you, my regrets and thanks for a delightful week end.*
>
> GORDON SLADE

He thrust the note into the pocket of his dinner jacket. Had Hugh Chesney sent for his senior clerk or was the excuse a smoke-screen to hide the real reason for the man's departure?

"Did Mr. Slade give you this letter, Miguel?"

"No, Señor. It was the servant, Juan. A few moments ago."

"Why didn't he bring it to me?"

"I do not know. Of a certainty I have something which is of importance to report, Señor."

"Shoot."

"It is about that same Juan. Since we caught him listening at your office door I have kept him in sight. In the plaza this afternoon a tall man who looked like a Texan cowboy spoke to him. They gave each other the *abrazo* with much slapping of the shoulders. Later a twisted paper slipped from hand to hand."

"Notice anything special about the stranger except that he was tall?"

"Three upper front teeth missing."

Joe, the Justice of the Peace. Had that paper been the cause of Kay's stifled scream? Was the Texan trying to extort money by threatening blackmail?

"After that did Juan return to the house?"

"Not at once, Señor. I joined him, we have become quite friendly. We stopped at several shops. He did not give the note there. A peon spoke to me and Juan went on, so quickly that I lost him."

"Has he a sweetheart among the maids at the house?"

"Oh, of a certainty, many. They quarrel among themselves for his attention. He is very handsome in a dark flashing way and a fairly good matador. He has fought often in the smaller *corridas*. You have seen him in his black-and-silver *charro* suit?"

"In many fights. He tries out our bulls. He'll get a chance to show his skill at the *fiesta* tomorrow. At what time did you see the Texan?"

"At about three. It was very hot."

"Were any of the house guests strolling about?"

"Señor Slade was buying a serape and was asking Señor Castello's advice about it. They separated and

Señor Slade rode off toward the ranch, Señor Castello returned to the house."

"They were both in the patio at five. Do you know which room Señor Castello is occupying?"

"*Sí, Señor.* Before I came Don Pasquale instructed me to learn the location of each guest. Señor Slade had the room at the head of the stairs. Señor Castello next and the room beyond is Herr Von Haas'. When I entered the corridor before dinner to raise the awnings I heard the last two talking English as if quarreling bitterly."

"Did they know you heard them?"

"Herr Von Haas came into the corridor and banged a door behind him. He stopped when he saw me and asked in Spanish if I spoke or understood English. I answered 'no.' He looked at me hard and went on."

"Did you understand what they said?"

"No. Only from their harsh voices did I know they were angry. Those lights are Señor Castello's. He is in his room now."

Hamilton's eyes followed the furtively pointed finger toward two windows directly across the patio from Kay's. Chiquita called that side of the house the bachelor barracks. Married guests were given the single adobe houses that faced the plaza. She and Tomás attended to the assignment of rooms.

His attention returned to the man beside him . . . *Mestizo,* undoubtedly. An upper-class white into whose blood-stream generations ago had crept the Inca strain. The Mexican of tomorrow. He claimed to be one of Pasquale's men—there was not a shadow of doubt of the Don's loyalty—and yet Kay was sure she had seen him in a church exchanging papers with the Mexican major who had been a rebel, was a rebel still, doubtless. To what would that add up? Was the twisted slip the Texan had given Juan one of those which had passed between Miguel and the major in the church? Could it be the cause of Kay's outcry? If this Miguel were a spy in the pay of foreign agents put here to check up on him, better let him play out his hand.

"If that is all, Señor, I will go," the man suggested.

"It isn't. I need you. Station yourself where you can see the door of Señor Castello's room. If he leaves it, report to me at once. I'll go in, change to dark clothes and return. I'll watch his windows from here. If he makes a move we can't miss him. Don't get the idea that I am in the least suspicious of Señor Castello's loyalty, Miguel. I have a personal reason for being interested in what he does."

"Of a certainty, I understand, Señor. I go at once."

How much did he understand, Hamilton questioned as he ran lightly up the broad stairs. Had others beside himself noticed Castello's smoldering eyes on Kay? He had wanted the tricky hidalgo at the hacienda where he could watch him not because of her but because he suspected him of being involved in the enterprise of unlawfully exporting material needed by the Government. He had him here . . . Now what? Had his meeting with Slade in the plaza been accident or was there bound up in it the reason for the unexpected departure of the Consul's clerk?

"Drex. Come in."

His sister's low voice stopped him as he tiptoed along the corridor. She stood in the doorway of her room. He had to pass that, then Kay's, before he reached his own.

"Can't stop to talk now, Chiquita. Dead with sleep." He gave an excellent imitation of an irrepressible yawn. "Want to be Little Bright-eyes for the *fiesta* tomorrow."

"Then you don't care to know why your wife cried?"

"You win." He drew her in and closed the door of the room behind them. "Don't call her my wife. She isn't, you know she isn't really. Sit down. Now spill it."

"She claims it was the altitude that took a crack at her tear ducts. I told her I knew where the alleged marriage took place and then—"

"Did you say 'alleged' to her? Did you let her believe that I didn't think the ceremony was real?"

"No, Drex. If you raise your voice like that she

may hear you in the next room. These old walls are thick but—"

"All right, all right. Let's get down to cases. Did you get at the real reason for her tears? Is she unhappy?"

"Yes. Unhappy because she hurled—that's her word—the announcement of the marriage at Edouard and thereby caused you to lose this estate and the woman you love. I suggested that she let you worry about that."

"Did you get the idea that the lad Bill Hewins cuts any ice in her unhappiness?"

Chiquita's laugh was like the sound of mellow bells. "Lucky I understand and speak American, that I'm not all Mexican, isn't it? If you mean is she in love with the aforementioned Hewins—if she is, she doesn't know it."

"Could a girl be in love with a man and *not* know it?"

"I've seen it happen. Also, at present, I am seeing a girl absolutely unaware that a certain man is mad about her. When you and Kay are together I can feel your love for her working below the surface like a chemical process which at any moment may blow up and betray you."

"That mustn't happen. The marriage is getting to be less and less of a nightmare to her, more and more like a fantastic dream. She can even laugh about it. One wrong move on my part and it might change to horror again. When she is ready for love, my love, I'll give her all she can possibly want. Meanwhile, forget it, Chiquita."

"Then guard your eyes. When you look at her they send little thrills along my veins. I didn't stop you to explain Kay's tears, I really wanted to warn you to watch Edouard Castello. At first I thought he was attracted to her as he is to every lovely girl he sees; now I think he's mad about her."

"But he knows she's married." His heart stopped. Perhaps Castello knew that she wasn't. Perhaps he knew something which he himself had been unable to find out when he had looked up Texas Joe in his own bailiwick. "He's supposed to be on his good behavior and it will have to be good. A word in the right place from me and exile again for him. This time for keeps."

"You don't think the fact that Kay is married will stop him from trying to get what he wants, do you? He's slipping. He used to play and run away. This time he's caught, desperately in love."

"Does that fact hurt you, Chiquita?" He followed her to the windows open on the balcony.

"Not now. Since I have seen Hugh Chesney's devotion to and defense of a worthless wife I know what a man's faithfulness can mean. How could she leave him?"

"Chiquita! Do you love the Consul?"

"Didn't you know it? I thought the whole world, but he, suspected. I've got to forget him. My Church wouldn't recognize a marriage with a divorced man. Don't look so troubled, Drex, dear. My life is full as it is. I'll crowd it fuller."

"I can't bear it, Chiquita, for you not to live life at its best."

"Don't worry; who knows, I may meet a countryman who will help me live it that way. Time is a powerful adjuster. I can't believe that I was ever so young and romantic that I could have been deceived by Edouard's love-making. I was. I might have been one of those neglected wives in fiction—and real life—if you hadn't interfered, Drex. I know now that it was what I had, not I, he wanted. I'm luckier than Amelia."

"Does she still love him?"

"I'm afraid so. The act you and she put on to make him jealous didn't work. He just didn't care. That was all I wanted to say, good— Who is that? Drex! Drex! A man is staggering across the patio!"

He was out of the room . . . Down the stairs. Switched on the patio light. He dashed to the figure lying face down on the flagging, turned him over. Miguel! Stabbed!

For a horrified instant he knelt there as if turned to stone. Don Pasquale's agent attacked, possibly murdered. Here. Had his chief discovered that he was a traitor? Had he heard that he had been seen slipping a paper to the bearded major in the church, or had Von Haas suspected that he had listened in on and understood his quarrel with Castello this afternoon and ordered him put out of the way? Had the assailant mistaken his man? "If your marriage is not speedily terminated your bridegroom will be missing," Castello had threatened Kay. Had that dagger thrust been intended for him? The patio light went out.

"Drex! Drex! Who is it?"

Chiquita's soft whisper was in his ears, her slender fingers clutched his shoulder. In her white frock she appeared like a ghost bending over him.

"Don't look! Go back to the house."

"I won't. Remember I lived through a revolution. Shall I call the servants to carry him in?"

"No one must know of this. The man came here to help me in—in a certain matter." He unfastened the stained waistcoat. His brain reeled for a split-second as he saw the handkerchief which had been stuffed over the wound. Miguel had made sure he left no bloody trail on his way to report to him.

Chiquita dropped to her knees beside him. "Listen! He's breathing! He's alive."

"I must get him into the house. Unless his life is threatened I won't call a doctor. We'll hide him till he can tell who stabbed him. If we can discover that, other lives may be saved."

"Yours, Drex?" The question was a strained whisper. "Do you think I don't realize that this may have been intended for you? We'll take him upstairs to my boudoir at the end of the corridor. Rosa is as good as a doctor for wounds like this. She will know if she can save his life without help. She has seen two revolutions. Lift his shoulders, I'll take his feet."

"He's too heavy—"

"Quick! We haven't a minute to spare."

It was amazing the swiftness and stillness with which they moved him. The fact that though tall he was thin to attenuation helped. Powerful emotion changed Chiquita from a delicately slender girl to a woman of almost superhuman strength. Once the sleepy chirp of a suddenly wakened bird stirred the drowsy quiet of the fragrant patio.

The only sounds inside the house were the scrape of a vine against the wall, the *tap, tap* of a leaf on a window. At the foot of the stairs he hoisted the wounded man over his shoulder like a sack, carried him up and laid him on a couch in the boudoir.

Half-awake, Rosa stumbled into the room in response to Chiquita's ring. Her heavy eyes came brilliantly alive, her withered mouth fell open, she crossed herself devoutly when she saw the colorless face, the limp figure.

"Mother of God! Trouble come all time in thees countree."

Chattering in Spanish she ran from the room, returned with a phial.

"A leetle of thees first on the lips then we tak' care of wound. *Bueno*, eet not so bad."

After that Hamilton helped when he could, which wasn't often. Chiquita and Rosa were expert nurses who had been trained in a tragic school.

In his room he changed the blood-stained white dinner coat . . . Back again. One hour. Two hours. Three. The crystal clock on the massive carved Spanish desk in Chiquita's boudoir ticked off the minutes as gaily as if no life hung in the balance, a life which if saved might prevent the loss of other lives.

Mostly he stood at the window looking down at the patio with its dusky pattern of palms, flower borders and pool; listening to bells calling the faithful to Mass; watching a golden meteor rocketing through a paling sky; waiting for the moment when the man on the couch might regain consciousness long enough to tell who had stabbed him. Faint pink kindled on the eastern horizon. The scent of flowers rose from below, the sickening odor of antiseptics came from behind him.

He thought of the most curious things: of Kay's enthusiasm for the wax figurines of Luis Hidalgo—he would buy some for her—remembered that Chiquita had brought his mother's jewels from the bank at his request. Decided that before he turned the hacienda and ranch over to his sister he must see that a half-dozen of the cottages were newly roofed. The spreading light above the mountains meant dawn. This was the hour when life so often slipped away. Miguel must live—

"Drex!"

He turned at his sister's soft whisper, her touch on his arm.

"Quick. He's conscious."

The man's glazed eyes were open. The blue lips moved when he knelt beside the couch.

"Señor. Your—*señora*—danger—black—and silver—" His eyes closed.

"Yes, Miguel. Yes. Danger for my *señora*. I got that. Black and silver, go on, man. Go *on*." His voice was hoarse with the effort to spur the lagging brain.

"Black and—silver—at bullfight—watch Consul."

He meant the Consul's sister of course. He had already warned him that Kay was in danger.

"I get it, Miguel. Who stabbed you? Tell me."

With all his will he tried to hold the man's attention to the answer.

"Señor—he—masked—came—lightning—quick —when—I—find—this."

He attempted to raise his clenched fist. The effort was too much. His eyes closed. His lips quivered. The faint light of consciousness flickered out.

Hamilton opened the tense fingers. In the palm of the hand lay a monocle with half a lens.

XXII

Kay knelt beside Carlotta on the cobblestoned floor of the chapel feverishly wondering what move to make —she hadn't counted on the presence of the Mexican major, if that black-and-silver figure were the man she thought him—while all the kneeling, praying men and women around her kept on kneeling and praying, the padre kept on intoning, red-cassocked boys kept on chanting in reply. She cast an occasional side glance toward the wall against which Joe the Texan still leaned. What thoughts, what plans were being hatched behind the eyes which sneaked after each person who entered or left the church?

She half closed her eyes and let them rove over the colorful walls, the praying congregation. It was happening to someone else. It couldn't be Kay Chesney kneeling here trying to decide how best to make herself known to the writer of that note. Having come this far she intended to find out what the man had to tell her or perish in the attempt . . . Perish. She was jittery enough now without having that word pop up like a jack-in-the-box. The man in black and silver was leaving. Thank heaven!

Carlotta touched her arm. She followed as the maid threaded her way between *rebosa-* and serape-shrouded figures to the great door. Something must be decided quickly. What? If only she could feel she was moving in a real world, and not as if her personality had split, as if her double were standing aside, totally without the flesh-and-blood quality of a living girl, watching with cool, critical detachment for her next move.

A lovely, lazy day was dawning outside the chapel. Faint, rosy light rested on the monks in their niches, touched their broken bodies with an unearthly beauty. Somewhere near a cock crowed lustily and from the distance another answered. Whatever she did must be done before daylight revealed who she was. Chiquita and Drex might be justly annoyed if she were discovered coming from church in a servant's clothes.

"Carlotta, I'm going back to the chapel."

"*Bueno, Señora.*" She fluttered her lashes; her teeth gleamed in a sly smile. "Ees eet el *señor* you wish to meet, there? That for w'y you come to Mass with me?"

The girl thought she had come to meet a lover. Could she make her understand?

"Listen carefully, Carlotta. I want to meet a man, but not for the reason you think. Did you notice two men leaning against the wall of the chapel?"

"*Sí, Señora*. I deed. They should have been on their knees."

"Sh-sh! Not so loud. Go home. If you meet the *señor* with black goggles over his eyes and he speaks to you, he may ask who was with you. Don't answer or if he persists tell him it was another maid. Understand?"

"*Sí, Señora*." Carlotta's low voice was husky with excitement. "I say to the *charro* een black and seelver —our Juan wear black an' seelver, w'en he fight—w'at you tell me."

"Right. Don't stop to speak to anyone. Keep your *rebosa* close around your head and go home."

"An' you spik to tall one?" She giggled. "Thees ees better than the pictures. *Gracias, Señora*. I hasten to do your bidding."

Kay thought, watching her go, have I dragged that girl into trouble? Will the black-goggled menace follow to find out who was with her? I mustn't move till she is out of sight. If my eyes ache from straining to see through the dusk what torture a blackout must be. How the minutes drag. I've always thought it a crime to wish time away as I am wanting it to hurry, hurry now.

At last. . . . Carlotta was lost in the crowd. Time for her own move in this fantastic game of human chess. Fantastic? Intrigue, deception and danger in the present state of the world were becoming alarmingly normal, weren't they?

Walk, do not run, to the nearest entrance; the reminder slowed her rapid steps. She peered from under a fold of the *rebosa* as she entered the chapel. The Texan still leaned against the wall. His rough dark hair only partially hid the deep creases across his forehead.

She drew a long, unsteady breath, whipped up her courage and approached him. She could see his black eyes narrow, his face split in the semitoothless grin she remembered.

"I'd know yo' even with that rig over yo' haid," he drawled. "I ain't ever fergot how proud yo' walked thet night at Casa Fresco."

Of course he wouldn't forget. Hadn't his boss reminded, "The marriage must be made to hold tight, Señores. Eet may pay us well." This looked like the first pay-off. A cutthroat like him wouldn't forget the location of a silver mine he figured was his loot. Wasn't she one potentially rich lode of that same mine?

"If you really have anything to tell—to sell—come outside where we can talk," she whispered.

"O.K., Marm."

He led the way to a narrow heavy-timbered side door, doubtless the one by which he and his pal had entered. Dawn had crept above the treetops to splash the heavens with deeper rose, but it was still pitchy-black near a clump of eucalyptus trees. The low chant of voices drifted from the chapel. The tom-toms of Indian drums throbbed faintly in the distance.

"Tell me here. Be quick! What's it all about? Blackmail or just a common, everyday holdup?"

"Nix, Marm, yo' got me wrong. Yo' don't think I'd hike miles to pull off a trick thet might land me in jail, do yo'?"

"Who was with you at first?"

"Him with goggles? He jest showed me the way here, he didn't say nothin' but he was curious to know why I come."

"Is he the Mexican major who was at Casa Fresco?"

"Nix, Marm. What ever made you ask thet? Did yo' bring the money?"

"Yes. But I don't pay till I am sure you have something to sell I want."

"Yo' don't think I'm a li'l ol' liar, do yo'?" His voice was injured innocence on the defense. "I got somethin' all right. Say, I like yo' spunk. I ain't got no use fer white-livered wimmin, no more'n I have fer them kind of hounds."

"I'm not interested in the kind of women or dogs you like. Go on. What have you to tell me?"

"Shore, Marm. I thot yo'd be willin' to pay good to larn thet I warn't no Justice of the Peace thet night at Casa Fresco."

Her spirit fanned wings of hope. As quickly folded them.

"You're lying. Mr. Hamilton inquired and found that your commission had been renewed."

He twisted the gallon hat she remembered between dirty big-knuckled hands. It was light enough now to see his burning black eyes, the gaps between his teeth. His awkward embarrassment was well done. The man was an actor. A fact to be remembered.

"I wus thet night, Marm, but I ain't now. I'm plumb ashamed to tell yo' thet there joinin' of yo' two warn't gen*uine*. Hit's my brother Joel what's the Justice of the Peace. Not me. I'm called Joe from bein' named Joshua."

Was it true? The labored beat of her heart threatened to choke her. She wanted so terribly to believe him.

"Then I'm not really married?" She had achieved a hoarse whisper.

"Not unless yo' got hitched to the fella since, Marm."

"Why didn't you tell me that night by the lake? Why?" Indignation restored her voice.

"I wus goin' to tell yo', shore I wus, but yo' didn't give me no chancet, Marm. Yo' run off as if the devil an' all hell wus at yo' heels. I wus all lickered up at the quick-lunch hand-out thet night an' we'n—"

"When that Mexican major told you what to do you were so afraid of him you were yellow enough to do it."

The vicious flash in his eyes stopped her heart . . . Idiot! Why anger him? It plunged on again when he grinned.

"Well, yo' see, Marm, 'twas like this. The Mex had told us 'fore then thet he'd got a score to pay off 'gainst thet gringo Hamilton—we all hed, so fur's thet went— he'd sicked the Border Patrol on our outfit, an' us jist a bunch of Texes tryin' to make an honest livin'—so w'en he dropped in on us we reckoned the Mex major would settle the score, but we shore were hornswoggled w'en we found out the way he aimed to git even. We didn't none of us know much w'at we were doin' an' it seemed like a rip-roarin' joke to hitch yo' two."

"Is unhitching us your idea of another joke?"

"Yo' shore got us wrong, Marm. The Mex, he's plumb ashamed too. He's ben thinkin' it over an' 'twas him thet planned I wus to put yo' wise, an' he writ out this paper fo' yo' so yo'll know we wus telling the truth." He took a folded sheet of foolscap from the pocket of his ragged coat.

"Where is he now?"

"On the other side of the Rio Grande, Marm. He figures he's safer there." He withdrew the paper when she reached for it.

"Nix. Yo' don't git it till yo' pays your money."

Too dark to read it here among the trees though it was almost as light as day in the plaza. Genuine or not, what difference did it make? Drex would get to the bottom of it. One thing she had discovered, that he and the Mexican major had been enemies before they met that night. Why hadn't he told her? Silly question; he hadn't recognized the man in that theatrical make-up, of course.

"Want it, Marm?"

"Yes. One hundred pesos was the price of your valuable information. Here it is."

She drew her purse from under the *rebosa* and counted out the money. He fingered the paper while he watched her greedily.

"Yo's gettin' the chance to marry the other fella, the fella in khaki I see yo' with, pretty cheap. Couldn't you give a leetle—more."

"I couldn't." She snatched the paper and flung the money at his feet. It scattered. Instinctively he stooped to pick it up. She pulled the *rebosa* close about her face and ran.

In the plaza she slipped from group to chattering group. Could she reach the house without being recognized? She hadn't realized that it was so far. Once she saw the servant Juan coming toward her and dodged behind an Indian with a straw pallet on his back. Once a bearded face set her heart galloping. For some inexplicable reason she didn't believe that the Mexican major was on the other side of the Rio Grande. She had a creepy feeling that he was stealing through the crowd looking for her.

It was daylight when she reached the side door

which she had left—it seemed years instead of hours ago. A hand twitched at her dress.

"*Gracias a Dios, Señora!*" Carlotta's voice was choked with tears. "I have been that fright. *El Patrón* was waiting when I came in. He ask eef I had seen you. Now w'at we do?"

Drex looking for her so early in the morning . . . What had happened?

"What did you tell him, Carlotta?"

"That I had not seen you seence las' night." She crossed herself. "Mother of God forgive me."

"Where is he now?"

"At hees coffee een patio."

Her chance to escape. She must examine the paper thrust into the front of her blouse before she explained to him. It might be—probably was—a fake; why raise his hopes until she was sure?

"Don't tell Señor Hamilton you've seen me, Carlotta. Bring breakfast to my balcony in half an hour and take away your clothes. I've just discovered that I'm starving."

Why did the old stairs have to squeak like a squeezed talking doll? . . . Someone moving in the corridor above? . . . No. . . . Nerves. . . . Just a plain attack of nerves. On tiptoes past Chiquita's door. Now her own.

She opened it cautiously. She allowed barely room to slide through, closed it carefully behind her.

"Why are you sneaking in, Kay?" a stern voice demanded.

Drex Hamilton followed his question into the room. He appeared superhumanly tall as he stood between the windows which opened on the balcony, made her think of an avenging deity. Lines she had never noticed before were etched between his nose and lips. He was furiously angry. No question about that.

"Put your adversary in the wrong first." Good old subconscious charged to her rescue and popped that tried-and-true bit of advice into her mind.

"Why are *you* sneaking into *my* room, Señor Hamilton?"

"I'm not sneaking." His fierce eyes caught at her breath as he pulled the *rebosa* from her head and shoulders. "Why are you wearing that? Where have you been? Answer."

"It isn't necessary to roar at me, *Jefe del Hogar*. I intend to tell all. But first, I've been away from the house for hours. If you think you can bear the suspense I'd like to change before we talk."

His hands were gentle on her shoulders.

"I'm sorry I crabbed, Kay. I've suffered the tortures of the damned. An hour ago I knocked at your door to tell you something of great importance. You didn't answer. I came in. You weren't here. I began prowling round the house thinking you might have gone for a walk. Half an hour ago I caught Carlotta slipping in. She swore she hadn't seen you since last night. I suspected then, now I know she was lying. Those are her clothes you have on, aren't they?"

His troubled eyes, the gravity of his voice disarmed her. He had responsibilities enough without worrying about her.

"These are Carlotta's clothes, Drex. I went to church with her. She isn't to blame for lying. I made her promise not to tell where I was. She'll bring my breakfast to the balcony in half an hour. Wait there for me until I change, will you? Then I'll tell the story of my young life to date. When you hear it—you'll be ready to jump over the moon."

He smiled in response to the gay note in her voice as she had hoped he would.

"It better be good if I'm to pull that stunt. I'm a little out of practice, but I'll do my darnedest to make the grade. I'll wait for you." He bent his head and kissed her gently on the lips. "I—I guess I went haywire. I began to think you had run away."

"I? Run away? Just where would I go?"

"Never mind. You're here. Change. Remember I'm waiting. Scram."

Her lips still throbbed from the touch of his, gentle as it had been. Why had he kissed her? She shivered under the shower. A knock! . . . Carlotta with breakfast. She opened the dressing-room door a crack to say,

"Come in." A stifled shriek. The maid had discovered Drex on the balcony. A deep rumble. He was speaking to her. Delicious aroma. Coffee. A sniffle. A series of sniffles . . . Repentant Carlotta collecting the clothing she had loaned. . . . What had *Jefe del Hogar* said to her? She had gone.

In frosty-white sharkskin slacks outfit she stopped a second before the mirror to color her lips lightly and add an unnecessary touch of powder to her nose. She twisted a white turban on her shining hair, drew the stems of three small lilies, which matched the flame-colored Mexican *huaraches* on her feet, through one of its folds and tucked a corresponding bunch into her belt. She shook her head at the looking-glass girl.

"You're stalling. You don't know how to tell him." She hastily picked up the folded paper she had flung on the dressing table when she had pulled off Carlotta's dress. That was the answer.

"I'm literally starving," she announced as she sank into the chair he drew out from the small table on the balcony. "Grapefruit. Bacon. Toast. Coffee. Hungry as I am, I'll share with you, Drex."

"Thanks. I've had my breakfast. What's that you're clutching?"

She was facing again the man who had come to her rescue at Casa Fresco, only this man's face was even whiter; his eyes burned deeper into her heart.

She made a desperate effort to hold her hand steady as she held out the paper, tried to keep her voice clear of emotion.

"Take it! Take it, Drex. It's your freedom and—and mine."

XXIII

A brightly plumaged bird lit on the tip of a shrub and poured forth his ecstatic morning greeting to the great god Sun.

Kay fervently wished she could appear as light-hearted. It was an effort to act unconcerned as she ate grapefruit, poured coffee, and followed Drex's every motion furtively. He hadn't spoken since her announcement of their freedom, had merely looked at her with eyes which probed her very soul as he took the paper so eagerly offered. One would think from the sternness of his face that her news had been bad instead of joyous.

He reread the statement, folded it and put it in the inner pocket of his coat. "Where did you get this remarkable document?" he asked, his eyes intent on the cigarette he was lighting.

She told of finding the twisted note in her jewel case, of her decision to follow it up, of her meeting with the Texan, of his explanation that now that he and the "Mex" were sober they were "plumb ashamed" of the trick they had played and were eager to repair it if they could, and of her headlong break for home with the precious statement in her possession. Better leave any mention of the man in black and silver out of the story at present, she decided. It might confuse the issue which was the value of that folded paper Drex had put in his pocket.

"Then you did scream last evening?" he asked as if that were a matter of paramount importance.

"Just—just half a scream."

"Why didn't you tell me about the note then and let me handle this?"

"That man Joe wrote that unless I came alone I wouldn't get it. I figured I was perfectly safe—"

"Good God, you're never perfectly safe."

She rose as if the same spring which had jerked him to his feet controlled her.

"What do you mean, Drex?"

He paced the length of the balcony and came back.

"Frightened you, didn't I? I'm sorry. Forget it. You're not in danger any more than—than Amelia or —Chiquita. Was Joe alone?"

"Not at first. There was a man leaning against the chapel wall beside him but he left before I spoke to the Texan."

"Who was he?"

"Joe said he was a stranger he picked up at the entrance to the hacienda who showed him the way to the church. I decided he had come for the bullfight, was perhaps an amateur matador in disguise. He wore black and silver—"

"Black and silver!"

"Yes, and black goggles. For one frantic minute I thought he was that horrible Mexican major—"

"Go on. Go on. What else did you notice?"

"That before he left the chapel he pulled a big straw sombrero low on his head as if to hide his face and I noticed the silver spurs on his high-heeled gaiter shoes. Drex! You're white. Was I right? Was he that vicious creature at Casa Fresco?"

He laid his hand over hers clutching his arm and gently straightened the tense fingers.

"I don't know what to think yet. I presume that this valuable document in my pocket wasn't a conscience gift. What did you pay for it?"

"One hundred pesos."

"You don't care how you waste money, do you?"

"What do you *mean?* That you think what is in that paper isn't true?"

"As true as that yarn about the repentance of those outlaws. I'm surprised that a girl of your intelligence could have believed it for a minute. Wanted to believe it, didn't you?"

"Of course I did. Not only for myself but for you too, Drex."

"Suppose you stop worrying about me. Suppose you let me slay my own dragons. I've been doing it for a good many years. Sorry to disappoint you, but it will take a court of law to break that marriage ceremony. Joe the Texan has no brother. I checked up on that guy from the cradle to the—sorry I can't say the grave, I'd like to know he was underground. Believe me?"

"You sound convincing. If it's true, nothing to do now but play our parts for the remainder of the two weeks, I presume."

"That discouraged voice gets me down. It isn't complimentary. Am I not a model husband?"

"I still can't take it as a joke, Drex. You were a bit low yourself a moment ago when you decided that that affidavit in your pocket was a fake. Now your spirit appears to be bobbing like a life-preserver on a choppy sea."

"Why not count on a happy solution of our personal problem? If we do it will be a lot more likely to work out that way than if we let Old Devil Defeat take over." He gently touched her lids with a fine white handkerchief.

"I don't like to see those gorgeous lashes wet. Stars in your eyes, sister. If you've finished breakfast, come along to my office. I have something to show you."

"Don't speak as if I were a disappointed child who must be amused and made happy, Drex. I'm really quite grown up."

"You're telling *me*. Come on. Have you forgotten this is *Fiesta* Day? I'll have to dress and be in the plaza in an hour. Did Chiquita find a costume for you?" They were on the stairs when he asked the question.

"A beauty. All green and glittery gold sequins plus a ravishing white mantilla. Wait till you see me in it. I'm near-Spanish. Do I keep it on for the bullfight this afternoon?"

"Sure. Come in. Take the chair by the table."

Instead of sitting down she crossed to the corner of the room and traced the design on the damascened breastplate of the suit of armor with one finger.

" 'Poor old fella.' He's like some of the movie houses here. All front and not much behind it. Someday I'll take a candid camera shot for my journal. Can't you think up a sensational story about him for me to add to the picture?"

"If you're yearning for melodrama here's a spot of it."

He touched a spring and a portion of the bookshelved wall swung forward. Kay peered over his shoulder.

"It's a room!"

"It was a monk's cell." He entered and drew her beside him. "See the panel at the farther end? It opens under the stairs. A secret exit and entrance which saved many a life. Years ago a skeleton was found here. Someone had gotten in and couldn't get out. Imagine the horror of finding oneself trapped. Sorry, I've driven the color from your face. It's a bit of hacienda history which only members of the family remember now. It couldn't happen again. There's no lock or catch on the inside of the exit door. This will make you forget tragedy."

He opened a safe and removed a large box beautifully inlaid with mother-of-pearl and gold.

"Come along out, Kay, and stop staring at the cell. Look at this."

He set the box on the table, unlocked it with a key he drew from his pocket and opened it. Kay drew an ecstatic breath.

"Drex! How gorgeous! Highlights in the world of jewels! Rubies! Emeralds! Sapphires! Topaz! Diamonds! Pearls! In sets. Reminds me of the House of Jewels at the late World's Fair. Are they your sister's?"

"No, mine. They were my mother's. She and her husband agreed that her property was to come to me as Chiquita would inherit the de la Cartina jewels which are fabulous. My step-father was a grand person. The jewels were one of his ways of expressing his appreciation and love for his wife. She deserved all he gave her. She was a great lady. Sweet, lovely, yet with a strength of character and gay courage which kept her chin up through some tragic tangles. You are like her. 'Her spirit spread a lovely light.' Curious how that line of Miguel's fits you both. We were great pals, my mother and I."

His eyes and smile were tender as if remembering a situation in which that same gay courage had played its part. Suddenly, irrelevantly, Kay fervently hoped that her son would speak of her with that same adoring tenderness when she was gone— "My mother and I." The words curled down in her heart like a kitten in a warm and friendly lap. He seemed boyish, as if there were no connection between him and the stern, white-faced man who had demanded, "Why are you sneaking in, Kay?"

As if her puzzled regard had brought him back to the present he picked up a string of pearls, large, perfectly matched, lustrous as only pearls can be.

"Wear these today. We're entertaining the Governor, politicos, a general or two, rich neighboring *hacendados* and their wives at luncheon. The women will wear few but gorgeous jewels. They'll have their eyes on you. Pearls have a bridish look. Like 'em?"

"Like them! Ever know a human female who didn't adore pearls?"

"Put them on."

"No, Drex."

"Rather have color? Take anything you like."

"Drex, *can't* you understand? *Won't* you understand? I don't want to wear any of them."

"Why?" His steady eyes on hers brought color to her cheeks.

"Because it isn't right."

"Any less 'right' than your presence in this house as my—as Señora Hamilton?"

"That's all wrong, too. My word. If the good Lord will get us out of this mix-up I'll be an angel for the rest of my life."

"I hope he doesn't. I'd hate like the dickens to live with an angel the rest of *my* life."

"Don't worry. You won't have to live with this one."

"No? Cockily sure you'll make the grade, aren't you?" Gravity replaced laughter in his eyes. "Don't hate me, do you?"

"Of course I don't. I like you. We could be great friends if—"

"Skip it. If a great friend asked you to do something to please him you'd do it, wouldn't you—or would you?"

"Of course I would."

"Then wear these. Bend your head." He flung the pearls about her neck. His fingers against her flesh as he fastened the diamond clasp sent tingles through her veins.

"Now that is nicely settled, let's on with the dance —in other words *fiesta*." He locked the jewel box, replaced it in the safe and swung the book-shelved wall into place.

"See how it's done, Kay? Here's the spring; touch it like this and out comes the wall." He closed the opening again.

"Anytime you feel a yen for the other jewels send out an SOS and they'll be yours. There's the phone. Wait a minute. May be for you. The Consul promised he would come today in time for the bullfight. He's bringing Johnny Shaw along. I like that boy. I forgot to tell you, your friend Gordon Slade returned to the Consulate last evening. Yes—She's here. It's for you, Kay."

At the table she picked up the phone.

"You! *Bill!* Where are you? In camp—wh-wh— what? Where did you see it—Yes, I presume that item you saw in 'Air Waves' referred to it—I didn't tell you because it isn't true—not exactly—I mean—I'll write and explain—of course I can explain it. Bill—*Bill*—"

She cradled the receiver. Her lids burned; her throat was dry. She answered the questioning eyes of the man who stood beside her chair.

"It—it was Bill."

"So I judged."

"He—he has seen an announcement of—of our —our—"

"Marriage?"

"Yes—in a Texas newspaper. He didn't believe it, at first."

"Does he now?"

"Don't be so wooden. I don't know. I couldn't explain over the telephone. He sounded furiously angry. Who would send that lie for publication?"

"Lie?"

"Of course it's a lie—really. Did—did *you* do it?"

"You seem to have forgotten, dear Lady Disdain, my determination to keep out of the spotlight. If you want to know who broadcast the news of that grotesque ceremony, page Señor Edouard Rafael Castello. Remember he is frothing at the mouth with eagerness to be announced as heir presumptive to the de la Cartina property. It will give him an A-1 financial standing."

"But, but he asked me to marry him. Why spread the story?"

"Perhaps it wasn't he, perhaps it was a reporter who thought it news. But just to put you wise, the demonic major, also, I suspect, that goggled man in black and silver with the Texan today and Señor Castello are the same person."

"Drex! It can't be true."

"If I didn't know it was true that veiled paragraph in the gossip column would prove it. Ever notice the twitch of Castello's left arm? It got out of control when I entered Casa Fresco and tipped me off as to the identity of the bearded gent. Before then I didn't know he was within miles of the Mexican border. He was drunk. The outlaws and rebels backing him were the gang about whom I had put the Border Patrol wise . . . A break for him. He could get even for that; incidentally he could count on the gang backing him in any deviltry, besides making such that I lost my stepfather's property by marrying a woman who was not Mexican."

"But why does the Texan's statement that the marriage was a fake prove it?"

"You answered that question when you reminded me that Castello had asked you to marry him. If Joe the Texan swears that he is not a Justice of the Peace, you're free, aren't you?"

"And you are no longer married to an American which means that he does not come into the de la Cartina property."

"He may think he'd rather have you than the estate, after which I can be conveniently bumped off and he'll be heir presumptive again."

"That's a cheery thought. I am here with you as your wife. He must believe that marriage is real."

"Can't you tell every time that cagey hidalgo looks at you that he knows the show you and I are putting on is a fake? When I see his eyes on you I have all I can do to keep my hands off his throat."

"But why was he with the Texan today dressed in that *charro* costume of black and silver?"

"That's something I intend to find out. You're a convincing actress. I've had my eye on you. I'm trusting you with my distrust of Castello. Don't let him get an inkling of the fact that I recognized him and remember this, if you see a man in black and silver coming, run, run as if the devil himself were after you. Better dress for the *fiesta,* pronto."

"Señor Castello won't get a hint from me that you have tied him up with the Casa Fresco horror. I still can't believe it. That warning to run will add to the festivity of the occasion." As he opened the door, she paused on the threshold and regarded him with a thoughtful frown.

"You've given me an idea."

"What idea?"

"Now you are frightened. Instead of being pursued I shall turn pursuer."

"What do you mean?"

"I'll be at the heels of every man in black and silver till I find out why he's there. *Buenos días, Señor.* It's been nice meeting you."

"Kay, come back."

She blew a kiss to him before she ran up the stairs.

XXIV

It was a shame that Hugh had missed this luncheon, Kay thought, as she looked about the great dining room which was used only on state occasions like the present. A staircase with intricate iron railing ran up one side to a gallery which went along a wall from which hung magnificent embroideries, on which three musicians, with marimba, violin and guitar played soft music. The ancient, richly carved black-walnut furniture, huge highboys and marvelous wall tapestries made a striking background for the frocks and the gay *charro* costumes of the men. The plates and goblets were of gold. There were tables in the patio for the younger guests.

Drex Hamilton, in green, heavily embroidered in gold and silver, loomed above her as she sat at one end of the long table beside Chiquita.

"The Governor is leaving, Kay; he wants to talk with you before he goes."

She rose hastily. "That has a chiller-diller sound as if I were summoned to court. What have I done?"

"Nothing but look like a million in that billowy green costume. The mantilla is a knockout on you and the pearls glow against your skin. Come on."

She valiantly resisted a childish impulse to slip her hand in his. Something in his voice made her suspect that the Governor had more to say than an appreciation of hospitality.

"His Excellency gave me the surprise of my life. I had pictured him fat, not streamlined; rather hard to look at, not one of the handsomest men I've met since I arrived in this country of super good-looking men."

"He's all right. Here he is. In my office."

A stout man in an orange-and-black *charro* suit, its seams on the verge of bursting from the pressure of imprisoned flesh, was gesticulating violently as he talked to the slim, frowning man in white duck:—

"Excellency, I said to him, 'Tax us as much as you like but don't give the land to those who will produce nothing.' I—"

"Pardon, Señor Devargano, I will listen later. Go now." The impassioned *hacendado* blinked furiously and stalked from the room.

The Governor touched Kay's hand with his lips. "Señora Hamilton, first I will offer my felicitations on your marriage—it is still recent enough for my reference to send the lovely color to your face, I see. You are a fortunate woman, Señora. I have known your husband for many years and I have for him the great affection and esteem."

Kay thought she had plumbed the depths of embarrassment before in regard to the farce she and Drex had staged, but this burned her up. What reply could she make without piling another lie on those that had gone before? The Governor spared her the effort as with only a second's pause for breath he continued gravely:—

"It is being said that Señor Hamilton is making ready to return to the United States permanently. I beg you to dissuade him, Señora. He is needed here. He has not only the point of view of the American way of life, he has also the sympathy with the leaders of Mexican thought which comes only with profound understanding of this country's needs and ideals. We want his help in our long-range planning. *Buenos días, Señora.*"

The head of the state had joined his staff waiting outside the office door before Kay had a chance to reply. She looked up at the man beside her, noted the sharp line between his brows, restrained an impulsive desire to smooth them out, before she asked:—

"Is that the problem you wanted to keep in the background for two weeks, Drex?"

"One of them. Why did he have to drag you into it? Why in thunder do you have to be dragged into every move I make?"

"I'll be glad to help in any way I can. Don't forget we're still in the same boat, Skipper."

The touch of gaiety in her voice relaxed the tense muscles of his jaw.

"Right. You'd better return to the dining room. I must see that the Governor gets away without being delayed by these fiery *hacendados* with their grievances. I was proud of your poise. Made me almost wish you were Mrs. Hamilton-for-good—not for-two-weeks." His grin robbed the words of any hint of sentiment.

"Poise! And I all the time thinking, 'It isn't real. I'm looking at a movie.' I warn you, the next time you are referred to as my husband I'll scream; then where will our act be?"

"You'll never blow up in your lines like that. You're too good an actress."

His laughing assurance was a touch too maddening. "Never say I didn't warn you," she flung over her shoulder as she turned away.

Kay was aware of the murmur of voices as in the late afternoon Chiquita and her house party took their seats on the shady side of the arena in the *Patrón*'s box. Her cheeks burned as she met curious eyes. She, as Señora Hamilton, apparently was still new. This sense of being an impostor was getting her down. Why spend a minute thinking of that when for the first time she was about to witness a real bullfight? If she managed to sit through this *corrida*, she would be willing to wager that the memory of it would satisfy her craving for local color for the rest of her life.

Better make notes of all the details for her journal. Mr. Small had promised to get moving pictures of it with her camera. If the three reels she had taken of the *fiesta* were a success she'd have a gorgeous record of dancing couples, shining sequins, brilliantly colored skirts, *charro* costumes and flashing eyes both male and female.

The slanting sun was highlighting the jagged tops of distant mountains, which loomed against a sky of sapphire. It blazed down on a group of old Indians huddled in their scarlet serapes, young peons in *fiesta* attire; even at a distance she could see the avid expectancy on those dark faces. A group in cowboy costumes roared out a ranchero song. A brass band in bolero jackets of green, red sashes and tight white pants, commenced to play the lively march "Guadalajara."

The shady side of the arena was crowded with visiting *hacendados* and their families. The heavily powdered women wore black with white flowers, towering mantillas and moved in an aura of mimosa and jasmine perfume. The men were gorgeous in scarlet, green, purple, black, white, orange *charro* costumes, heavily embroidered in gold and silver, with revolver holsters of beautifully carved leather and elaborately monogrammed sombreros prominently displayed.

The air echoed with *"mi amigo," "mi paisano."* She heard Spanish, French, English words. She knew from what she had already seen of Mexican society that in conversation these people were cultured, gay, even profound, that deep within they were upheld by a heritage of spiritual strength. Sophisticated as they

were, one sensed a touch of the mystic which went
back to the age of Aztec rites. She had heard that a
bullfight was one of the most elegant spectacles in the
world with its colorful costumes, trumpets, parades,
flags and matadors. She could well believe it.

She relaxed with a long-drawn breath of relief.
Heavenly to rest for a minute and feel that no effort
was required of her. She had been on the move con-
stantly since long before daybreak. She surreptitiously
slipped her feet out of gold sandals. She had danced
their soles thin in the plaza with men of different na-
tionalities whom she had met socially in the town, who
had come to the *fiesta* as guests of neighboring *hacendados*, if persons who lived acres and acres apart could
be called neighbors. If only she could as easily dispose
of the lace mantilla. The unaccustomed weight of the
high comb which supported it tired her head.

Her thoughts drifted back. There had been two
men in black and silver in the crowd. She remembered
them because, like many of the dancers, they wore
masks and because neither one had asked her to dance.
In defiance of Drex's warning she had given one an
opportunity to speak to her as she stopped at a stall,
which had been set up at a side of the plaza, where
an old woman was carrying on a brisk trade with tortillas which sizzled upon a primitive griddle. The other
was selecting beautiful colored candles which were a
specialty of the region, when she lingered near him.
Both had quickly stopped bargaining and moved away
at her approach. Drex had the wires crossed. It had
been made painfully plain to her that she had no lure
for the *caballeros* in black and silver.

If he were wrong about them he might be about
Edouard Rafael Castello. She had danced three times
with him. His gorgeous white-and-gold costume had
eliminated him at once from the black-and-silver menace. Where wàs Von Haas? Unless he had been one of
the masked dancers he had not been present at the
fiesta.

He had been sporting about her fiery reply to him
that evening at the Cantina—the memory of it still
sent a rush of embarrassment to her head—had teased

her in his heavy way, had called her "Miss Liberty, late of Bedloe's Island."

"Like it, Señora?"

The voice brought Kay's thoughts back from the memory of Von Haas. A little chill crept up her spine and coasted down as her eyes met the narrowed eyes of the man in the seat beside her. Was Drex right? Were the Mexican major and Edouard Rafael Castello one and the same person?

"Like it? I love it," she replied gaily even as she wondered why he had changed from the *charro* regalia to impeccably tailored white duck when every other man in sight was in some sort of musical-comedy costume. Perhaps he thought that his white sombrero, with its heavy embroidered monogram, and his gold-mounted quirt kept him in *fiesta* character.

"You are making progress in our customs as well as in our language, Señora. In that billowy costume you look the part of a chatelaine of a great hacienda. The white mantilla lends you a real dignity."

"*Muchas gracias, Señor.* Lend is the word. This being Chiquita's frock, the real dignity of which you approve must have come with it. I have no ambition to be the chatelaine of a great hacienda."

"*Quién sabe?* Not of this one perhaps but—ah, Von Haas, as usual *simpático* with the customs of the country."

"*Mi amigo,* why not? I love your country." The man's expression had not been changed by so much as a flicker by the sarcasm of Castello's voice. "I dress for the *fiesta* as my host requested. *Un gran caballero.* Am I not perfect?"

Von Haas straightened his already straight shoulders and made a gesture to call attention to his costume. Kay's heart caught. Had he been masked that she had not recognized him before? Garment for garment it was the same costume worn by the man who had leaned against the chapel wall beside the Texan this morning. His leather pants were skin-tight; his black jacket, bound and lavishly embroidered in silver, was short, presumably that he might reach with ease the ornate revolver holster hanging from a red sash. Silver spurs glistened at the high heels of *vaquero* boots. The broad black sombrero in his hand was heavily embroidered to match his jacket.

Drex's voice ran along the sound track of her mind. "Remember, Kay, if you see a man in black and silver coming, run, run as if the devil himself were after you."

As if in some uncanny way her thoughts had summoned him, Hamilton dropped into the seat beside her.

"How's it going, Kay? I haven't had a chance to dance with you. Have you had all the partners you wanted?"

"More. I've played the field. This is the most gorgeous spectacle I've ever seen."

"Glad you like the setup. We do them rather well, here. Watch the matador every minute. His is a violent and hazardous profession. His success depends on the perfect co-ordination of eye and movement. A slight mistake in judgment and he pays for it with a severe goring if not with his life. Don't shiver. This man is one of the aces though his bull was removed alive at his last fight, which is a terrible disgrace. He'll have to get this one or he's through."

"That shiver was excitement, not fear. Did you get the Governor off on time?"

"Yes. Boy, oh, boy, only a set of quints could adequately cover the ground I've covered today. I missed your brother. He's a tower of strength on an occasion like this."

"Hasn't he come?"

"No. Detained at the office probably. These are hectic days for an American Consul. There may be a message at the house when we get back. Listen. The fanfare. Now the band is playing 'The Diane.' That's regulation music for the opening of a bullfight in Mexico. The show is on."

A mounted man in black saluted . . . Disappeared. Came the *matador* in blue and gold. *Toreros. Picadores* on heavily padded horses. *Banderilleros* on foot. A vicious, young black bull rushed with a roar into the arena. *Toreros* flicked capes. *Banderilleros* stuck darts into the furious animal.

To Kay, time after that summed up to a confusion of color, motion, sounds, smells, a heart stunting back and forth from its normal location to her throat, blood prickling with icy chills, cheeks burning with excitement. Eyes closed more often than open. Once she glanced at Chiquita and Amelia Mansilla, who were eager, glowing with pleasurable excitement. How could they like it? It was horrible to see a creature tortured. A hand caught hers and held it tight. She smiled through stiff lips at the man beside her, whispered:—

"I—I'm all right, Drex. I—I won't disgrace you. Why are the people screaming, yelling and shaking their fists?" She rose as he sprang to his feet.

"The matador didn't kill the bull after nine sword thrusts. Second time he's lost out. He's slinking away. His goose is cooked."

"What will happen now?"

"Sit down, darling. Juan will have his chance. Here he comes. In green and gold—my colors—usually he wears black and silver. See him swagger. Here comes the bull. Ugly as they make 'em. Take it easy, Kay. Remember it's all in the day's work to those men in the arena."

He tightened his grip on her hand. She was tempted to close her eyes. . . . Resisted. This time she must look and listen or later she wouldn't know what the cheers, hisses and yells meant.

A picador down! A toreador coaxed the bull away. Stumbled! He was down. On his feet again. Too late to retreat. He backed against the wall. Crossed his arms over his terrified face. The bull charged. She shut her eyes tight.

"He's safe, Kay," Drex whispered.

"What—what happened? I—I didn't look."

"The horns were so long they crashed into the wall each side of the toreador's head and he slipped from under." She sensed his quick glance at her. "Can you stand any more?"

"Of—of course I c—can." She smiled reassurance. If he realized that the last word was a frightened gulp he would never again think she had a winner's heart.

It seemed as if she lived through an eternity of

graceful, deliberate passes with the cape, of pirouettes and steps before Juan, the matador, received his sword, before he advanced to kill the frantic animal stuck with three pairs of gaily flagged darts till he looked like an enormous pincushion on parade.

She stood it without a murmur when the man in green and gold buried his sword to the hilt in the vitals of the bull who stood with forefeet planted; but when blood began to gush from the animal's mouth, she turned and hid her face against Hamilton's shoulder.

"Savages! It—it isn't fair," she whispered brokenly. "That poor creature didn't have a chance, he didn't know what it was—all—about."

"Sh, darling, that subject is loaded with dynamite in this company." Even the tender pressure of his hand on hers, his low "Stars in your eyes, sister," didn't mitigate the surge of shame which enveloped her like a flame. She lifted her head as if his shoulder had suddenly gone red-hot.

"I—I'm sorry. Terribly sorry I welshed."

"Don't worry. You weren't noticed; everyone was yelling like mad. That was a beautiful thrust. Juan will be getting delusions of grandeur."

"I don't wonder with all this acclaim. It's deafening."

"All right now? Let me look at you."

She smiled as she met his anxious eyes. "Just one hundred per cent perfect."

"I'll have to leave, Kay. Should have been in a dozen other places but couldn't let you go through this alone. Rest when you get home. I'll let you know the moment your brother arrives."

For some time after she reached her room her stomach put on an act which would have made an aviation test seem child's play. It took all her will power to thrust the gory events of the bullfight from the screen of her mind. To help get her thoughts in hand she worked up an argument for the defense.

"Of course it's horrible and bloody," she told an imaginary audience at home, "and elemental because death is always hovering in the arena waiting for a chance to strike, but is it, I wonder, as revolting as to see two men trying to bludgeon and beat each other into unconsciousness? There's something not quite civilized in that."

Later, gowned in a lilac mist of tulle dotted with silver sequins, she entered the patio where Chiquita in filmy black, Amelia in white with her amazing emeralds, Mrs. Small in gauzy blue, Von Haas, Castello, Charles Small and Hamilton in white evening clothes, were assembled before dinner.

"O.K. now?" Drex asked in the voice of a conspirator.

"O.K. I made notes of my impressions for my journal. That helped me get my grip. As I thought back, I decided that I would hate to meet 'our Juan' in the dark if he didn't like me. His 'perfect co-ordination of eye and movement' turned my blood to liquid air—that's the coldest thing I can think of at this moment. If he could handle a sword with such lightning thrusts, fancy what he could do with a slim, keen dagger. Ooch! It makes me shiver to think of it. Do you agree with me, or don't you? You started to say something and stopped."

"It was what you said about Juan and a dagger which gave me an idea."

"Not to have undesirable guests despatched by him, I hope?"

"That's an idea, too. Better be good. Watch your step, sister." He had matched the lightness of her voice. "Glad you're wearing the pearls. They were made for you."

"But, Drex—"

"I phoned the Consulate. They said your brother had started in his car with Johnny Shaw at the wheel. They were to stop at Casa Blanca for a package Blanche wanted to send to Jill. They ought to show up soon. Don't worry."

As he crossed the patio Charles Small, his face scrubbed, shining, rosy as a baby's, spoke to her.

"Did I hear the word worry, Kay? That is as out of place in this heavenly spot as—er—er—Smoking Mirror." His eyes rested on Von Haas, who was fastening Chiquita's pearl bracelet. "I still think the name fits the man beside our hostess. Did you like the show? I got some swell movies of it for you."

"Like the bullfight! Yes and no. Once is as good as a feast for me. I can't believe that I ever could shout with laughter as the audience shouted at some of the things that happened there. There is too much cruelty in the present world to find any sort of torture funny."

"Many of the people there laughed to stave off tears. The therapeutic value of laughter is inestimable when problems seem unsolvable, when tragedy stalks every human in the world today and the light of peace in the forest of doubt is as elusive as a will-o'-the-wisp. We'd better laugh all we can while the laughing is good. Now that my little sermon is off my chest, what say we go in to dinner?"

Kay slipped her hand under his arm. "I loved your little sermon." She lowered her voice. "You still believe that Smoking Mirror is a menace?"

"A menace and how. Of course Drex had a reason for inviting him here. That boy makes his moves with the skill of an expert chess player, but I wish he hadn't felt that Von Haas was a necessary pawn in his game. I sniff a crisis in the air." He laughed and patted her hand.

"Your eyes are as big as those enormous dark topazes Amelia wears sometimes. That crisis stuff is doubtless a twinge of indigestion, warning me not to eat tomatoes stuffed with baby shrimp if they are served tonight. Great Scott, I love 'em. Don't you?"

Kay acknowledged that she did while her thoughts were busy with his prophecy of a crisis in the air, his distrust of Von Haas.

She thought of it again when, after dinner, she stood by the great window of the modern drawing room to comply with Chiquita's request for a song. Four servants with guitars and worn violins had appeared as suddenly as if summoned by a rub of Aladdin's lamp.

Someone called for the Mexican "Home Sweet Home." As she sang her thoughts raced back to the evening at the Cantina; instinctively her eyes sought Von Haas. He was standing at one side of the enormous fireplace. As the song ended he applauded and suggested:—

"Now the song of your country."

"No. Not—" she broke off as Tomás touched Drex on the shoulder. Something had happened to Hugh; she knew it. She took a step forward. . . . Stopped. Johnny Shaw, dusty, bedraggled, panting, paused in the doorway. A dark bruise on his forehead accentuated the livid whiteness of his face.

"Drex! Drex! They've got the Consul!" he called breathlessly.

Hamilton gripped his shoulder.

"Take it easy, Johnny. Who's got the Consul?"

"Bandits."

XXV

"Sit down, Johnny. Don't try to talk till you get your breath."

"But—but—I must, Drex." Shaw's eyes, aflame with excitement, roamed from face to face of the startled occupants of the room.

Hamilton spoke in Spanish to the butler, whose cheeks were wrinkled in accordion pleats of fright.

"*Sí, Patrón. Sí Patrón, todas,*" Tomá muttered and hurried from the room.

"Now, Johnny, get on with your story. I've ordered the hacienda police to report here at once and we'll get after the bandits. The rest of you better sit down and relax. Kay, come here."

He put his arm about her shoulders. He wanted to make light of her brother's capture but he couldn't, the situation had too many tragic possibilities. He shifted his position that he might watch Von Haas. Had he applied the spark which might set off an explosion? Was this one of the foreign agent's moves to stir up trouble with the country at the north which was running a dangerously high temperature because of recent indignities? The kidnaping of its Consul by bandits wouldn't be likely to reduce the fever.

"Slade hadn't arrived at the office at the hour we had planned to start." Johnny Shaw's face was still colorless. "The Chief hesitated about leaving, but as Gordon had phoned he was on his way and there were two clerks at the office, we started. Mrs.—the former Mrs. Chesney had asked him to stop at Casa Blanca to get a present for Jill."

"Is Blanche staying at the house?"

"Yes, Kay. Your brother's been living at the Consulate. We got the package and started for the hacienda. I drove; he dozed—you could see he was about at the end of his tether emotionally, poor old fella. We were tooling along when someone ran into the road just ahead. I ground on the brakes with a suddenness that jolted the Chief wide-awake and drove my upper teeth through my lips. The guy evidently had been saying a prayer at a roadside cross and was picking up a stone to add to the cairn at the foot of the shrine to show he had said a prayer."

"A trap," Charles Small growled. His "crisis" had proved to be a premonition and not indigestion, Kay thought.

Hamilton furtively observed Von Haas. His skin was pasty. It had the appearance of having been stretched tight over the bone formation. His pale eyes, intent on Johnny Shaw, had receded into dark caverns. His expression betrayed him. It confirmed the suspicion that foreign agents were behind the kidnaping. Even Mexican bandits, bold as they were, would be squeamish about touching an American Consul.

"I cussed the darn fool to the limit; he'd scared me stiff," Johnny Shaw declared angrily. "The Chief was letting go in Spanish when four masked men rode out of the underbrush, leveled rifles and by signs ordered him out of the car. They didn't speak during the holdup; that's why I think they weren't Mexicans. I tumbled out ready to fight but the Chief ordered me back, whispered: 'Get to the hacienda, quick,' got out, mounted the extra horse they had and rode off with them." He sprang to his feet.

"What are we waiting here for? Something may be happening to him at this min—ute—" His boyish voice broke.

"Johnny! Johnny! You don't think—Drex! Why don't you do something?"

"Steady, Kay. Your brother won't be hurt. It's a trick to get ransom. We know that, don't we Edouard?" He caught the blaze of hate in Castello's eyes as they flashed to Von Haas.

"We do. Proceedings will now go forward according to the stereotyped plan. It's about time for the ransom note to appear—and here it is," he added, as gray-faced Tomás appeared in the doorway.

"How did this come?" Hamilton picked up a dirty paper from the silver tray the butler presented. The servant mumbled an answer.

"A masked horseman flung it down at the door," Hamilton translated for Kay's benefit. "They get bold, these bandits."

"Please—please read it aloud in English, Drex," Kay pleaded.

"Take it easy. Just remember this threat is a gigantic bluff. Here's the gist of it:—

" *'Unless this messenger brings us thirty thousand pesos by dawn Señor C——will be shot at the hour of noon.'* "

"Noon. It's midnight now. Drex! What can we do?"

"Stars in your eyes, sister. Listen. Hear those sounds? The hacienda constabulary is at the door. Every mother's son of them is crazy to get in a lick at those bandits. I'll have to change these clothes. Tomás, send Juan to my room."

"Celebrating after his victory," he translated the butler's murmur. "O.K. I won't be a minute."

It seemed to Kay that hours passed instead of the few minutes ticked off by the crystal clock before he was in the hall in riding clothes strapping a holster to his hip.

"Kay, come to the door with me. You'll feel better when you see the escort."

Her throat was dry and tight. It was with difficulty she forced her voice through stiff lips. "Drex! Be careful, yourself."

"Sure, I'll be careful. Come along. You come too, Johnny."

A dozen mounted men on high Mexican saddles waited before the great door of the house . . . Dark men. Dashingly handsome in green-velvet waistcoats over scarlet shirts, tight leather pants and *vaquero* boots with jingling silver spurs. Their holsters glistened with gold and silver. Carbines lay across their knees. A truck laden with camp material had a uniformed man at the wheel. A beautiful, shining bay was led up to Hamilton. Before he mounted he directed:—

"Don't let Von Haas out of your sight, Johnny. Stick to him like a burr. I'll bet a hundred to one his master mind is behind this. Chin up, sister, we'll have your brother here, if not in time for breakfast, soon. You see, we are prepared to camp if necessary." He swung into the saddle. Gave an order in Spanish and touched spurs to his horse.

"What did he say, Johnny?" Kay whispered.

" 'Keep your guns fully loaded, men. We are going into bandit country.' "

Side by side Kay and Johnny Shaw strained their ears to listen till the last jingle died away in the stillness of the night. She gripped his arm.

"What can we do to help?"

"Stick like a burr to Von Haas, them's orders. Come on. You don't go in heavy for rouge, do you? Pinch your cheeks, they're chalky. Atta gal. All set? Let's see what's doing on the drawing-room front. Drex is a grand guy. We've got to help him."

Kay took three steps to Johnny's one as they crossed the great hall. He is a grand guy, she thought. Why haven't I let him know I appreciated his tenderness and consideration? If only he comes back safe I'll show him after this. He might have saved his fortune that night at Casa Fresco and let that hideous Mexican major—who really was—

"What you shivering for?" Johnny Shaw demanded. "They'll come through all right. I'll bet there was a machine gun or two under the camp equipment in that truck."

"N—nerves, just plain nerves, I reckon. Those police looked—looked invincible, didn't you think so, Johnny?"

"Human dynamos loaded with TNT. Gosh, I'd hate to come up against them."

Kay had the same curious feeling that it was all happening to someone else as her eyes swept round Chiquita's charming room which had been so gay less than an hour before and now seemed all tension and fear.

"Oh, here you are, Kay. Don't worry. No harm will come to your brother. It would be too cruel. God wouldn't let it happen."

Kay had only time to wonder at the passionate breathlessness of Chiquita's protest before a voice came from the doorway.

"What do you mean? Why should harm come to my dad—?" Jill's high-pitched, frightened question broke on the last word. A big tear rolled down her cheek. She stood on the threshold in pink peppermint-candy striped pajamas. One hand clutched a book; the other gripped the collar of the Dalmatian who was looking from face to face as if trying to decide which person present had brought the sob to his little mistress's voice.

Kay dropped to her knees and put her arm about the child. "No harm will come to Daddy, Jill. Drex has gone to meet him." Surprisingly the statement brought peace to her own frightened heart.

"Drexy has gone? Then Daddy will be safe." The child drew a long sobbing breath and smiled through tears. She twitched the silky ears of the black-and-white dog beside her.

"We bet on Drexy every time, sure do, don't we, Mr. Pickwick?" The Dalmatian barked and rose on his hind feet to lick her face.

"Stop it, you tickle." She smiled engagingly at her aunt. "I brought *Alice*. I thought you'd like to read me to sleep, Kay."

"I'd love it. Good night, everybody."

"Can I help?" Kay shook her head in answer to Chiquita's tender voice.

"Thanks, no. I'll stay with Jill until she gets to sleep. If—you hear anything—I—I'll be in my room. *Buenas noches.*"

Beeny met them at the head of the stairs. Her eyes resembled nothing so much as chunks of obsidian in white-porcelain settings.

"My stars, Miss Jill, you done give me de scare of my life, sure did. W'at yo' go to run downstairs fer, w'en I jest slipped out de room fer a minute?"

"I heard something an' thought I'd 'vestigate. Come on, Mr. Pickwick." Jill ran ahead into her room, jumped and plumped into the middle of the great bed, the dog with her. The Negress caught Kay's arm.

"There's queer things agoin' on in this house, sure am, Miss Kay." Her eyes rolled alarmingly. Each *s* in her whisper hissed. "Dat dog he know too, he go to de do' at end of corridor an' he jest stan' dere, head on one side lak he's awonderin'. Dere's someone terrible sick in dat room, sure is."

"Sick! You're imagining it, Beeny."

"Oh, no I ain't, Miss Kay. I smelled antipepseptics too, sure did. That Indian woman, Rosa, she keep goin' in an' out there an' w'en she caught me listenin' outside—I wus jest int'rested, Miss Kay, I wusn't tryin' to nose out nothin', sure wasn't—she swore at me somethin' terrible in Spanish, she sure did."

"You shouldn't be listening at doors, Beeny. Stay here while I read to Jill. When she gets sleepy, I'll slip away."

In a chair beside the bed Kay read in a voice calculated to induce sleep in a confirmed insomniac. Beeny touched her on the shoulder.

"Dat honey chile, she's dropped off, sure has."

Kay nodded and tiptoed out. In her room she changed from the gauzy evening frock to the pink lounge coat. On the balcony she dropped to her knees and folded her arms on top of the iron rail. This was the first moment she had had in which to really think since Drex had ridden away with his men. How still the night was . . . How cool and sweet the air. How dark and mysterious the heavens. Its stars were glittering jewels. Its wisps of clouds were gossamer scarves.

It was all happening to someone else. Curious how that strange feeling persisted. Bandits couldn't be threatening Hugh's life, luring Drex into danger. Apparently they could. They might seem like a bad dream but those armed men who had ridden away from the door a short time ago had given it a horrible reality. "I'll bet there was a machine gun or two under the camp equipment," Johnny had said.

What could she do to help? She sniffed . . . Cigarette smoke. Drifting upward from the patio. The smoker must be under the balcony. Would it by any chance be Von Haas? Drex had told Johnny not to let the man out of his sight. Holding her breath for fear it might stir a leaf and disclose her presence she pressed closer to the iron railing. Just below a voice said:—

"The office. Midnight."

An answering murmur. It sounded like *"Sí, Señor"*; she couldn't be sure. Followed faint sounds of feet across the patio. Silence. Silence pulsing with mystery. Creepy with tragedy to come?

She sank back on her heels. "The office. Midnight." Who was meeting whom? Why the office?

She closed her eyes and visualized the room as she had seen it when Drex had been showing her his mother's jewels.

"Jewels!" Someone knew that Chiquita had brought them from the bank. Someone was taking advantage of the absence of Drex and the police to steal them. Perhaps Hugh's kidnaping had been planned for the very purpose of drawing them away.

What could she do about it? If she could only contact Johnny. The jewels were in a safe behind the books near the corner where the suit of armor—

The suit of armor! What a break to have that flash on the screen of memory. She glanced at the clock on a stand beside her bed. . . . Just eleven-thirty. The voice had said, "The office. Midnight." Would there be time to get there before the two who had planned a meeting? There must be!

She started to unclasp the pearls. No. The feel of

them about her throat gave her courage. She pulled on a black swim suit. Tossed away the skirt. No room for that within the armor. Hadn't Drex said she was a tight fit in the rancho pants? She tucked a tiny electric torch deep into the V of the bodice, slipped on the pink lounge coat. Flung it off. What would she do with it when she reached the office? No shoes, either. She'd have to go as she was, fervently praying that she would not be seen in this abbreviated costume. If she met anyone she'd say she was going for a midnight swim in the pool to quiet her racketing nerves while she waited for news of Hugh. Not a minute to waste imagining what might happen. "By audacity alone are high things accomplished," she reminded herself and stepped into the corridor. Listened.

Spooky quiet. Why did the stairs have to creak as she ran down? The office seemed miles away. The door at last.

She pressed her face against it and listened. Not a sound inside. She opened it, closed it cautiously. She was in. Now for the—

Something touched her bare arm. Her heart stopped. Her body turned to ice. A hand pressed hard against her mouth.

XXVI

"Kay! *You?*"

It was Johnny Shaw's hoarse whisper, Johnny's hand dropping from her mouth to her bare shoulder.

"For the love of Pete! Are you nake—haven't you got anything on?"

"Yes and no," she whispered back and in spite of, perhaps because of, emotional tension had all she could do to swallow a hysterical giggle.

Lips close to his ear she told what she had overheard, her plan to hide in the armor that she might prevent, if she could, the theft of the jewels.

"Yeah! I heard 'em too; that's why I'm here. One of 'em was Von Haas. Remember Drex told me to shadow him? I didn't know about the jewels." He threw a dim light around the room. She caught his hand:—

"Don't! They may be watching outside!"

"It's O.K. Someone took the precaution to close the shutters and draw the heavy hangings across the windows. Did you mean you're planning to crawl into that thing in the corner? You're crazy."

"Watch me."

She tiptoed forward in the path made by the dim light he threw on the thick rug and stepped cautiously behind and into the suit of armor and slipped her hands into the steel gauntlets.

"Gosh! Kay! *Gosh.*" His frightened eyes seemed almost to touch hers they were so close to the helmet. "Is it safe? Suppose the guys see you?"

"Can you?" she whispered.

"Nope. O.K. I guess you know what you're doing." He wiped beads of sweat from his forehead. "I'll beat it. I'll hide somewhere outside this room and stand guard. If you're in danger, yell. Yell like the devil. If the Chief or Hamilton knew I was letting you do this they'd swish me in boiling oil. Listen! Someone's fumbling at the door."

"Scram, Johnny. Or you may be caught."

Even to her own ears her voice sounded sepulchral. Johnny's gulp was proof that the spooky effect had registered.

"Too late. Have to take my chance behind the—" His voice faded out.

Behind what? . . . Behind *what?* she wondered frantically and listened till her eardrums felt strained to bursting. . . . No sound in the room. . . . No faint step to show which way he had gone. Her chattering teeth sounded like a spatter of machine-gun fire. If she didn't watch out her shivers of nerves would shake "Poor Old Fella" till her presence was revealed; then where would she be?

Why hadn't she told Johnny about the monk's cell behind the bookshelves with its secret doors? He might have hidden there and been within call. Perhaps he was safer where he'd gone, wherever that was. It seemed already as if she had been standing in the armor for hours. "Time marches on"; if only it would break into quickstep. She must stop thinking about danger to herself. Bandits were holding Hugh for ransom. Suppose Drex were hurt while trying to rescue him? She would never forgive herself for not having let him know how greatly she appreciated—

The sound of a door being cautiously opened stopped her heart. Forever? It felt now as if it never would go again. A man was setting a large flashlight upright on the table. Hair like a silver-gilt cap. Von Haas! Her heart leaped back on the job thumping like an Indian tom-tom. It seemed as if he must hear it as he paced the floor. Twice he passed close to the suit of armor. Once he stopped in front of it as if listening. Walked away.

"Enter." She heard the low whisper. "You took your time coming, Juan." The last sentence sounded nearer.

Juan a thief? He must have told Von Haas about the jewels. Kay's world whirled and steadied: Juan who had made a name and reputation for himself this afternoon a common thief. Incredible.

"*Sí*, Señor, I tak' my time. You give me too mucha to do. Last night I stab the waiter who call heemself Miguel, w'en he come into your room an' search yo' bags. You say yo' find he Don Pasquale's man. He w'at yo' call double-cross yo'. He run downstairs. I saw heem fall een patio before I w'at yo' call beat eet. Where he gone? That w'at I lak to know. No one say notin'. Eet too quiet. Mucha too quiet. Eet mak' me fright."

Miguel had disappeared? Kay thought of Beeny's story about the sick person in the room at the end of the corridor and she thought of Drex's answer when she had said she would hate to meet the victorious matador in the dark. "It's given me an idea." Had he suspected then that Juan had stabbed Miguel? She'd better stop wondering and listen.

"You, frightened! You're being paid for what you do, aren't you?"

"*Sí*, Señor, beeg pay, but p'raps I lak my head on

my shoulders better. Eef *El Patrón* hear I tell yo' w'en
Señor Consul leave ceety so bandits seize heem, p'raps
some Mex bandit who do not lak me, because he bet
pesos on odder matador, tell. I be locked up in jail
—I never fight no more in *corrida*—*sí?* Me, Juan, who
mak' beeg name today."

"*You* a matador, losing your nerve. That's a joke.
There are no Mexicans in the gang which has taken
the U. S. Consul into the mountains. They're Texans—
but who but you and I knows that? Stop your whining
and tell me how you managed it."

If only her memory were made of flypaper that
the words they were saying would stick. She could
see Juan now, could watch his dark, handsome face,
his wicked eyes. He was no longer picturesque. His
clothes were cheap, modern. The bright reds and purples of his shirt and tie shrieked for attention. Green
glass set in a heavy gold ring on his little finger shone
like a *Go* signal.

"I deed w'at yo' tell me, Señor." He had summoned a touch of arrogance to bolster his tottering
courage. "I called Señora Chesney from the phone in
the plaza office thees mornin' w'ile *fiesta* bein' made.
She tell me the hour the Consul start."

Blanche had betrayed her husband. Much as she
disliked her, she hadn't believed she could fall so low.
Kay thrust aside thought of her. Juan was speaking
again:—

"The Texan without some teeth who gif me letter
for Señora Hamilton—"

"Who sent her a letter?"

"I have the words not so good, Herr—"

"Don't say my name. Go on."

"Eet was not a letter; eet was a tweest of paper
with writing. Me, I put eet among the Señora's jewels
myself."

"Where did the Texan get the paper?"

"*Naturalmente* I not know. He gav' me pesos; I
put paper where he ask."

Von Haas was sitting on the arm of the big chair
at the table now, facing the armor. Kay saw his pale
eyes contract to steel points.

"So—o you're a double-crosser, too. You'll take pay from anyone, eh, Juan? I'll have to see what can be done about that."

It had been a vainglorious matador who had jauntily faced a maddened bull; it was a cringing peon who replied to the smooth voice with its undertone of brutal threat.

"*Sí* Señor, w'y not, I ask you. I do your work good, vera good. I keel for yo'. I need pesos, mucha pesos. I hav' tree women. They tak' mucha moneys. Yo' tell me I help my countree eef I help you mak' the fellas odder side of Rio Grande mad at eet. I help yo'. Texan he tell me I help *El Patrón* eef I put the tweested paper in hees *señora's* jewel casket; I help heem. Why yo' mad 'bout that? Eet ees the same Texan who tol' yo' 'bout the marriage of Señor Hamilton an' Mees Chesney at Casa Fresco. Yo' pay heem mucha pesos for that story for yo' paper an' now—"

"Shut up, you fool. Something moved. There's someone in the room."

Had they heard Johnny? Kay's blood congealed. . . . No. They were on their feet staring at the corner. Her corner. What would she do? What would she say if—

The bookshelved wall swung forward with a suddenness that made her jump and set the armor swaying. A man appeared from behind it.

"*Buenas noches, Señores,*" greeted Edouard Rafael Castello jauntily. "You made the strategic mistake of dropping this in the hall, Von Haas."

He flung to a chair the black-and-white checked sports coat. If Kay had doubted Drex when he told her that Castello had been the bearded, goggled major at Casa Fresco, she knew now by the way this man twirled the automatic in his hand that they were one and the same.

"Arms up, Juan! Keep your hands out of your pockets, Von Haas. We've come to the pay-off. I discovered last week that you are responsible for the story of the marriage of the *hacendado* and the lady in that scandalous 'Air Waves'. I arrived behind the book-wall, luckily, just in time to hear Juan tell how you procured certain information." His Oxonian accent was at its perfection.

Von Haas shrugged. "Why this virtuous pose, *mi amigo?* You, who as a matter of patriotism—you assured me—bargained with me to sell your country's metal abroad. You, who bribed a clerk in the U. S. Consul's office to cover-up for you and your gang of Texas outlaws."

"What I do is my affair. I'm operating in my own country in a way I believe will help; the money from that metal is going toward a righteous cause. What's more, I don't intend to stand by and see its honor smirched, its pledges to the friendly neighbor on its northern border broken by the kidnaping of one of its consuls. What switched you from your scheme to carry off Miss Chesney herself? Think I didn't know that you feared her influence after her appeal to reason at the Cantina? Think I haven't watched your every move? Think I haven't known that you are working against the best interest of Mexico? That you are pushing forward in every underground way possible your fifth-column activities?"

" 'My country' act; it is amusing, Señor Castello. You talk of honor, you who at pistol's point force a man and girl to marry that you may inherit a fortune. You knew the cutthroat who mumbled the ceremony hadn't had a license for years. You sent óne of the outlaws with whom you lived and stole and murdered to threaten and bribe an official to swear that the man's license had been renewed. Don't speak till I am through. You can't deny this. I have it in black and white from the man Joe, himself. Oh, I paid for it, handsomely. We 'fifth columnists' have money. What's more, this morning in the chapel he showed me the retraction you had ordered him to hand over to the girl. Now that you covet her you intend to prove the marriage wasn't legal and—"

"Leave her out of this." The hoarse interruption came at last.

"Why, *mi amigo?* Can't you bear for the world to know she's living with a man to whom she isn't legally—*Juan!*"

Something bright, shining, flew through the air and struck Castello in the breast. The automatic he had leveled dropped. He fell. Von Haas' laugh was low, brutal.

"*Ach!* The pay-off. Your knife is as true as your sword, Juan." He bent down. "Straight in the heart. A bull and a man in the same day. You'll be a great matador, if you keep your mouth closed. If you don't . . ." The pause was loaded with dire portent. "Stop cringing. Help me drag what is left of Señor Edouard Rafael Castello behind that open wall. We'll shut him in. They'll be a long time find—What's that sound outside? That jingle."

"The hacienda police, Señor! They have come back! They find us with heem—I go but first I take my knife."

Running footsteps. . . . A softly closed door. . . . Darkness. . . . Kay shut her teeth hard in her lips to steady them. Would the ice in her veins ever melt? Had Johnny Shaw heard and seen what she had heard and seen? If he had she would know these last few minutes hadn't been a horrific nightmare.

"Johnny! Johnny!" she whispered. No answer . . . Where was he? Had he followed the others from the room? If Juan or Von Haas were to dodge back for safety they would find her, would know she had overheard. Then what? She would be spirited off where she could never tell the truth about what had happened.

She must get away, quickly. Why wouldn't her hands slip out of the gauntlets when every second counted? Were they cramped to uselessness? Terror shook her. The hair at her temples was wet. Suppose they came back and she never had a chance to tell what she knew.

"Steady." Drex's voice echoing through her memory, the strong pressure of his hand on hers, were as real as if he were beside her. "No more jitters, sister. Of course you can't free your hands when you're shaking like a leaf in a breeze." He would say that to her. She must get away. The information she had might save countless lives.

The realization steadied her. Cleared her confused

mind. Cautiously she moved her hands. Free. So was she. She drew the tiny electric flash from the front of her swim suit. Stepped from behind the armor into a spot of light. She followed the gleam till it rested on a still body. Could she help? She bent down. Drew back with a shudder. The only way she could help now was to get her information to Drex.

Footsteps in the hall. What could she find to cover her in case she were seen. She flashed her light about the room. Von Haas' sports coat Castello had flung into a chair. She slipped her arms into it. The book-shelved wall was still open . . . Out that way. Suppose she were trapped in the cell. Idiot! Hadn't Drex said there was no lock or catch on the further door now?

Up the stairs. Reaching her room without having been seen would always remain one of the inexplicable mysteries of her life. Her heart was pounding like a prisoner beating against the bars of a steel cage as she entered and cautiously closed the door behind her. She flung off the sports jacket, belted a blue lounge coat and thrust her bare feet into silver mules.

No light yet. She could concentrate better in the dark. She must remember every word that had been said by the three men. Von Haas had accused, "You bribed a clerk in the U. S. Consul's office." Gordon had confided to her, "Here I can save my salary and there's always the hope of a chance to make a little something . . ." He had broken off quickly. The two sentences together revealed his treachery. Castello had a curious sense of honor. He would unlawfully sell his country's goods but would not stand by and see its national pledges broken.

Voices in the patio. The hacienda police had returned. Had they rescued Hugh? It was the first time she had thought of him since she entered the office. Had the clock stopped? Its illuminated face told her that but an hour had passed since she looked at it before. She had lived a lifetime in that suit of armor. Why had the rescue party returned so soon? Had they been too late to ransom Hugh?

She tiptoed to the balcony. Was it possible that this perfection could be part of the same night which had held the moments of horror downstairs? A single lovely star was caught in the surface of the pool. The air was sweet with the scent of gardenias. No sound broke the stillness save the soft sighs of palm fronds in slow-motion. . . .

Voices again. Curiously hushed. The patio sprang into light. She leaned far over the railing. Men. Men carrying something. A stretcher. The hacienda police. They had gone to rescue her brother. A hand of steel gripped her heart. Could it be—

"Oh, God! Don't let it be Hugh," she whispered. "Don't let it be Hugh."

XXVII

Drex Hamilton rode through the clear mountain air under a sky as thick with golden stars as a field over-run with wild marigolds. He visualized Kay's white face at the bullfight, remembered his passionate desire to hold her close in his arms till the show was over. She hadn't needed him. She had made a smiling comeback. Her voice had held a hint of self-mockery when she had said of Juan, "Fancy what he could do with a slim, keen dagger."

Her words had flashed a series of pictures with sound effects on the screen of memory. Ghastly white Miguel trying to speak: "Señor—he masked—came lightning—quick." He had known then what he had subconsciously suspected, that Juan had stabbed Don Pasquale's head man. Had he been spying when Miguel had found the broken monocle which would be evidence that Von Haas had attacked his chief?

Where was Juan now? Tomás had said he was "celebrating" his victory. Was he, or was he at more of his murderous work?

The leader of the police pulled up beside him, pointed. *"El Señor* Consul—ees eet not heem?"

Retrospection faded out into a close-up of the

present. He stared ahead at the figure seated on a stone, silhouetted against a ghostly tumble-down house.

"Sure, he's sitting pretty on that boulder, smoking his pipe. What do you know about that?" As he slid from the saddle Hugh Chesney greeted him with a grin.

"I take it that Johnny Shaw burned up the road getting to you, Drex. Hope you didn't stop to collect the thirty thousand pesos demanded. They won't be needed this trip."

"Are you hurt?"

"Not even a scratch." He tapped his pipe against the rock, slipped it into a pocket and rose slowly. "Relax, Drex. You're white enough to be a spooky resident of this spooky outfit. I'm a bit stiff that's all. The mountain air is right off the ice."

"Thank the Lord for the ghost town instead of a hacienda back in the mountains which is reputed to be the headquarters of a bandit chief. It's a break you're all right. My imagination had you tied, gagged and slugged unconscious. Recognize the bandits?"

"No bandit chief behind this. The guys were Texans. No other men ride as they ride with rifles across their saddle horns, or wear their gallon hats as they wear them. I was stationed on the border long enough to learn that. Bandanas hid the lower part of their faces and they used sign language entirely. Unless I miss my guess, it was part of the Scorpion gang."

"Did you sense Castello's expert touch?"

"No. More likely it's that of his running mate, Van Haas. Since I've been sitting here I've figured that the gang had been hired by a foreign agent to kidnap me, that when I was well hidden the story would be spread that Mexicans had pulled the boner and out the window would go the friendship the U. S. has for this country—that's what they thought—knowing that emotions and tempers in the U. S. are taut as violin strings. Which result certain Governments would give their eyeteeth—if they have eyeteeth, not fangs—to have happen."

"But why leave you doing the Ancient Mariner stunt here? I don't get it."

"The cagey agent who planned the scoop didn't

count upon his cutthroats letting Johnny Shaw get away, nor upon the hacienda police following quickly. The air is so clear that the jingle of spurs carries far. The kidnapers were playing dumb but I could see they were not dead. They went into a huddle to decide what to do.

"Then I got busy, talked to them like a Dutch uncle—and you bet I didn't use sign language—told them I knew they were Texans, that their numbers were already up because of the fake marriage they had pulled off at Casa Fresco—I could see that registered—and suggested that if the legal machinery of the U. S. once caught them they'd be ground to powder. They gathered the trend of my remarks, untied me and dumped me off here. Lord, I wonder if I'll ever feel warm again."

"Hop into the truck, Consul. We'll make record time getting you to the house and something hot to drink."

"No, Drex. Let your man drive me to town. My presence there in the morning will put the kibosh on the kidnaping yarn if it has started. I must get back. I have been ordered to Washington at once. The Department is moving another Consulate outfit down from the border to take over. Thank God for the chance to break away from this place which is haunted by memories of Blanche. I had intended to stay with you tonight only long enough to tell Kay of my change of plans. I'm taking Jill and Beeny along. My sister Sally has arrived in Washington and wants the child. It will be an ideal arrangement; I can see my daughter every day. Rather leaves Kay out on a limb—but orders are orders."

"What d'you mean, on a limb? She'll be with me, won't she?"

"If she decides to stay. Deep down in your heart, Drex, how much faith have you in that Casa Fresco ceremony?"

He thought of the paper Kay had bought from Joe the Texan, remembered with what eager assurance she had produced it that morning on her balcony, and he thought of the slimy county official who had shown him the records and sworn on oath that the Texan's commission as Justice of the Peace had been renewed.

"I have faith enough in it to keep her in my house for the present—but not sufficient faith to claim her as my wife. I'm nearly through my G-man consignment—" He told quickly of the stabbing of Miguel, of the broken monocle. "It won't take me long to run down the men I want. After that I shall devote my entire time to straightening out the melodramatic tangle in which Kay and I are caught."

"It will take some straightening out. If only she hadn't announced the marriage as she did. She wrote me what happened."

"Kay isn't to blame. The responsibility is entirely mine. The simplest way to settle it will be to come out with the whole story. Romantic melodrama. Unbelievable as it is, it's true. Boy, how the public will eat it up. Perhaps for a week it will provide a colorful respite from war and destruction; then an enemy big shot may drop from the sky and it will be forgotten in a new sensation. Does that satisfy you, Consul?"

Hugh Chesney's hand closed hard on his arm.

"You're a grand guy, Drex. The fact that I persuaded Kay to come here, and in coming she got mixed up in that Casa Fresco affair, has been like a spot skinned raw on my consciousness which wouldn't heal. Now, perhaps, it will grow a scar tissue. I'd better get going if I'm to beat rumor. The dame travels fast."

Hamilton glanced at his wrist watch. "It's not quite midnight. You'll make it."

He gave directions to the driver of the truck. Watched the man pull a cover from a machine gun and lay it across the shoulders of Hugh Chesney on the seat beside him.

"All set? Get going! Good luck, Consul. I'll see you before you leave."

"Make it quick. I'll be gone in forty-eight hours. Send Jill and Beeny along tomorrow without fail. I'd like to see Kay."

"I'd like to see Kay." The words accompanied Drex as he rode back to the house. What would she say, what would she do, when he told her that her brother was returning to his own country? Could he hold her here with him until he had completed his arrangements to turn over the hacienda and ranch that he might become an active resident of the United States?

Would his conscience allow him to do that? Why not? His life was his own. Suppose the Governor, Chiquita, the padre, even the high-ups in Washington, argued that his place was here—what did that prove? Did it make it imperative that he stay? Not a chance. If his marriage to Kay was legal—as he hoped and prayed it was—the de la Cartina estate was no longer his. No obligation there. If Chiquita did not marry—of course she would—there was always Edouard Rafael Castello to inherit. He would hate like thunder to see him in command. Why the dog-in-the-manger stuff? He didn't want the estate himself, did he? Why worry? He wouldn't be here to see the tricky *caballero* carry on.

As he entered the drive he was whistling softly with satisfaction engendered by the picture of himself on his native soil.

"Help! Help!" The muffled shout shattered his dream. The hacienda police sprang from their saddles and dashed toward the four men struggling between the great gates. A short, stout, grotesque figure in lurid red-and-white–striped pajamas doubled and went down with a grunt as a fist took him below the belt.

"Drex! Drex! Get these guys! Juan! Von Haas! They've killed . . ." A vicious hand on Johnny Shaw's throat choked off the sentence.

Killed . . . The word stopped Hamilton's heart. Kay? He tore his thoughts free from the paralyzing suggestion. There was work to do here.

"Bring those men to my office," he ordered the police who had dragged Von Haas and Juan from Johnny Shaw and Charles Small, who groggy, but full of fight, was still in the ring. "Shut up, Von Haas; you'll be given a chance to talk later. Watch Juan's wrist, men. He parks knives in his sleeves."

He put his arm about Johnny Shaw's shoulders as he led the way into the house. As he snapped on the light in the office, the boy caught his arm.

"Look, Drex! I told you—" His voice choked in a convulsive gulp.

"Edouard! Edouard!" Hamilton whispered incredulously as he bent over the body on the floor. He straightened and looked at the ghastly, shaking Indian, in his blinding reds and purples, being held upright by two scornful police—who, only a few hours before, had swaggered victoriously from the arena.

"Your knife again, Juan. I'm beginning to recognize your touch. You stabbed the waiter Miguel, didn't you? No answer expected. Von Haas, that swelling eye won't help you when you face a magistrate tomorrow. Even the friendship this country has had for yours won't keep you here after this. You're through and all agents of your breed." He gave an order in Spanish to the police.

He waited until Von Haas and Juan had been pushed and dragged from the room before he spoke to the four men standing like statues each side of the door. They saluted and hurried away.

"They've gone for a stretcher on which to—to carry Señor Castello's body across the patio to his room. Small, put something on over those pajamas; come back and tell the men where to—to take him, will you? I must go at once to Chiquita."

"Sure, Drex, sure." Small turned his back on the still figure on the floor. "Couldn't sleep. Thought I heard someone prowling down here; that's how I come to be mixed up in this mess. Didn't stop for a robe for fear I might waken the wife, then she'd insist on going with me. Saw Von Haas and Juan gum-shoeing out of the office with Johnny skulking at their heels. I got into the fight, pronto." He massaged his paunch tenderly. "I paid this score with a left to Von Haas' eye. I'll be in the hall by the time the police come. Our fighting was done out by the gates. I don't believe it disturbed anyone in the house."

As he left the room Johnny Shaw clutched Hamilton's arm. "Drex! Drex! What's happened to Kay?"

"To Kay? Have you gone crazy? What do you mean?"

"She—she hid in th—that armor. She overheard

someone—I heard them too, agreeing to meet here at midnight—and got the cockeyed idea they were after your jewels. Said she was going to watch them."

"In *that!* Are you sure she was here, Johnny?"

"I saw her step into it."

"Good God, did she see that horrible thing happen?"

"She must have. I was behind one of the hangings; I couldn't see but I heard. I've got a lot to tell you, Drex, and Kay can confirm it unless she fainted. Gosh, look at the opening in the wall. First time I've seen it. Did she go that way?"

"It's the way I'm going—" As the police entered with a stretcher he added, "After they take Castello out better get back to your room, Johnny. You're about all in."

He waited until the men with their burden had crossed the hall before he entered the onetime cell . . . Nothing disturbed there. Crazy child, Kay, to think she could protect those jewels. He took the stairs three at a time. Tried to discipline his pumping heart, his hard-drawn breath when he reached the upper corridor. He would frighten her to death if she saw him like this. She would think he had tragic news of her brother.

Before he could knock she pulled open the door. Her room was dark. Her face was colorless in the light from the corridor.

"I heard you! I heard you!" She caught his arm and shook it. "Drex! Drex! Is Hugh safe? It wasn't he—they were carrying—"

"He's safe. Unharmed." He closed the door. Snapped on the light with one hand, then with an arm about her drew her into the room.

"I'm, I'm so thank—" She hid her face against his shoulder and sobbed as she had sobbed one night not so long ago.

"Cry it out, darling," he comforted, with his lips against her hair. "We found the Consul sitting on a log beside the road smoking his pipe. The bandits had—" He stared at the heap of black-and-white checks on the chaise longue.

"Where have you been? What have you been doing, Kay?" He gripped her arm. "Has Von Haas been here? I'd know that checked coat if I saw it at the Pole. Why did he come to this room with you?" He cleared his hoarse voice. "Answer! Make it fast."

He had not known that tear-drenched lashes could dry so quickly, that eyes like brown-velvet pansies could kindle to scorching flame.

"What do you mean? What are you daring to think?" She wrenched her arm free.

Common sense, which the sight of that coat had bombed to smithereens, shifted into its accustomed pattern. What he had thought for one demented instant she never would know.

"Take it easy, Kay. I went haywire from surprise for a minute, that's all. Relax on the chaise longue while I tell you what happened to your brother." He plumped up a cushion invitingly.

She shook her head and perched on the edge of a chair. She looked pathetically slight and young against the dark wood of its intricately carved tall back; her face was colorless, her brown eyes enormous.

"Now that I know Hugh is safe, I must talk first —before I forget. Don't interrupt me. I want to tell what I saw, what I heard. Get a pencil and paper from the desk. Take down what I say. It's tragically important. Hurry. Are you ready?"

"Yes. Go on." The sooner she had it off her mind the sooner the color would come back to her strained face.

Hands locked tight in her lap she told of her thoughts, her actions from the time he had ridden away from the door. When she came to the moment when she had leaned over Castello and realized that she could do nothing for him, she shuddered but went on with her story.

"I wore that coat so I wouldn't be seen as I dashed up the stairs. Señor Castello brought it to the office. Von Haas left it when he ran. Believe it or not, he hasn't been near this room."

She still angrily resented his crazy "Has Von Haas been here?" Could he convince her that the furious question had been a cockeyed backfire from the constant anxiety he had had as to her safety since the night the Cantina waiter had warned him of danger to her?

"Forget it, Kay, please. Sometime I'll explain so you will understand."

"Will anyone believe that I really heard what I've just told you?"

"Don't worry about that. Johnny Shaw was behind a hanging. He will swear to the truth of all you've told me. You have done much for Mexico. Stretch out on the chaise longue, Kay, please. I have a lot to tell you and I can't think while you sit there rigid as one of the stone monks outside the chapel."

"I'll relax here. I promise." She rested her head against the tall back of the chair. "Go on. Talk. It's your turn. Why did Hugh return to the Consulate instead of coming here?"

He told her of finding her brother free and placidly smoking, of his theory as to the reason for the kidnaping, of his summons to Washington; that Jill and Beeny were to join him at once and that he wanted to see her.

"My car is here. I'll drive them to town," she proposed eagerly.

"When Mrs. Small knows what has happened—as she will in a few hours—she and her husband will leave. Jill and Beeny can go with them. You'd better take dog and luggage. This will be a house of mourning for days—Chiquita and Amelia are the nearest relatives Edouard had, but there are many distant ones who will swarm on this hacienda. I shall be glad to have you out of it. You've had more than one person's share of melodrama since you arrived in this country. If it is true, as you heard Von Haas accuse Castello tonight, that the official at the county seat was bribed to swear that the commission of Justice of the Peace for Joe the Texan had been renewed when it hadn't, you're free as air."

"You're free too."

"Yes—I'm free."

"And you'll have the estate and—and the girl you want to marry." She smiled through tears. "I—I ought not to be happy after listening in on that act of

villainy downstairs—but—but I feel as if I had been
released from jail."

"*Jail!* Is that what this hacienda, your marriage
to me, have meant? You overwhelm me with your
compliments, Miss Chesney. I'll give orders for your
car to be at the door at nine. It would be wise to get
away before the relatives begin to arrive and greet you
as my wife." He turned on the threshold.

"By the way, better not marry Bill Hewins till
I've checked up on this last report on Joe, onetime
Justice of the Peace. You'll hear from me."

"Wait, Drex. The pearls." She put her hand to her
throat to unfasten the necklace.

"Keep them as a souvenir of your little adventure
in matrimony. Good-by."

Motionless she stood in the middle of the room
staring at the heavy door he had closed softly behind
him.

Why had he gone like that? His eyes had been a
burning blue, his voice keen and sharp and cold as
steel. Couldn't he see that she was happy for him even
more than for herself? Didn't he realize that she liked
him better than any man she had met in her whole
life? Why should he? She had taken his decency, tenderness, generosity for granted, hadn't she? Why had
she let him go—she might never see him again—without telling him that with all her heart she thanked
him for saving her from what so easily might have
been tragedy at Casa Fresco.

Why was she standing here like a graven image?
She must stop him. She must tell him.

She pulled open the door. Her lips parted . . .
Shut tight. Lucky she hadn't spoken. She closed her
eyes. Opened them. No mistake. Drex *was* standing at
the head of the stairs; Amelia Mansilla *was* in his arms.
The great emerald on her white hand at the back of
his neck glittered like an evil eye. Evidently he had
told her he was free.

She stepped into the room and leaned against the
door she had closed behind her.

"That tears it," she whispered and tilted up her
chin. "Stars in your eyes, sister. Get busy packing."

XXVIII

Seen from the porch of the Inn the Texas camp was a patchwork of sun-gilded roads, dark shapes which were barracks, mess halls, classrooms, hospitals, recreation centers, swaying trees, fluttering Stars-and-Stripes. Above it, high up, in and out of whipped-cream fluffs of cloud, against a sky of della Robbia blue, beneath a brassy noon sun, a plane circled with cautious movements. Perched on the railing Kay Chesney watched the maneuvers.

"It's marvelous, Bill. Like a mammoth silver bird. Are you learning to fly a ship like that?"

"Yep. 'Keep 'em flying' is the Army Air Corps slogan." He laid his arm in its khaki sleeve across the shoulders of her green cardigan, rested his blond head against her shining copper-color hair and tilted up her chin.

"Keep your eyes on it. Watch. Here comes the first one."

A dark spot against the sky. Another. More coming thick and fast. A shower of parachutes unfolding slowly, majestically, like the blossoms of a night-blooming cereus.

"Are you going to do *that?*"

"Sure I'm going to do *that*. What d'ye think I'm here for? See the other plane coming in? It's a demonstration flight. Did you catch the wing dip? Every move is a signal to the camp that it is not an enemy plane come to lay a couple of eggs. Watch! Now the pilot will set off a rocket! Here it comes!"

"What did it mean, Bill?" From the open window behind them came a radioed voice telling of bombs diving, of homes shattered.

"That the plane is on friendly business. If the pilot hadn't let go with it his ship might have been blown to kingdom come—theoretically—by the antiair-

241

craft guns." He banged down the window and shut off the voice.

"It's the most thrilling sight I've seen since I arrived at the Inn a week ago and there hasn't been a dull moment, either." She freed herself from his encircling arm . . . Colored faintly as he grinned:—

"My mistake. Thought for a minute happy days were here again."

"Not those days, Bill, but perhaps happier ones for you."

"What about yourself? Not in love with that guy you married, are you?"

She straightened his black tie, caught his arms, looked up into his brown eyes and administered a rebuking shake.

"It wasn't a marriage in any sense of the word, Bill."

"Oh yeah? You both believed that that ceremony was straight goods, didn't you? Was your *hacendado* wood or stone that it 'wasn't a marriage in any sense of the word'?"

"Bill Hewins!" Her face was scarlet. "Sometimes I think you've grown darn common since you joined the army."

"Camp life has a way of making one realize the elemental facts of life."

"I stopped off at this camp on my way home to tell you the whole story. Don't you understand yet what happened?"

"It's too fantastic a yarn to understand. Sure you didn't dream it?"

"Has this last week been wasted? I didn't dream it. You read the story of the marriage of the *hacendado* and the lady in that poisonous 'Air Waves,' didn't you?"

"I did. I guess it really happened. The experience has done something to you, Kay. You're quite a different person, I've noticed."

"But a much nicer person, wouldn't you say that, Bill?"

"The old wheedle. You won't get a dream-girl line from me. You've been spoiled by those guitar-strumming *caballeros*. To get back to that wasted week.

Haven't you sung every evening at the recreation center? Haven't you acquired a stag line which if laid end to end would reach from here to the border? Even the cute trick at the hostess house says you give out a sort of glow; that's a lot for one pretty girl to say about another."

"I like her very much, Bill. I hope . . ."

"Don't say it. No come-on matrimonial line from me at present. Not until I'm back in civic circulation. Think you can bear up under that blow?"

"I'll do my best. When I get home I'll plunge into Defense work. That will help me bear my blighted life."

"You sure are a knockout when you turn on the charm, Kay. There's enough here to keep me too busy to think of the past or of much beyond the immediate present. This training not only teaches a man to shoot, fly, use mechanized material, it trains him to understand complicated instructions, to carry them out with speed and precision, in short to keep his eye on the ball every minute. Now having got that off my chest I'm back to normal. When you leave here will you head straight for good old Mass.-there-she-stands-God-bless-her?"

"I've planned to stop in Washington. Hugh wants me to see Jill in her new home."

"I'm glad he could break away from surroundings which must have become unendurable. What became of the clerk at the Consulate who did a little business on the side? Saw a short write-up about him in a Texas paper."

"That's a minor tragedy. He'll never be taken back into the service. I had a letter from him yesterday. He wrote that he felt he owed me an explanation of his leaving me the night he took me to the Cantina—"

"The night you waved the Red, White and Blue?"

"Yes. Joe the Texan called him outside to hold him up for hush money. Gordon knew that the Scorpion gang was behind the unlawful export of metal, but he hadn't the least suspicion that Señor Castello was the head and front of the enterprise, ably aided and abetted by Von Haas. He admitted that he had taken money as cover-up man, wanted me to know that he would regret it all his life."

"Made a tragic mess of that same life, didn't he? What did a few more bucks get him but disgrace? Where's Blanche?"

"New York. It makes me heartsick when I think of what she has done to Hugh's life."

"If you ask me, a woman like her is better out of a man's life than in it. I think she's given Hugh a break. Having delivered this profound conclusion, I'll shove along."

"Aren't you staying for lunch? You said you had procured leave so we could spend my last day here together. My bags are packed except for a very special spectator-sports costume I've kept out for our date this afternoon. I'm leaving early tomorrow to the tune of 'I can't get 'em up, I can't get 'em up, I can't get 'em up in the morning.' You haven't forgotten have you?"

"You bet I haven't. This last week has been heaven." He cleared his gruff voice. "You offered to take some truck I've brought back to the family. I'll get it together and bring it this afternoon. Got to write a few explanatory notes to go with it so they'll be sure to know what the queer things—serapes, *rebosas,* et cetera —are for. I'll be here with your car in time for tea, then we'll step out for the evening—and how. I'll be seeing you."

She watched him, straight, tall, snappy in his khaki uniform, cap cockily aslant on his fair hair, until he was out of sight; impatiently dashed a mist from her eyes. "You're not getting sentimental about Bill at this late date, I hope, Miss Chesney," she flouted herself.

The sun was slanting when dressed for Bill's party she faced the long mirror in her room. There was nothing more becoming to her coloring than white, she decided, and the twist of snowy turban gave the last perfect touch. The emerald-green shoes and stockings which matched her bag were ultra, but effective. Too bad she hadn't a smashing big ring to complete the color scheme.

Quite suddenly between her eyes and the looking-glass girl glittered a tray of jewels. She heard Drex's voice: "Anytime you feel a yen for the others send out an SOS and they'll be yours."

On a sudden impulse she unlocked her alligator-skin dressing case. Tried not to see the glittering diamond circlet in the same white-satin–lined box as she drew out the lustrous string of pearls. "Keep them as a souvenir of your little adventure in matrimony," Drex had said.

She remembered his face as he had spoken, remembered the edge in his voice. She had been too miserably unhappy then to insist upon his taking them. The horror of what she had seen such a short time before, the realization of how near she had been to personal tragedy, still held her in their numbing spell. She had expected to give the necklace—and ring—to him in the morning when he said good-by, but he hadn't come; only Chiquita had bid her a tender Godspeed. She thought of the time since, of how each day she had expected to receive word as to the validity of the commission of Texas Joe as Justice of the Peace—but no word had come.

Impulsively she clasped the pearls about her throat. Why not wear them? They were much safer on her neck than in her bag. Bill would cross-examine her about them. . . . So what? She could say they were costume, couldn't she? She couldn't. She was through with deception. If Bill asked her she would tell him the truth.

She glanced at her watch. Too early for him; she'd wait in the garden. Why had she allowed her thoughts to drift back to Drex and the days at the hacienda, she wondered, as she left the room. She felt again as she had when she had seen him at the head of the stairs with Amelia Mansilla in his arms, a sense that the world had smashed into infinitesimal glittering bits and left her swinging in space, the only living thing in a spinning universe.

The garden was a square between the red-roofed house and a low hedge beyond which were a putting green, a pool and tennis courts.

Because it was too early for the regular afternoon-tea addicts she had her choice of tables, and because it reminded her of the flower border in the patio at the Consulate she chose one under a huge green-and-white umbrella in a corner fragrant with the scent of pink roses and Madonna lilies.

Her eyes were on a silver ship stunting in the distance when she heard a footstep. "Bill," she said without turning, "when you can do that you'll be good and I mean good."

"I'm not Bill," reminded a voice which brought her to her feet. "Remember me? I'm the man you half-married."

"Drex!" she said under her breath. Then as if to assure herself that she was awake, was really seeing his deeply blue eyes, the dark gravity of his face, she repeated, *"Drex!"*

"That's the name. Glad you haven't forgotten it. Better sit down. Sorry I startled you."

"I'm, I'm not st—startled." In spite of her spirited denial she was glad of the support of the chair. She gripped her bag with white-knuckled fingers. She had a perfectly insane urge to fling herself into his arms, to tell him that nothing in the world mattered now that he was here. Instead she said:—

"I—I was expecting Bill and—"

"So I gathered. He isn't coming."

"How do you know?"

"Isn't there a seat beyond the hedge? I keep hitting my head against this confounded umbrella. Come on, let's look." He led her through an opening and sat on the bench beside her.

"This is better. We're safe from curious eyes for a short time at least. You appear nervous. Not afraid of me, I hope."

"Of course not. Why isn't Bill coming?"

"I had a long talk with him after I arrived in camp at noon. We'll order later." He waved away the smiling mulatto girl, in a uniform as brightly pink as her lips, who had suddenly appeared in the break in the hedge. Waited until the screen door of the house banged before he asked:—

"Forgotten I told you I would let you know the truth about Texas Joe's commission?"

"No, but I thought *you* had."

"Not for a minute. When you heard Von Haas

accuse Castello of bribery of a county official you heard the truth. He was after the de la Cartina fortune. Later he wanted you and sent Texas Joe with that paper to tell you the truth. I don't believe that Edouard, rotten as he had been, intended you to pay one hundred pesos for it; that was a little business deal of Joe's. It took me two days, these last two, to drag a confession from the aforementioned slimy official, but I got it. That Casa Fresco ceremony was a fake."

"I'm thankful—"

"I know it. You needn't tell me again."

"You might let me finish and say 'for you as well as myself.' "

"I know that, too. We'll close that chapter and begin another."

"Tell me what happened after I left. Did Miguel live? Was he able to tell you who attacked him?"

"Yes. It was he you saw in church. It was Von Haas, bearded and goggled, with him, not the onetime Mexican major. They did exchange slips of paper. Von Haas knocked out Don Pasquale—to prevent any chance of his stopping the roll of the *camiónes* that night. Thanks to Slade's cigarette case I got in my warning first. There was a message in that from Castello. He had it dropped into the patio at Casa Blanca figuring that you would return it to its owner."

"What a network of conspiracy. What a dangerous game both you and Miguel were playing."

"I came through safe. When Von Haas discovered that he had been fooled by Don Pasquale's head man, he ordered Juan to put him out of the way. For that, the foreign agent has been deported. You've heard about Gordon Slade. I suspected he was the cover-up man from the beginning. Unlawful exporting is washed-up and I've been released from further G-man activities with an *abrazo* and a kiss on both cheeks. Johnny Shaw has asked permission to leave the consular service to join the air corps. Interested to know what I plan to do next?"

"Of course, Drex. Don't speak to me as if we were mortal enemies. Now that that Casa Fresco nightmare is over why can't we be friends?"

"Nothing like that between you and me. We might stretch a point and call ourselves friendly neighbors. I have decided to stay in Mexico. I've given in. There was too great a pressure on all sides for me to go my own way with an easy conscience."

"Will you take the name de la Cartina? Will you become a citizen?"

"No. The law has been adjusted to allow Chiquita to make over to me half of the estate. I don't want it, but she won't have it any other way. I keep my name, my citizenship and—my wife."

"But, Drex. You're not—have you already married Amelia?"

"You'd like to think that, wouldn't you? You saw her in my arms, didn't you? I heard your gasp of surprise when you stood at the door of your room. I had just told her of Castello's death. She fainted. I caught her. She loved him, you see. Any other questions?"

She hadn't known that a voice could be so cold when eyes were so burningly blue. "Only one. Then we'll close this chapter too and—forever. How will you explain my presence at your hacienda as—as Mrs.-Hamilton-for-two-weeks?"

What had she said to set those sparks of laughter in his eyes, to change his voice from frost to caressing tenderness?

"Why explain? Already the fact of our sudden alleged marriage has been forgotten in the excitement of recent world-shaking events. Even the wedding presents stopped coming. You never knew that a lot arrived. I didn't intend you to be made more unhappy than you were. When inquiries were made for you I said your brother was unexpectedly leaving Mexico, and that you were helping them get away. True, wasn't it?"

"Yes. Thank goodness that something is true. But what will you say now?"

"I'll leave it as it is at present. You see, I'm on my way to Washington."

"Really, Drex? So am I. Can't we go together? It would be fun."

"Miss Chesney, you aren't by any chance proposing to me, are you?"

"Was he wood or stone?" Bill had demanded.

Wood? Stone? The ardent light in his eyes set her heart stunting in her throat. Quite suddenly her shattered world was whole again.

"Want me to?"

"If you look at me like that again you'll be kissed and kissed hard. I do *not* want you to propose to me. I'm asking you to marry me."

"Drex! You're not asking me because I—I lived in your house and—"

"Because I feel I must make an honest woman of you? Come here—you darling."

He caught her in his arms, kissed her throat, her eyes, her lips.

"What do you think now?" he asked huskily.

"Something tells me you—you are asking me because you love me. I—"

"Just a minute before you say anything more." He released her. The sharp lines between his brows were chiseled deep.

"I want you to realize what you are promising if you consent to marry me. Years in a country not your own. Later, perhaps, we could repatriate ourselves; perhaps never. Remember what you answered when I asked you if you could make your home in Mexico? I do. I've thought of little else since I decided to stay. You said, 'Leave my own country? I couldn't. I wouldn't.' Even if you say, again, 'I wouldn't' it will not change my decision to stay in Mexico."

She stood motionless, eyes on him. He was right. She must stop and think; but she couldn't consider anything but the heavenly sense of his nearness when she was in his arms. She thought of her homeland, of her inherited love for it and pride in its greatness, of what she had meant to do, of how she had meant to count in it, and she remembered her words to her brother: "I wanted to be sure that what I felt for Bill was the until-death-do-us-part sort of love—his kisses left me quite cold—" Kisses. Liquid fire ran through her veins as she thought of Drex's lips on hers as they had been a moment ago.

"Well?" he prompted. "Well?"

She promised with steady eyes on his:—

" 'Whither thou goest I will go and whither thou lodgest I will lodge, thy people—' "

He caught her close in his arms.

"Say you'll marry me, now, within an hour; then we'll go to Washington together."

"Within an hour! Are you crazy?"

"Perhaps, with happiness since the moment you looked up at me and said, 'Drex!' For the first time I thought you might love me a fraction as much as I love you, but there was still the hurdle of changing your country to take. I have loved you since that night at Casa Fresco. Will you marry me now?"

"But, Drex—"

"Just a minute. The white frock and pearls are perfect for a bride. I've interviewed the camp chaplain; I have the license *and* I have another ring."

"You were sure of me."

"Come here. I can't talk when you are so far away. I wasn't sure. I had my fingers crossed. My car is at the gate. I'll order your bags put in while we have tea here. I've arranged with Bill and his girl friend —they'll be our witnesses—to take your car and meet us at the chaplain's after reveille. All right with you, Kay?"

"Such executive ability is wasted on a mere marriage ceremony. Nothing short of a hemisphere to manage is worthy of your genius, *Jefe del Hogar*," she mocked with unsteady gaiety.

She met his eyes; he was so boyishly jubilant, so adoringly tender—and yet the hair at his temples hadn't been frosted a week ago. He was taking on responsibilities he didn't want, giving up a life he desired because he believed the other was his work. She would help him and love him all her life.

"All right with me, Drex."

He kissed her tenderly before he turned to the dusky, pink-frocked maid teetering in giggling uncertainty in the opening of the hedge.

"Tea for two," he ordered, "and make it fast. We have a date."